Dear Reader,

You know the saying. Old soldiers never die, they just fade away. Or in my case, they turn to a life of murder and mayhem—purely fictional, of course.

I'm thrilled to return to my military roots in this novel and the one to follow in the Cleo North series. As a squadron, base and wing commander, I saw firsthand the expertise air force special agents brought to their always demanding, often gruesome investigations. As an author, I want to portray their dedication and gritty determination to safeguard air force people and property.

I hope you enjoy this glimpse into the world of undercover agents, past and present!

All my best,

Merline Lovelace

Also by MERLINE LOVELACE

THE FIRST MISTAKE
UNTAMED
A SAVAGE BEAUTY
THE CAPTAIN'S WOMAN
THE COLONEL'S DAUGHTER
THE HORSE SOLDIER

And watch for the next book in this
action-packed new series

THE LAST BULLET

Coming June 2005

MERLINE LOVELACE

THE MIDDLE SIN

MIRA®

ISBN 0-7783-2172-X

THE MIDDLE SIN

Copyright © 2005 by Merline Lovelace.

www.MIRABooks.com

Printed in U.S.A.

To Marie and Tom, best friends and fellow travelers. Here's to many more great adventures together.

ACKNOWLEDGMENTS

With special thanks to:

Lieutenant Colonel Eddie Howard, USAF, for his OSI expertise, quick reads and even quicker wit. The bad guys better watch their step!

And to the men and women in uniform who get the bombs, bullets and combat boots where they're needed, when they're needed. As the saying goes, amateurs talk tactics, professionals talk logistics.

1

Cleo lunged at her attacker.

He was huge, six-foot-six of solid muscle wrapped in black leather pants and a sleeveless leather vest that displayed a half acre or so of hairy chest.

The scumbag had come at Cleo from behind just as she'd entered a locker room ripe with the acrid tang of sweat and the heat of a mid-April Dallas morning. When he'd whipped an arm around her throat, she'd managed to ram her butt into his midsection and catapult him over her shoulder.

Now she was on the offensive. Launching herself through the air, Cleo angled her attack so her knee hit square in his gut. The breath exploded from his lungs. His lips curled over his teeth. Under the tattoos decorating his bald skull, he went as white as a week-old corpse.

But before Cleo could take advantage of her momentary mastery, he contracted his stomach. The muscles under her knee snapped together like coiled springs and almost bounced her right off the hulking giant.

Cursing, she dove forward. The heel of her hand was an inch from his nose when he threw up an arm. Deflecting her blow, he heaved his hips upward and tossed her off like a pesky spaniel. She landed hard enough to water her eyes.

"Dammit, Goose!"

The bald Goliath grinned and made a grab for her. "You're getting soft, North."

This was what she paid him for, Cleo reminded herself grimly as they writhed across the concrete floor. Why she'd turned to him after leaving the air force and starting up her own security-consulting firm. She *wanted* Goose to toss her on her head occasionally—or try to. A girl had to stay on her toes in this business.

Jamming her booted foot against the floor for leverage, Cleo heaved to one side and slammed Goose into a row of metal lockers. Wedged against the unyielding steel, he lost just enough of his maneuverability for her to hook an ankle over his and bring him down. She had his wrist in a death grip and was attempting to shove it up between his massive shoulder blades when the cell phone clipped to her waist pinged.

Cleo froze. It was a special ring tone, one she recognized immediately. Goose recognized it, too. He shot a look of sudden terror over his shoulder.

"That's Mae. For God's sake, don't answer it!"

Struggling for breath, she hunkered back on her heels. Mae was her part-time office manager. The sixtyish retired accountant had recently developed a severe case of the hots for the muscled giant pinned between Cleo's thighs.

The cell phone rang again. Short. Sharp. Impatient. She could feel Goose start to tremble beneath her. Mae did that to people.

Surrendering to the inevitable, Cleo unhooked her leg and slid off her trainer's rump. "I'd better take it. You know she only uses this signal in emergencies."

Goose rolled over, his face scrunched in earnest entreaty. "Don't tell her you're with me!"

"She knows we had a training session scheduled. Which *would* have taken place in the gym on a nice, soft rubber pad if my rat-faced trainer hadn't decided to jump me in the women's locker room!"

"You think you're gonna land on a rubber pad out there in the real world, woman?"

Resisting the urge to flip him the bird, she flipped up the phone instead. "It's me, Mae. What's happening?"

"I just took a call from a potential client. He says it's urgent."

"He who?"

"Marcus Sloan."

Cleo's stomach did a quick roll. The image that leapt into her mind was tall, dark and drop-dead gorgeous. Not to mention obscenely rich.

She'd first encountered Marc Sloan four months ago in Santa Fe, while working a case. Sloan had promised to call Cleo and follow up on his not-very-subtle invitations to get her into the sack during those weeks in Santa Fe. After four months of nothing, now it was urgent?

"I told him you'd return his call," Mae announced in her crisp, no-nonsense way. Without missing a breath, she switched gears. "Is Goose with you?"

"Goose?"

Cleo glanced at her hulking trainer. At the mention of his name, he made frantic no-no-no signs with his hands.

"Yes, he's here."

"Put him on."

Smirking, she held out the phone. "Remember this next time you decide to jump me in a women's locker room."

His scowl promised far more lethal tactics in the future. Folding her arms, Cleo listened with unabashed enjoyment to his side of the conversation.

"Hi, Mae. Yes. Yes." A long pause. "No."

Another pause, punctuated by heavy looks aimed at Cleo, followed by a startled exclamation.

"Good God, no!"

Her eyes widened. Was that a blush crawling up Goose's size-twenty-two neck? It was!

"I'm outta here," he said, thrusting the phone back at her. "Got a job down in Mexico I've been dragging my tail on. It just moved up to number-one priority."

His face as red as the heart on his left biceps, he rushed out of the locker room. Grinning, Cleo put the phone to her ear.

"Goose is about to set a new world record for departing Dallas. What did you say to him?"

Mae huffed into the phone. "I merely suggested he doesn't need to pick up bimbos at biker bars to get his knob polished."

Cleo choked.

"There are more mature women available who might be willing to perform that task," the retired accountant finished.

She wasn't going to *touch* that one.

"Speaking of mature women," Mae added. "You need to call your stepmother. She left a message saying she wants your advice on new wallpaper for the guest room."

With a little thump, all the fun went out of Cleo's morning.

For years, it had just been her and her father. Her mother had died when Cleo was only three, and her dad's job as a hydrologist with the U.S. Agency for International Development had taken both father and daughter all over the world. Cleo had ridden her first shaggy pony in Nepal, started school in Brazil and learned to drive in Bangkok.

Patrick North had returned to the States at frequent intervals during Cleo's years at the University of Texas. Once she'd joined the military and qualified as an agent with the Air Force Office of Special Investigations, though, he was off again.

Not long after Cleo had finished her stint in the air force, a bout of angina had brought him back to his native Texas and into retirement. Cleo had chosen Dallas as the base for her security-consulting firm primarily to keep an eye on him. Then, almost a year ago, big, bluff Patrick North had fallen hard for a woman he'd met at a dance at the seniors' center. Wanda was petite, perky, and the bane of Cleo's existence.

Her dad was happy, she reminded herself sternly. That's all that mattered. But Cleo would rather walk barefoot across a sea of razor blades than go wallpaper-hunting with a woman who dithered for twenty minutes before she could decide between French or Italian dressing on her salad.

"Do me a favor," she begged Mae. "Call Wanda and tell her I'm on a case."

"Sorry, dear. I tee off in thirty minutes. I'm not getting sucked into that discussion. Besides, you're not on a case."

"I might be," Cleo retorted, "once you get around to giving me Marc Sloan's number."

A moment later, she punched in the long-distance number. The voice that answered was young and flavored with a soft, rolling accent that hinted at mint juleps and magnolias.

"Sloan Enterprises. May I help you?"

"This is Cleo North. I'm returning Mr. Sloan's call."

"Hold, please."

She was handed off to the next echelon of palace guard. This one sounded older, crisper and more difficult to get around.

"I'm Diane Walker, Mr. Sloan's executive assistant. I'm sorry, but I don't show you on the call log, Ms. North."

"Not my problem. He called me."

"If this is in regard to a personal matter, Mr. Sloan has entrusted me to handle his affairs."

Impatient now, Cleo put a bite into her reply. "I repeat, Ms. Walker, Mr. Sloan called me. My business is with him."

Any notion that the sophisticated executive was calling to pick up where they'd left off a few months ago evaporated ten seconds after he came on the line.

"Hello, Cleo." It was the same sexy baritone she remembered. "Thanks for getting back to me."

"Hello, Marc. How's Alex?"

The last time she'd seen Sloan's twin, the retired air force colonel had been slumped over his desk, blood oozing from the neat hole in his skull.

"He's walking. Slowly and with a cane, but walking."

"Good to hear. What can I do for you?"

"One of my assistants hasn't shown up for work this week. I'm worried about her and would like you to find her. How soon can you get to Charleston?"

Normally, Cleo went through a detailed intake interview before accepting a job or a new client. But Sloan's timing was perfect. He'd caught her just coming off another job and faced with the grim prospect of going wallpaper shopping with Waffling Wanda.

"I can fly out this afternoon."

"That's what I was hoping. My private jet is already in the air. It'll be on the ground at Love Field in an hour."

He was pretty damned sure of himself. Then again, you don't take a company onto the Fortune 500 list by being faint of heart. Which reminded Cleo...

"We haven't discussed fees."

A smile crept into his voice. "Whatever they are, Brown Eyes, you're worth it."

Little shivers danced down Cleo's spine. She could almost feel the crush of Sloan's mouth on hers.

The man was one hell of a kisser. Not as good as Jack Donovan, she admitted, but Cleo and Special Agent Donovan had yet to figure out what they had going between them. Besides careers that included getting shot at every so often and intermittent sessions of world-class sex, that is.

At the rate things were going, they might *never* figure out just why the heck the air started steaming whenever they got within ten feet of each other. Donovan had e-mailed her exactly three times in the past four months and then only to tell her he was still untangling the web of treason and deceit they'd uncovered in Santa Fe.

Cleo had never been one to sit around and wait. For men *or* for jobs.

"See you this afternoon," she told Sloan.

When Cleo arrived back at the north-Dallas condo that served as her residence and home office, Mae was out whacking golf balls around the country club's manicured fairways. Unfortunately, she'd left Doreen behind to man the office.

Doreen was Wavering Wanda's niece by marriage, which made her Cleo's step-cousin-in-law, or something like that. When the dot.com company Doreen had worked for folded, Wanda had begged Cleo to hire the girl. Just until she could find other employment.

The "girl" was thirty-seven, had a laugh like a constipated hyena and was addicted to *The Simpsons* cartoon series. She was also a near genius when it came to electronic gadgetry. Go figure.

When Cleo let herself into her condo, Bart Simpson was doing his thing on the big-screen TV in the living room. Doreen was doing hers on the couch. She lay sprawled on the creamy Natuzzi leather, cackling away. For this Cleo paid her twice what she'd earned at the dot.com.

She managed to drag her attention away from the TV long enough to lift her head. "Hey, cuz."

"Hey, Doreen. What are you doing here? I thought you had a job interview this morning."

"I went, I saw, I passed."

Cleo swallowed a groan. She was beginning to suspect Doreen would remain on her payroll indefinitely. Or until all *Simpsons* reruns went off the air.

Her groan slid into a gulp when she spied the shiny little cylinder sitting on the kitchen counter. It looked like an ordinary penlight, but she knew better than to touch it. Doreen's toys could shock, burn or otherwise severely injure the uninitiated.

"What's this?" she asked warily.

"A forever light."

"Oooo-kay."

Pushing off the sofa, her step-cousin-in-law ambled over. She was a big woman, topping Cleo's five-eight by two inches and her weight by at least a hundred pounds. The fact that she squeezed all those dimpled pounds into stretch leggings and a T-shirt emblazoned with Bart's face didn't exactly increase her employment opportunities.

Enthusiasm kindled in her eyes as she fondled her latest creation. "I bought it at Wal-Mart and did some tinkering."

"What kind of tinkering?"

"Nothing much. I just installed a high-intensity LED bulb and some miniature, solid-state circuitry that extends the battery life into infinity."

When she flicked the switch, a beam of light stabbed across the kitchen. It was so bright and intense Cleo had to fling up an arm to keep from being blinded.

"I also coated the outer case in polyurethane." Doreen flicked the switch to Off. "This baby is waterproof, tamperproof and shatterproof. You can drop it down a Pennsylvania coal-mine shaft and it'll still send up a stream of light visible to the astronauts on the space station."

"Right," Cleo muttered, cautiously lowering her arm. "I'll give 'em a signal next time I'm at the bottom of a mine shaft."

At Doreen's insistence, she clipped the penlight to her keychain and went to throw a few things in an overnight bag. Her years jaunting around the world with her dad had taught her to travel light. Her tour in the military had taught her to pare the essentials down even more.

Learning to cram a month's worth of necessities into a light carryall was one of the more useful skills she'd honed in the air force. Her training as an investigative agent was another real plus. The rest...

Well, the rest was up for debate. She certainly could have done without the eighty-seven layers of supervision. And all those rules and regulations were a real pain in the ass. Looking back, though, those years in uniform had been worth the effort.

She'd joined the service right out of college, had been selected for training as a special agent with the Air Force Office of Special Investigations. She'd surprised herself by acing every school and specialized course the OSI had sent her to. Given her fluency in languages and globetrotting childhood, Cleo had expected to specialize in the spook stuff. Counterintelligence. Risk assessment. Overseas force protection.

But OSI policy dictated that recruits receive training in *all* aspects of law enforcement and security. As a consequence, she'd investigated everything from illegal-arms sales to sex crimes and murders. She'd also rotated through white-collar crime, fraud and computer ops before plunging into the shadow world of spies and secret agents.

For most of those years in the field, she'd had to blend into the background. Her regular uniform had been jeans and military-spec Oakley boots, with a nine millimeter SIG Sauer semiautomatic tucked into an ankle or underarm holster. Now that she was in business for herself, she still worked primarily in jeans, but paired them with cashmere turtlenecks or silk tanks topped by hand-tailored blazers. She also preferred the new ten millimeter Glock to the SIG.

The Glock went into a special side pocket in her carryall. Since she didn't know how long it would take her to find Sloan's missing employee, she tossed in another pair of slacks and a couple more tops. Also a clingy spandex dress in a vivid jungle print. *Not* because the dress showed off the trim one-twenty she was down to these days. Simply because she preferred to travel prepared for any eventuality.

Several pairs of the lace-trimmed Brazilian Boxers she'd just discovered in a pricy boutique, her favorite Dallas Cowboys sleep shirt and a few toiletries rounded out the list of personal necessities.

Her professional gear was already packed and ready in a flyaway kit. In addition to her digital camera and laptop, she'd take along the usual complement of electronic sweeps, listening devices and satellite-link communications. She doubted she'd need them on a missing-person case but had learned to go in prepared for anything.

Doreen was back on the sofa, snorting and cackling, when Cleo passed through the living room on her way to the garage.

"Call your aunt for me, would you? Tell her I'm going out of town on a job and can't talk wallpaper with her."

"Oh, jeez," Doreen groaned. "Hasn't she finished redecorating your dad's place?"

"Evidently not."

"She'll try to rope me into this wallpaper waltz. I know she will."

"Better you than me."

"You owe me for this one, cuz."

Almost giddy at the reprieve, Cleo climbed behind the wheel of her black MG. Her father was always after her to buy something a little more solid, like a Humvee or an Abrams tank. Either one, Patrick claimed, would be more appropriate, given Cleo's road techniques. Since he'd been the one to instruct her in the fine art of guerrilla driving in the first place, she had so far ignored his advice.

The "forever" light thunked against the dash as she zipped through traffic on the Dallas North Tollway. The usual smog hung over the city, not as bad as in L.A. or D.C., but gray enough to almost obscure the skyscrapers poking up from the plains. Turning off the toll road and onto Mockingbird Lane, she wound through an older part of the city and enjoyed a real Texas spring for a few blocks. Daffodils poked through cedar chips raked neatly in beds. Redbuds flowered in shades of magenta, hot pink and pearly white. The occasional dogwood showered snowy petals on shaded lawns. Gradually, the fifties-era bungalows gave way to what used to be Dallas's main airport.

Nice of Marc Sloan to send his private jet to Love Field instead of big, sprawling Dallas-Fort Worth International. Love was a good half hour closer to Cleo's condo and much more accessible to private jets.

The one that waited for her was a Gulfstream V. She didn't track the private-jet industry in any detail but knew enough about the business to guess this baby sold for a cool forty or fifty million. As the pilot informed her when she'd strapped in, the sleek, twin-engine jet could cruise at 51,000 feet and fly nonstop from Tokyo to New York.

They were only going from Texas to South Carolina, but Cleo lolled in leather-coated luxury all the way. A male flight attendant offered her a choice of champagnes and a selection of imported hams and cheeses. Since she was technically on the job, Cleo passed up the champagne but did serious damage to two crusty baguettes, several thick slices of Parma ham and a wedge of smoked Danish gouda, all lavishly spread with sweet French mustard.

After surreptitiously loosening her black leather belt a notch, she flipped up her laptop to review her file on Marc Sloan. She'd gathered most of the data when she'd headed up to Santa Fe to investigate his brother. The more personal tidbits had been added after she'd mistaken Marc for his twin and ended up in the man's arms. Scrolling slowly, she skimmed the file on the Sloan twins.

The boys had been adopted at birth by a career army officer and renowned scholar of ancient warfare. Marcus, Cleo had learned, was named for the Roman general Marcus Aurelius, and his brother Alexander for the Greek conqueror. Both sons had followed their father into the military. Alex had put twenty-plus years into the air force. Marc had opted out of the navy after completing his four-year service commitment and went to work for Northrop Grumman Ship Systems Division. A few years later, he'd left Northrop to form his own company.

Sloan Engineering had started small, with a navy contract to reengineer amphibious assault ships, and had grown steadily. A few years later the company had burst into the big time with an innovative design to retrofit ocean-going cargo vessels and significantly reduce NOx emissions— whatever the heck those were. Evidently Sloan had cornered the market on NOx's. *Forbes* magazine put his estimated current assets at somewhere between four and five billion.

He hadn't been quite as successful in his personal life. Or maybe he'd been *too* successful. At the ripe old age of forty-five, Marc Sloan had racked up two ex-wives and a string of "just friends" that stretched from Washington, D.C., to Hollywood, with a few international beauties tossed in here and there for variety.

Cleo was still digesting the eye-popping details of his last divorce settlement when the pilot announced they were on final approach. Shutting down her laptop, she enjoyed an aerial view of Charleston as the pilot swooped into a private airport just north of the city. The hatch whirred down a moment later and let in a blast of warm April air.

Cleo gathered her things and poked her head into the cockpit. "Thanks for the ride."

"Anytime, Ms. North."

She wished!

A limo with Sloan Engineering's logo etched in gold and marine blue whisked her into Charleston. The city was as muggy and charming as she remembered from a brief visit years ago.

Palm trees rustled, showy rhododendrons blossomed everywhere, and the perfume of camellias battled with the distinct tang of the sea. The salty scent grew stronger as the limo glided over the bridge spanning the Cooper River just a few miles north of where it joined with the Ashley to flow into the sea. Fifteen minutes later the driver pulled up at Sloan Engineering's corporate headquarters.

The building's exterior was impressive—seven or eight stories of glass with just enough wrought iron and architectural detail to give it a Low Country flavor. But the atrium lobby stole Cleo's breath.

It featured palmettos, a cascading waterfall and a freestanding world globe at least three stories tall. Little red lights moving around the globe represented ships built or retrofitted by Sloan Engineering, or so the discreet plaque at the base of the globe informed her.

"Ms. North?"

Cleo recognized the polite, magnolia-tinted drawl from her earlier call. "Yes."

"Would you come with me, please? Mr. Sloan is expecting you."

A glass-enclosed elevator zinged them upward, giving Cleo a bird's-eye view of the globe and all those red dots.

"Right this way."

She followed the young woman into a suite of offices redolent with the scents of polished mahogany and the calla lilies massed in a tall vase. Depositing her carryall and laptop in the outer office, Cleo entered the inner sanctum and was greeted by Sloan's executive assistant.

Diane Walker proved to be a trim, well-groomed forty or so, with honey-colored hair cut in a chin-length bob. The suit was Chanel, the shoes were Ferragamo and the eyes were coolly assessing as she shook Cleo's hand.

"This way, Ms. North. Marc's waiting for you."

Marc, huh? Curious, Cleo probed a bit. "Have you been with Sloan Engineering long, Ms. Walker?"

"Almost fifteen years. Marc and I were both at Northrop. I left when he did."

So she'd gotten into Sloan Engineering on the ground floor. If the woman took part of her salary in stock options, it was no wonder she could afford Chanel.

"Ms. North is here," she announced, ushering Cleo into an office the size of Rhode Island. The executive seated at a marble slab of a desk rose and came to greet her.

"Hello, Cleo."

Oh, man!

Oh-man-oh-man-oh-man!

She remembered the chiseled jaw. The smoke-gray eyes. The black hair threaded with silver at the temples. She even recalled the sexy little Kirk Douglas dimple in his chin. She'd forgotten the impact the sum of the parts could have on her respiratory system, though.

Struggling to recall just why the heck she'd

turned down Sloan's repeated invitations to join him for dinner or bed or both, she turned her head and took his kiss on her cheek.

Amusement leapt into his face, but he followed her lead and kept it to a light brush of his lips across first one cheek, then the other.

Very European. Very polite.

Very sexy.

This was business, Cleo reminded herself. She tended to be flexible when it came to rules and regulations. But letting a client get her all hot and bothered before they'd established the parameters of the case was a stretch, even for her.

Declining offers of coffee or a cool drink, she followed Sloan and his executive assistant to the armchairs grouped beside a wall of windows. The floor-to-ceiling sheets of glass were set at angles to give panoramic views of Charleston harbor. Historic Fort Sumter sat smack in the middle of the harbor, with the Stars and Stripes flying above its ramparts. The sight was poignant, considering the first shots of the war that almost ripped the Union apart were fired at those same ramparts.

Dragging her gaze from the view, Cleo rummaged in her purse and dug out a small black notebook. During her years as an air force special agent, she'd had access to the world's most sophisticated computers and anticrime databases. Since going into business for herself, Cleo had kept abreast of the latest security techniques and equipment. Doreen, despite her nails-on-chalkboard laugh, was as good with computers as she was with electronic gadgets. Yet the basic tool for any cop, investigative agent or security specialist was and probably always would be a little black notebook.

Pen at the ready, she got down to business. "Why don't you tell me about this missing employee?"

2

"Her name's Patricia Jackson," Sloan informed Cleo. "She goes by Trish."

"Trish. Got it."

"She's worked here a little over two years."

"Prior to that?"

Sloan turned to his executive assistant.

"Trish had no previous work experience," Walker explained. "I hired her right out of business school."

"Okay. How about the personal details? Age, marital status, place of birth."

"Her parents live in a small town about a hundred miles from here. As far as I know, that's where she was born. She's single and has just turned twenty-two."

Sloan's brow hiked. He looked surprised, or as

surprised as a man who controlled a multibillion-dollar corporation would allow himself to look.

His assistant noted the reaction with a flicker of something that could have been amusement. Or disdain. It was gone before Cleo could decide which.

"Yes, Marc, she's only twenty-two."

"What does Trish do here?"

"General office work," Walker replied. "Typing, filing, answering the phone. Lately I've been letting her manage Marc's schedule."

"When did you last see her?"

"Friday afternoon. No, make that Friday evening. Marc and I were tied up in a meeting, so I asked her to cover the phones. She left just after seven."

This was Thursday. Trish had been missing almost a week. Not good, Cleo thought.

"When she didn't show up for work Monday morning," Walker continued, "I wasn't unduly alarmed. She's a good worker and bright as they come, but..."

"Yes?"

"Well..."

There it was again. That subtle shift of emotions. The woman didn't look at Marc this time, but Cleo was picking up definite vibes.

"Trish has been known to party hard on occasion," Walker finished.

"Only one occasion we know of," Sloan put in with a wry twist of his lips. "It was an office party. On my yacht. Trish drank too much, got seasick as well as drunk and passed out in my stateroom. We didn't see her for two days after we made harbor."

"So what makes you think she isn't just off somewhere, recovering from another party?"

"When she didn't show Tuesday morning, I called her apartment and got no answer." A crease formed between Walker's perfectly penciled brows. "I drove out to her place and convinced the manager of her apartment complex to let me in. I found her purse, her keys, her car and her very hungry cat."

Uh-oh. The cat was a dead giveaway. No self-respecting feline lover would go off for a week without making arrangements for her pet.

"I brought the cat back to the office with me, got Marc's authorization to bypass the company security codes and had my folks start calling the personal phone numbers stored in Trish's office computer. They called everyone in it. Acquaintances, relatives, former instructors, the pet store where she purchased special flea collars. No one's seen or heard from her since last Friday."

Sloan picked it up from there. "That's when I spoke to her parents and suggested they file a missing-person report. I also called the Charleston chief of police. He's a friend."

"Have the police searched Trish's apartment?"

"They went through it yesterday—Wednesday—afternoon. I'm told they dusted for prints and sprayed the place with luminol."

The prints would take a while to run. The luminol would have highlighted blood spatters instantly.

"Anything show up?"

"No. The detective assigned to the case is following up now on the calls Diane and her people made."

Cleo waited a beat or two. "That's it?"

"That's it."

"Just out of curiosity, why did you call me in so soon? The police haven't had time to work the case yet."

Sloan's eyes went as hard as slate. "Chief Benton gave me the statistics. The chances of finding a missing or abducted woman alive diminish by a factor of ten with every twenty-four hours she's gone. I don't like the odds."

Neither did Cleo, although there was nothing to indicate the missing employee had been abducted or otherwise harmed.

Yet.

"Tell me more about Trish's personal life," she prompted. "Hobbies. Tastes in food or music. Friends—boy, girl or in between."

"She's gone to lunch with the others here in the office a number of times," Walker related, "but hasn't really grown close to anyone. One of her coworkers, Heather Dalton, says she thinks Trish has been seeing someone lately but doesn't know who. Her only hobby I know of is collecting starfish. She had one shellacked and keeps it on her desk."

Cleo duly noted the starfish, then flipped her notebook shut and checked her watch. It was still early afternoon. Plenty of time to poke around.

"I'd like to talk to Trish's co-workers, then go through the apartment myself. I'll need a vehicle."

Walker nodded. "I've got one of the company cars waiting for you. I also have Trish's house keys. I picked them up yesterday."

"Good. I'll also need a city map, a printout of her address book and a recent photo."

"I have those ready, too," Ms. Super Efficiency responded. "And I've booked you a suite at the Hilton Waterfront."

That worked for Cleo. Not for Sloan, though.

"Cancel the suite, Diane. Ms. North can use the corporate guest house."

"The Hilton is more convenient to Trish's neighborhood."

"Cancel the suite."

The tone was even, but the order unmistakably boss to employee. After an infinitesimal pause, Walker's expression clicked into neutral.

"Very well. I'll get a keycard for the guest house."

Cleo waited until the other woman had departed the office to ask the question hovering at the back of her suspicious investigator's mind. "Is there something going on here you haven't told me about?"

"What do you mean?"

"Between you and Trish?"

His aristocratic features assumed a haughty air. "I make it a point never to mix business with pleasure."

"Care to tell me why Ms. Jackson ended up in your cabin aboard your yacht, then?"

Grimacing, he climbed down off his high horse. "All right, it's true Trish developed something of a crush on me when she first came to work at Sloan Engineering. She was young and impressionable. That night on the yacht was...awkward. But I was in the middle of divorce negotiations at the time. I wasn't about to up the stakes by getting involved with one of my employees."

"Yeah, I read about those stakes." Cleo waggled her brows. "Twelve thousand a month for maintenance?"

His shrug said he could afford it.

"Which reminds me. We still haven't discussed fees for my services."

"What's your going rate?"

She didn't hesitate. "For a missing-person locate, two hundred an hour, plus expenses. With a twenty-thousand-dollar bonus when I find her."

"Done."

Cleo swallowed a grin. Actually, her going rate depended a whole lot on the client. She'd accepted more than one case over the years for a token fee of a dollar. One, she recalled, involved finding a missing hamster for her seven-year-old neighbor. Another lasted months and ripped a hole in her heart, but in the end she'd managed to take down the sick pervert who'd assaulted and raped a seventy-nine-year-old Alzheimer's patient. Those clients who could afford it, though, paid well for her services.

Marc Sloan could afford it.

"I've instructed Diane to cut a check for your retainer," he told her. "She has it waiting for you."

"Efficient woman, your Diane."

"Yes, she is."

There didn't seem to be much to add to that, so Cleo slung her purse over her shoulder. "I'd better get to work. I'll keep you posted on my progress."

Nodding, Sloan took her elbow and escorted her to the door. His hand slid up her blazer sleeve in an almost-caress, but he didn't press things.

That was pretty much okay with Cleo.

True, she hadn't had sex since Santa Fe. Also true, she'd probably made a serious error in judgment by letting Jack Donovan jump her bones during that particular gig. Or maybe she'd jumped his. She wasn't quite sure at this point. In any case, four months was a long time to go with only a couple of e-mails to hold her hormones in check.

They were certainly humming now. Handsome, sexy billionaires could do that. Particularly *this* handsome, sexy billionaire. Sternly ignoring the tingle his touch generated, Cleo eased out of his hold.

"I'll see you later."

"Yes, you will."

The murmured exchange was low and obviously intended to be private, but Diane was too well tuned to Marc's voice to miss it. Due to years of practice she managed not to frown, but the manila envelope she'd just retrieved from her desk crumpled in her fingers.

He had his hands on her. Already.

Damn him!

Pain spilled through her lungs, so swift and sharp she couldn't breathe. How many times would she have to stand on the sidelines and watch him make these same moves? How many women was he going to tumble into bed before he got tired of the game?

And it *was* a game—one she'd seen him play again and again through the years. She couldn't count the number of charge accounts she'd opened for the latest flavor of the month, or the endless orders she'd placed at the jeweler who handled all Marc's business.

You'd think he would have learned after the debacle of his first marriage. He'd still been struggling to win contracts for their fledgling company at the time, attempting to break into the lucrative defense market. Betsy had almost milked both Marc *and* Sloan Engineering dry.

Had the idiot taken the lesson to heart? Had he once considered going for substance instead of sex?

Ha! He wouldn't recognize substance if it kicked him in the balls, which was exactly what Diane ached to do at this moment.

Somehow she managed to swallow the corrosive combination of anger, hurt and sheer frustration at his obtuseness. Dredging up her best professional smile, she handed over the envelope.

"This contains the keys to a company SUV. It's the white Cadillac Escalade in slot number three on the first floor of the parking garage. The envelope also holds the key to Trish's apartment. We obtained her parents' permission to enter her residence if necessary. Our corporate attorneys tell us their consent doesn't constitute legal authority, since Trish is an adult, but Marc's not worried about the legalities at this point."

"So I gathered."

"I've also got a map of Charleston, a key card for the guest house, directions to Trish's apartment, the printout of her address book and the photo you requested." She picked up a folder and slid out a color eight-by-ten. "I retrieved it from the personnel files, increased the size and printed it out."

The photo made Diane's chest squeeze. The woman—girl, really—who smiled up from the photo was so very young. Round-cheeked and dimpled, she looked at the world through eager eyes. Her sandy hair was shaped in a pixie cut that gave her a look of gamine innocence.

Had Trish's girlish infatuation for her boss spilled over into passion? Had she and Marc become involved? The possibility gnawed at Diane's insides as she passed the photo to the tall, trim brunette she suspected was Marc's latest quarry.

"Thanks. Now, if you'll introduce me to her friend, Heather..."

3

It didn't take Cleo long to confirm that neither Heather Dalton nor any of Trish's other co-workers had a clue where the missing woman might be.

As Diane had indicated, Trish Jackson was apparently friendly and outgoing but didn't socialize much with folks from the office. Maybe because she lived across the Ashley River, where the rent was more reasonable than in historic downtown Charleston.

Cleo made the drive during nonrush hour, yet it still ate up a good twenty minutes, partly due to the wrong turns she made while negotiating the downtown's rabbit warren of streets. Even with OnStar chirping out directions, she missed the onramp for the first bridge across the Ashley. The second took her within sight of the Charleston Police Department. Keeping a wary eye on the bridge traffic, she skimmed the list of contacts Diane had provided, punched in the number of the detective working the missing-person case and introduced herself.

Sloan's friendship with the chief of police had paved the way. Instead of resenting the fact that the engineering executive had brought in hired help, Detective Lafayette Devereaux agreed to compare notes with Cleo at nine the following morning.

"Assuming there's anything to compare," he said in a deep bass drawl that resonated like a ket-tledrum. "So far I'm coming up empty."

"Maybe one of us will get lucky."

"It happens."

"See you tomorrow."

Flipping the phone shut, Cleo concentrated on maneuvering the Escalade through the heavy traf-fic. Her father would approve, she thought. The vehicle was almost six thousand pounds of leather and burled-wood luxury.

Trish's apartment was located in a large com-plex a half mile or so from a shopping mall. Al-though not as high rent as the downtown area, the place still looked pricy for a recent business col-lege grad. Sloan must pay his office help as well as he did his ex-wives and security consultants, Cleo mused as she pulled into the slot assigned to Trish's apartment.

Reaching into her gear bag, she extracted a set of rubber gloves and her digital camera. No sense adding to the mélange of prints the police were sifting through. Or contaminating possible evidence if, in fact, Trish Jackson turned up as a victim.

This was the grunt work of any investigation. Gathering information. Recording impressions. Separating the merely interesting from the potentially useful. As Cleo had learned during her years as an air force investigative agent, this initial phase required diligence, patience and morbid curiosity. Camera, gloves and notebook at the ready, she let herself into the apartment.

The first thing that hit her was the musty odor of closed windows and used kitty litter. The combination wasn't as bad as the stench at some of the crime scenes she'd been called to. She wouldn't ever forget the lieutenant who'd choked to death while indulging in a little autoerotic whacking off. He'd hooked a rope over a door jamb and leaned into it to heighten his orgasm.

He must have had one heck of a ride, seeing as he'd passed out, slumped to his knees and strangled himself. Unfortunately, he'd also been on two weeks' leave at the time. His putrefying corpse hadn't been discovered until the folks in the adjoining apartment had complained of the stink coming through the air vents.

Since the police had already searched Trish's apartment, Cleo didn't anticipate finding any putrefying corpses. What she did find was neat, bright and cheerful. A counter with two cane-backed stools separated the closet-size kitchen from the more generous living-sleeping area. A platform bed backed by colorful pillows occupied a raised dais and doubled as extra seating.

Evidence of Trish's hobby showed in the prints of starfish hung over the sofa and the framed specimens arranged on little easels on the coffee table. Along with the starfish, Trish had collected an assortment of unique and colorful seashells. Those she displayed in a glass apothecary jar in her bathroom.

The bathroom was almost as large as the living area, with a nice-size oval tub. Cleo poked through the bathroom cabinets and found plenty of dental floss, over-the-counter cold remedies, aspirin and Tampax, as well as a box of birth-control patches.

Making a note of the OB-GYN who'd prescribed the patches, Cleo looked for further evidence to support the feeling among Trish's co-workers that she was seeing someone. If she was, she didn't have any photos of him in the packet of recently developed pictures Cleo found in the nightstand. They were mostly shots of starfish, although one snagged Cleo's instant interest.

"Well, well," she murmured. "What have we here?"

The photo showed a trail made by two sets of bare-toed footprints in wet, glistening sand. One set was relatively small and dainty, the other considerably larger.

Unfortunately, the camera had been aimed at a low angle that cut off most of the surrounding scenery. All that showed were sandy dunes, a curving stretch of shore and a portion of a pier in the distance.

Laying the photo on the bed, Cleo snapped a duplicate with her digital camera. There was a chance—a remote chance—she could match that bit of shoreline to satellite imagery of the Charleston area.

Doreen had loaded Cleo's laptop with a program she'd constructed using NASA's Geophysical Satellite Imaging Database. The program was supposed to be able to compare a description or picture of just about any topographical feature on the surface of the earth to the imagery in the database and extrapolate precise longitude and latitude. The only time Cleo had tried to use the program, though, it had directed her to a used car lot instead of the dry gulch she'd been searching for.

But what the heck. She didn't have anything to lose by giving it another shot. She got the address of the MotoPhoto lab that had developed the photo from the package, in case Trish had dropped off another roll when she picked this one up.

From the bedroom area Cleo moved to the kitchen. She spent another half hour poking through drawers, peering into cupboards, jotting down brands and labels. In one of the cupboards, she spotted a pink plastic child's bucket and shovel. Washed clean, it was probably last used when Trish went hunting for her shells and starfish.

The thirty-two-ounce plastic water jug next to the bucket held more interest for Cleo. She recognized the distinctive logo instantly.

"Going to Weight Watchers, are you?"

Cleo had sucked on a water jug just like this one in a futile attempt to shave off the extra pounds she'd put on after leaving the air force. After several months, she'd jettisoned that effort and hired Goose to whip her into shape instead. With a twinge of sympathy for a fellow warrior in the battle of the bulge, she made a note to call Information for the nearest Weight Watchers clinic.

Abandoning the cupboards, she searched the fridge and the trash can. She found a receipt in the trash indicating Trish shopped for her food and personal items at a local Wal-Mart Super Center, but not much else of immediate use.

After the kitchen she turned to the some-assembly-required computer stand that served as Trish's home office. The answering machine yielded only increasingly concerned messages from Diane Walker and Trish's parents. The home computer showed a checking-account balance of four hundred and twenty-six dollars, with no unusual withdrawals or deposits. The bank had also issued her a Visa card. Cleo would check with Detective Devereaux in the morning to see if he'd obtained a record of charges.

The mid-April afternoon had turned steamy by the time she locked the apartment door behind her. Her linen-blend blazer was showing the effects of the muggy heat. Tossing the wrinkled jacket into the back seat, she spent an unproductive twenty minutes with the apartment-complex manager.

The woman vaguely remembered Trish from when she'd moved in a little less than a year ago, but that was it. Security-camera sweeps of the common areas outside her apartment didn't help. No unusual traffic in or out of the apartment. No unfamiliar vehicles parked for long stretches of time in the slots near hers.

Phone calls to local numbers listed in the address book printout produced no leads. Most of them had already been contacted, first by Diane, then by the police. The MotoPhoto that had developed the starfish pix had no unclaimed rolls of film waiting for Trish. No one at the Wal-Mart Super Center remembered her face or her name.

Cleo's butt was dragging as she wove her way through the Wal-Mart parking lot toward the Escalade. Her abrupt encounter with the concrete floor of the locker room this morning was starting to make itself felt.

She was tempted to call it a day but decided to tie up one loose end. Easing into the SUV, she turned the air conditioner on full blast while she called for information on Weight Watchers clinics. She was in luck. The nearest location was only a few blocks from Trish's apartment complex and had a meeting scheduled to begin in a half hour.

The clinic was jammed. Long lines of men and women just coming off work waited to weigh in and get their cards stamped. Cleo worked her way to the front of the line and ignored the electronic scale.

"I'm Cleo North." She slid her P.I. license to the attendant behind the counter. "I'm looking for a woman by the name of Patricia Jackson. She's dropped out of sight and her family's worried about her."

"I'm sorry, I don't…"

"You might know her by the nickname Trish."

"Oh! Trish. She hasn't been in for several weeks. Not since…"

The woman clicked a few keys on her computer and squinted at the screen through the reading glasses perched on the end of her nose.

"Not since April 1."

A little crease formed between the attendant's brows. She pursed her lips, peered at the screen and swung her gaze back to Cleo.

"Did you say Trish is in some kind of trouble?"

"We don't know. She's disappeared. Why? Is there something in the computer about her?"

"I, uh, better get my supervisor."

An investigator who played by the book would wait patiently until the woman returned and then convince the supervisor of the gravity of the situation. One of the reasons Cleo and the air force had parted ways, though, was her tendency to bend, stretch or otherwise torque the rules.

She glanced through the glass window, saw

Counter Woman in consultation with Supervisor Lady, and leaned across the counter to sneak a peek.

She left the clinic a few minutes later, armed with the information that Weight Watchers had suspended Trish from its weight-loss program due to her stated belief she might be pregnant.

Chewing on her lower lip, Cleo made for the SUV. As much as she wanted to find Sloan's missing employee safe and unharmed, she didn't like the picture that was beginning to form.

She hoped to God this wasn't another Laci Peterson or Cherica Adams situation. Peterson's husband had been charged with murdering his wife and her unborn child. Adams's boyfriend, an ex-football player for the Carolina Panthers, was serving hard time for his role in the execution-style murder of his pregnant girlfriend. The bastard had arranged to have her killed to avoid paying child support. Doctors had saved the baby, but Cherica died a month later.

As yet there wasn't any evidence linking Trish's disappearance to her possible pregnancy, but Cleo's instincts were starting to rear their ugly heads.

The sun was a flaming red ball hanging just above the harbor when Cleo turned into the alley that led to Sloan Engineering's corporate guest house.

The two-story brick-and-stucco residence was located in the area depicted on the city map as High Battery. The slick little brochure tucked inside the folder with the key-card informed Cleo that the guest residence once served as stables and carriage house for a wealthy rice planter whose town residence was one of Charleston's showplaces. After the key card snicked in the lock and Cleo stepped inside, she felt her eyes pop.

"Whoa!"

Somehow she suspected the horses hadn't enjoyed this elegant mix of heart-pine flooring, washed-brick walls and exposed beam ceilings. Her boot heels sinking in what felt like two inches of carpet runner, she dropped her carryall and went exploring.

The downstairs included a living room furnished with period antiques and high-tech entertainment systems, a dining room with a well-stocked bar encased in an early-nineteenth-century sideboard, and a kitchen with, among many other shiny gizmos, the only appliance Cleo considered absolutely essential. After giving the coffeemaker a friendly pat, she took her bag upstairs.

The choice was between a monster of a suite at the front of the carriage house, complete with four-poster and Jacuzzi tub, or a smaller suite at the rear overlooking a handkerchief-size garden. The garden won hands down.

Drawn by the music of water splashing into the three-tiered, pineapple-topped stone fountain below, Cleo pushed open the French doors and plopped into one of the rocking chairs that marched along the balcony. Feathery ferns dripped from hanging pots and stirred in the breeze. The rocking chair creaked like an old friend. For a few moments she shelved her gathering concerns about Trish Jackson and simply soaked in the perfume of the evening.

"Now, this," she murmured, squeaking away, "is the way to live."

"I think so, too."

The amused drawl came from behind her. Her boot heels hit the porch floor with a thump. Some security expert she was. She hadn't bothered to check the guest house's alarm system, much less set it.

If all intruders came packaged the way Marc Sloan did, though, she might just leave the door wide open during her stay in Charleston. Forget Pierce Brosnan. In this setting, with the breeze ruffling his dark hair and his white dress shirt open at the neck, he was Rhett Butler incarnate. All he needed was a pencil-thin mustache to complete the image.

"I saw your car parked outside the carriage house," he said with a smile that was obviously intended to excuse his unauthorized entry. It worked for Cleo. "Thought I'd stroll over and see if you had everything you needed."

"Stroll over?"

"I live in the main residence just across the alley. I had the carriage house renovated to use as guest quarters when I bought the estate."

"Convenient."

"At times."

"This being one of them?"

"This being one of them."

In the deepening shadows she could barely make out the glint in his eyes. It was there, though. Too bad Cleo couldn't follow up on it. With a sigh of real regret, she pushed out of the rocking chair.

"Do you recall what you said this morning about not mixing business with pleasure?"

"Yes."

"Same goes."

Despite her liberal approach to rules in general, she did adhere to her own set of professional ethics. Jumping in the sack with a client the first day on the job was a definite no-no, particularly when she was starting to get a goosey feel about said client's exact relationship to his missing employee.

She needed to probe that relationship a little more but wanted to see Marc's face when she did. Casually, she slapped at a mosquito feasting on the underside of her arm.

"The natives are getting restless. Let's go inside and I'll give you an update on my afternoon activities."

"Why don't you update me over dinner?" he suggested as they took the stairs to the first floor. "My chef's prepared sugarcane shrimp in your honor. It's a local specialty and one of his best dishes."

Sugarcane shrimp sounded too good to pass

up. Adding spice to the dish was the opportunity to see Marc Sloan in his native habitat.

"Give me fifteen minutes to get unpacked and clean up."

"Just wander across the alley whenever you're ready."

She was ready in considerably less than fifteen minutes but used the spare time for a quick call to her father. Crossing her fingers that Patrick would pick up instead of his bride, Cleo hit speed dial.

The gods were conspiring against her. Wanda not only answered, she was still waffling over wallpaper.

"I just can't make up my mind whether to go with a print or a stripe for the guest room."

Surprise, surprise.

"What do you think, Cleo?"

"Why don't you hang a sample of each on opposite walls and see which works best for you?"

"I suppose I could do that. Although…"

Cleo smothered a sigh.

"Your father really likes the country-French mural sample I brought home. It doesn't go with the rest of the house, though."

Cleo had to smile at that. After a lifetime of travel, Patrick North had filled his retirement home with mementoes that included everything from an Egyptian obelisk to a water buffalo head. Oscar the water buffalo got relegated to the attic soon after Wanda moved in, but none of Patrick's remaining *objets de junk* would go with stripes, prints *or* country-French murals. For a moment, Cleo felt something dangerously close to sympathy for her stepmother.

"When will you be home?" Wanda asked.

"I'm not sure."

"Well, there's nothing pressing about this. I'll wait until you get back to Dallas to pick out the paper."

"Oh. Okay."

"Your dad just came upstairs. Here he is."

He picked up, wheezing a little. "Hey, kiddo."

"Hiya, Pop." Cleo hid her instant worry behind a breezy irreverence. "Sounds like you're puffing. Are you hitting the chocolate fudge sauce again?"

"Not hardly. Wanda's got me counting fat grams *and* carbs *and* calories. All I eat these days are raw carrots and ice cubes."

She knew that wasn't true but had to give her stepmother points for trying to curb her father's hearty appetite.

"What are you doing in Charleston?"

"Working a locate."

"Sounds pretty tame compared to some of your recent cases."

"It is."

So far, anyway.

"You sure you're feeling okay, Pop?"

He heaved a melodramatic sigh. "One little heart cramp, and a man can't even huff without everyone reaching for the nitro."

"Just take it easy, okay? And don't down too many Viagras."

It was a measure of their unique relationship that Patrick only laughed. He would no more discuss his love life with Cleo than she would hers with him.

Not that she had anything to discuss these days. The Texas Ranger outfielder she'd gotten involved with shortly after leaving the air force was now only a distant memory. The lawyer she'd been dating off and on for most of the last year had also bitten the dust.

Things had heated up considerably when Special Agent Jack Donovan had appeared in Santa Fe a few months ago. The embers were still alive, but fading fast.

"Come over when you get home," her father instructed. "We'll fire up the grill and do ribs."

"How about we do chicken or fish?"

"Whatever. *Tachi-dao*, kiddo."

"*Tachi-dao*, Pop."

They'd adopted the phrase years ago. Roughly translated, it meant *sharp sword* in the language of the Ryukyu Islands. Patrick had extracted the phrase from an ancient proverb that advised travelers to maintain vigilance and keep a sharp sword. For father and daughter, it was shorthand for *take care, stay safe, I love you*. The two simple words always put a smile in Cleo's heart.

It stayed with her as she headed downstairs and across the alley to Marc Sloan's house.

4

Crossing the passageway between the former carriage house and the main residence took Cleo from the merely elegant to the exquisite. She wasn't real up on formal gardens and colonial architecture, but the brickwork in the path leading through the roses and gardenias was as intricate as the leaded fanlights over the windows.

Marc met her at the front door, which happened to be at the side of the house. Wide brick steps led up to a porch flanked by Doric columns that soared for three stories and supported the upper piazzas. Inside the door was a circular staircase that spiraled upward with no visible means of support.

"The house was built in 1825," Marc said in answer to her question. "The original owner was a rice planter with considerable property upriver.

His father was one of the signers of the Declaration of Independence."

"No kidding?"

"No kidding. Interestingly, the owner's grandson was a cadet at the Citadel. Rumor has it he was one of the kids who took aim at a Union supply ship entering the harbor in January 1861, thus participating in the first barrage of the War of Succession. My father would have appreciated the irony," he added dryly. "The general was a connoisseur of such historical paradoxes."

The comment triggered a memory of a similar remark he'd made in Santa Fe. Evidently neither Marc nor his twin harbored warm, cuddly memories of the man who'd adopted them at birth.

"Would you like a drink before dinner? I mixed a pitcher of martinis but have been known to pour a mean Scarlett O'Hara."

"What is it, aside from redundant?"

"Southern Comfort with a splash of cranberry juice and a twist of lime. Delicious to look at, but tart and potent. Very much like you."

"Why, thank you, sir."

Batting her lashes, she did her best Texas-girl hair fluff. It was an acquired skill, since Cleo had only taken up permanent residence in the Lone Star State after leaving the air force.

"I'll have a martini. Straight up, with a twist."

Marc swept a hand toward a high-ceilinged room across the foyer. "The bar is in the music room."

Her brow hitched, but when she stepped into

the long hall she saw it really *was* a music room, complete with a cluster of lyre-backed chairs, music stands and a harp, for God's sake. The instrument was one of those big jobbers, taller than Cleo, with two thousand or so keys running down its spine or neck or whatever it was called.

"Do you play?" she asked, trying to picture Sloan with the harp between his knees.

"I take a stab at it occasionally." A grin slashed across his face. "When I'm feeling really pissed about life in general and marriage in particular. My first wife insisted we purchase the harp with the house. She thought it added to the ambience. I pluck the strings every once in a while as a reminder of what ambience can do to a marriage."

It wasn't the best lead-in, but Cleo grabbed it, anyway. While Marc gently swirled the contents of a sleek Baccarat martini pitcher, she dropped her bombshell.

"Speaking of relationships, I found out this afternoon Trish might be pregnant."

The pitcher stilled in mid-swirl. Slate-gray eyes locked on her face. "And you're wondering if the baby is mine?"

"The possibility occurred to me."

"Yes, I can see how it might."

The pitcher made another slow swirl. Filling two long-stemmed glasses, Sloan skewered an olive for one, swiped a lemon twist around the rim of the other, and carried both to where Cleo stood beside the harp.

"If Trish *is* pregnant, I'm not the father of her child." Tipping his head in a brief, mocking salute, he hoisted his glass. "Cheers."

Cleo did the same.

As the Tanqueray went down, though, Sloan's mockery disappeared. His brow creasing, he gave the toothpick spearing his olive a little flick. "Maybe when you find the father, you'll find Trish."

"Maybe."

"Where do you plan to look next?"

"I'm still working the basics. Phone bills. Grocery receipts. Doctor and pharmacy records."

"I thought medical records were confidential."

"They are, except in certain instances. The Health Privacy Act passed after 9/11 included provisions for obtaining information regarding possible crime victims."

Actually, the main provisions of the act had been aimed at gathering information on suspected terrorists, but terrorism wasn't Cleo's concern at the moment.

"The missing-persons report Trish's parents filed should give me access to her health records. I'm going to pick up a copy tomorrow morning, when I meet with the detective working the case."

"What time's your meeting?"

"Nine."

"I'll give Chief Benton another call later and make sure his detective affords you full cooperation."

"He sounded cooperative enough when I

spoke to him this afternoon. I'll let you know if I need help."

He got the message. Mr. Take-Charge Executive backed off, yielding his place to Smooth, Handsome Rich Guy.

"Point taken," he said with a smile every bit as potent as the gin.

The martini put Cleo in a mellow mood, but the sugarcane shrimp melted her into a puddle of mindless ecstasy.

Threaded on cane skewers and char-grilled with a tequila, honey and lime juice glaze, the succulent morsels melted in her mouth. They were served with jasmine rice and a long, stemmy vegetable that looked like a cross between asparagus and broccoli. Cleo wasn't into veggies as a rule, but these weren't bad. Not bad at all.

After dinner there was coffee and a wicked crème brûlée served on the screened-in piazza with a spectacular view of the harbor and a floodlit Fort Sumter. Sloan took the conversation from his brother's slow recovery from the bullet in his skull and the deal his assailant had cut with the feds, to some of his firm's latest projects.

"We just won a contract to convert Atlantic-class container vessels to SL-31-class ships. We're going to modify the hull and add additional power from a diesel-generated electric motor. It'll reduce the container capacity from four thousand TEU to just a little more than three."

"And that's good?"

"It is when the reduction is accompanied by a corresponding increase in speed from eighteen to twenty-one knots. Getting cargo where it's needed faster is the name of the game these days, particularly with our military forces engaged in hot spots around the globe."

That Cleo could understand. Her years in the air force had taken her to several of those hot spots.

"How much of your business is defense-related?"

"Almost eighty percent at present. Afghanistan and Iraq dramatically upped the demand for cargo vessels to augment the military's prepositioned fleet."

No surprise there. They talked about the war for a while, drawing on their separate military perspectives, before Cleo set aside her coffee cup.

"It's getting late. We both have busy days tomorrow. I'd better make it a night."

Sloan walked her through the gardens and across the alley to the carriage house. Cleo was all too aware of the warmth of his hand on her elbow—and the brush of his mouth over hers when they reached the door.

She was tempted to take him up on the unspoken offer that came with the kiss. Lord, she was tempted! He tasted of caramel crème brûlée, dark coffee and *very* hot, very interested male. She was already mentally kicking herself in the butt when she eased away.

"Thanks for dinner, Marc."

"You're welcome." Amusement added another

layer to his rich baritone. "You do realize we're going take this to the next stage one of these days?"

"I realize the possibility exists. I'll see you tomorrow."

Marc parted with her at the door. Reluctantly.

The contrast between Cleo North's enticing exterior and clever mind had intrigued him from the first moment they'd met. The subsequent discovery that she'd suspected his twin of murder had taken some of the edge from that fascination. But then she'd turned around and helped prove Alex's innocence. A woman of many facets, Ms. Cleopatra North.

He'd only needed a few moments with her this afternoon to feel the spark again. He still wanted her, and he was a man who got what he wanted. One way or another.

Shoving his hands in his slacks pockets, he whistled a few bars from *Aïda* and retraced his steps.

5

An annoying little ping dragged Cleo from sleep. She poked her head out from under silky cotton sheets and fumbled for the phone on the bedside stand. Since the stand was antique and almost as wide across as her kitchen table at home, it took her a couple of attempts to find the source of the irritating chirp.

Scowling at the light bars slanting through the plantation shutters, she stabbed the Talk button and jammed the instrument against her ear. She didn't do mornings well. Given the choice, she didn't do them at all. Not until she'd downed her third or fourth cup of coffee, anyway.

"What?"

The snarl produced a stark silence on the other end of the line. She gave it a couple of seconds. This happened a lot.

"Ms. North?"

She didn't recognize the voice. Propping herself up on one elbow, she tempered her tone to a semi-growl.

"Yeah. Who's this?"

"Thomas Gerard, Mr. Sloan's chef. He advised me you have a nine o'clock appointment this morning and suggested I call to ascertain your wishes regarding breakfast."

She was ready to tell him she didn't do breakfast when he said the magic words.

"I've prepared my special blend of cinnamon mocha café au lait."

That was close enough to real coffee to get her attention. What followed made her feel almost cheerful.

"I've also baked a fresh batch of croissants to accompany the eggs Florentine. Or, of course, you may order any other dish you prefer."

If this guy's eggs came anywhere close to his shrimp, Cleo wanted in. "Croissants and eggs Florentine sound good."

"Shall I have a table set on the piazza? The view is quite lovely in the mornings."

"Whatever Mr. Sloan wants."

"Mr. Sloan is out for his morning run. He'll join you when he returns."

"Then the piazza it is. Put the coffeepot on the table, please. I'll be there in ten minutes."

Driven by the beast inside that craved caffeine, she reduced her already minimal morning routine to the absolute essentials. Her shower took all of six minutes. Pulling on jeans and a red tank top, she wrapped her hair in a mango-colored towel and thrust her feet into flip-flops. A few quick swipes with a toothbrush banished the overnight fuzz, but flossing would have to wait until she fed the monster.

Although it was barely seven-thirty, the warm April sun had already coaxed a heady perfume from the gardenias lining the brick walk. The star-shaped white blossoms had massed so thick they almost obscured the dark, glossy foliage. Cleo sniffed appreciatively, but it wasn't until she dropped into one of the wrought-iron chairs on the piazza and gulped down her first cup that all systems became fully functional.

One of Mr. Gerard's minions materialized with a basket of croissants that still had steam rising from it. Cleo devoured two before the eggs Florentine appeared. Ordinarily, she wasn't into spinach for breakfast—or any other meal, for that matter. Last night's adventure with the broccoli-asparagus had her reconsidering her general philosophy regarding green stuff.

This particular green stuff went down like ambrosia of the gods. The grated Gruyere cheese and white sauce topping the spinach helped. So did the thick slab of sugar-cured ham and sweet green grapes that accompanied the dish. She had just popped another grape into her mouth when Marc strolled onto the piazza.

Cleo almost choked. Smooth, Handsome Rich Guy was gone. So was Mr. Take-Charge Executive. In their place was Sweaty Hunk. He wore an old gray sweatshirt with the sleeves ripped out and running shorts that showed long stretches of hairy thigh. Cleo couldn't remember the last time she'd seen so much glistening male muscle.

Wait. Yes, she could. Four months ago in Santa Fe, to be exact. And the slimeball had zinged off only a couple of e-mails since.

Pasting on a smile, she tipped Sweaty Hunk a greeting. "Morning. How was your run?"

"Too short, but I've got a meeting with some Japanese investors to get to. How was your breakfast?"

"There aren't enough superlatives in the English language to describe Mr. Gerard. Whatever you pay him, you should double it."

"I have. Twice."

Dragging up a corner of the towel draped around his neck, Sloan swiped his forehead. "Mind if I join you? I'll sit downwind."

She waved an airy hand. "It's your piazza."

His buns hadn't even touched wrought iron before the same efficient minion who'd served Cleo appeared with his breakfast and a fresh pot of coffee. High test this time, thank God. This au-lait business was okay but didn't produce quite the same kick as the real stuff. She helped herself to another cup while Sloan poured skim milk into his cereal and sprinkled Sweet 'n Low on the flakes.

"What's this? Croissants and poached eggs for me, Special K for you?"

"Fine wine and gourmet meals are all part of the plan. It won't work if I put on a paunch in the process, though."

She figured she knew the answer, but asked the question, anyway. "Okay, I'll bite. What plan?"

"To finesse you into bed," he confirmed between crunchy spoonfuls.

Cleo tapped a fingernail against her cup. "Interesting that you waited until one of your employees went missing to implement this plan."

"Alex needed me," he said, making no excuses.

She knew his twin's recovery and rehab had consumed Sloan for a good chunk of the past few months, just as debriefing the traitor who'd shot Alex had consumed a certain air force special agent. But it was comforting to know at least *one* of them had moved getting Cleo into the sack up a notch on their agendas.

She clicked her nail against the cup again, wondering why she balked at letting Sloan press ahead with his scheme to seduce her. Maybe after she'd answered the questions swirling around in her mind about his relationship to Trish Jackson, she'd rethink this business about not getting involved with clients. A girl could only go so long before her batteries lost their juice.

"Hello, Marc."

The greeting floated from inside the house. Diane Walker floated out a few seconds later.

"I brought the contract by for you—"

Ms. Super Efficiency stopped abruptly just inside the tall double doors opening onto the piazza. Her glance cut from her employer, sprawled at his ease in shorts and sweatshirt, to Cleo, all cuddly in mango towel turban and flip-flops.

"Excuse me." A touch of frost coated the words. "Is this an inconvenient time to go over the Mitsubishi contract before your meeting with the Japanese investors?"

"Not at all. Cleo and I are just finishing breakfast. Come join us."

"Thank you, but I've already eaten." She unbent enough to produce a cool smile. "I'll have some coffee, though."

While Sloan signaled for another cup, Cleo pushed back her chair. "I'll leave you two to Mitsubishi. I have to hustle to make my appointment with Detective Devereaux."

Her shower shoes slapping on the tiles, she made her way toward the door at the end of the piazza.

Diane fought for control as she followed the woman's progress. Acid rolled around her stomach, every bit as corrosive as the compounds Sloan Engineering's dry-dock workers used to clean the hulls of ocean-going cargo vessels. Somehow, she managed to keep it out of her voice as she swung her gaze to the man opposite her.

"Another conquest, Marc?"

"Not yet."

He flicked a glance at the retreating figure. A smile played at the corners of his lips.

"Soon, though."

She might as well be invisible, Diane thought on a wave of resentment so bitter it closed her throat. She'd worked with the man for fifteen years, had loved him desperately for almost as long, and he still didn't see her.

She'd chucked a fat pension at Northrop to help him start Sloan Engineering. They'd built the company together, from the ground up. Along the way, she'd tamed her frizzy curls into a sleek bob, had gone for LASIK surgery to get rid of the glasses that used to perch at the end of her nose, and learned to dress like a model. An older, more mature model, maybe, but one who still turned heads when she walked into a room.

Every head but Marc's. If the fool would look at her, just *look* at her, he might see the living, breathing woman behind the machine that ran his office.

But, no! His tastes ran to younger, brighter, bolder women.

Like this Cleo North.

The acid took another roll and rose in Diane's throat. She fought it down. All these years she'd watched Marc move from one quarry to the next, almost without taking a breath in between. She'd learned to mask her feelings, was so good at it he never suspected her frustration and pain each time he moved in on new prey.

But she was getting tired of standing in the shadows, watching him bag trophy after trophy. And God knew she wasn't getting any younger.

Maybe it was time she updated her résumé, she thought with a pain that was like a knife blade through her heart. She'd put everything she had into Sloan Engineering. Mentally. Physically. Financially. But she'd be damned if she'd stand by, twiddling her thumbs, while Marc went after yet another prize. Pulling the thick contract from her briefcase, she slapped it on the table.

"Page twelve—clause 16C needs to be revised to include the latest welding estimates."

Five minutes after meeting Detective Sergeant Lafayette Devereaux, Cleo had discovered he was directly descended from South Carolina's most notorious black pirate and had once served in the same Special Ops unit as her personal trainer.

"Yeah, I talked to Goose last night, after I made the connection between you two."

The drawl was down-home southern. The smile came with a display of blindingly white teeth.

"Just out of curiosity," Cleo asked, "how did you make that connection?"

"Goose and I keep in touch."

That's all he would say. The Special Ops guys were like that, she remembered from her air force days. Most communicated in monosyllabic grunts that could convey anything from sexual ecstasy to the imminent demise of whoever they happened to have in their crosshairs.

"So what have you got on Trish Jackson?" she asked, helping herself to a doughnut from the green-and-white box Devereaux nudged across his desk. She'd waged a fierce battle with the snap on her jeans after pigging out last night and this morning, but these were Krispy Kremes.

"Still nothing," the detective replied. "I'm almost through making calls and about to start pounding on neighbors' doors again."

"How about going with me to pound on a couple of doctors' doors first?"

"What doctors and why?"

"I found out Trish may be pregnant."

The genial smile fell off Devereaux's face. "How did you get that?"

"I spotted a Weight Watchers water jug in her kitchen and checked with the clinic in her neighborhood. Turns out she had to drop out of the program due to a possible pregnancy."

"I'll be damned." Devereaux inhaled the remains of his chocolate-sprinkle combo and swiped a few stray crumbs from his shirtfront. "Goose said you were good."

"He did?"

Basking in those rare words of praise, Cleo munched her way through a maple glaze. "I'm hoping Trish consulted with either her family practitioner or OB-GYN," she said between bites. "The doc could give us a lead to the father."

"Who in turn could give us a lead to Ms. Jackson's whereabouts."

"Exactamundo."

Devereaux flipped through the printout on his desk. "I didn't see her physicians' names in her computer address book. Must have missed them."

"No sweat. I got 'em off the prescriptions in her medicine chest."

"We're good to go, then."

Lifting his bulk from his chair, the detective snagged his seersucker sport coat. Cleo started out of the office, hesitated and swung back for another maple glaze.

Trish was evidently a healthy young woman. She hadn't visited her family doctor in more than a year. She had, however, brought a urine sample into her OB-GYN to verify the results of a home-pregnancy test just a few days before she went missing.

"She waited for the results," the nurse related after Detective Devereaux charmed her with his dazzling smile and a copy of the missing-persons report. "She seemed more excited than apprehensive when they came back positive."

"Did she share any information about the father? Like a name or an address?"

"Not that I recall. We ask for a detailed medical history of both parents to determine whether or not there might be complications during pregnancy. The patient usually supplies that information prior to her first prenatal visit with Dr. Rasmussen. Trish might have called the father, though. She was certainly eager to share her news with someone."

"Excuse me?"

"She asked to use the phone here at my station to make a quick call. I went to take the vitals on another patient, so I didn't catch any of the conversation."

Cleo and Devereaux exchanged a quick glance. The detective would have to get a subpoena to obtain an official phone-company record of all calls made from this number. There was a faster way, thank goodness—one Cleo resorted to frequently in her line of work.

"Does this clinic pay the phone bill electronically?" she asked the nurse.

"I think so. Yes, I'm sure we do."

"Good. Your office administrator can go online and print us out a list of all calls made from this number."

List in hand, Cleo and Devereaux manned their cell phones. Most of the calls made from the nurses' station at the approximate time of Trish's appointment were traced to labs, medical suppliers or patients, who verified conversations with Dr. Rasmussen's nurse on the date in question. None, Cleo noted, traced back to Marc Sloan, Diane Walker or Sloan Engineering.

Only one number came up blank. The service at that number had been deactivated a few days ago. Prior to deactivation, it had been registered to Frank Helms at 312 Harbor Drive, Unit 6B.

When Dr. Rasmussen's nurse confirmed they had no patient by the name of Helms or one who listed him as a contact, Cleo and Devereaux headed back to the Charleston PD to run a check on the man.

A name alone wasn't enough for a NCIC check. The National Crime Information Center database required a minimum of two identifiers, such as date of birth or social security number. But Devereaux could—and did—run him through the Charleston police department's records bureau.

The screen produced no hits.

Strangely, a check of various non-crime-related databases came up blank as well. A detailed search was impossible without a social security number, but still it was odd that a sweep of credit bureaus, utility accounts and the DMV returned no one with that name and address.

"Looks like we've got us a mystery boy here," Devereaux commented.

"Looks like," Cleo agreed, trying to ignore the last doughnut. The damned thing sat in a pool of hardened grease, shouting *Cleo, Cleo, Cleo*.

"Harbor Drive is only a few blocks from here. Pricey neighborhood for a guy with no apparent financial assets. Want to ride along while I canvass the neighbors?"

Cleo did better than ride along. Fueled by another injection of sugar and grease, she worked the residences to the east of Frank Helms's waterfront condo while Lafayette worked the west.

A woman in red spandex and a sweatband answered the second bell Cleo rang. The jogger didn't recognize Trish from the photo but remembered the man who'd rented the condo two doors down from hers.

"He pretty much kept to himself. I only spoke to him a couple of times, at the mail center. He had a definite accent. British-sounding, although he looked more…"

"More?"

"More exotic. Olive skin. Dark eyes."

Cleo jotted down the details, took the woman's name and phone number, and compared notes with Devereaux. He'd turned up almost the same information.

A visit to the agency that managed the property produced even more intriguing results. Seems British-Accent Guy had rented the condo fully furnished and paid the hefty security deposit in cash. He'd also plunked down three months' advance rent.

"He was new in town," the agent explained, fidgeting in his plush leather chair. "Said he needed a place right away. The condo was available for immediate occupancy. The owner keeps the utilities in his name and turned on for just that reason. So I, uh…"

"So you pocketed a hefty lease-signing bonus and ran only a cursory background check," Devereaux finished dryly. "I don't suppose you followed up when the financial references Mr. Helms supplied came back as unknown or unavailable."

"Well..."

"Christ! What rock have you been living under since 9/11? Don't you get even a little suspicious when a man slaps down a wad of cash and provides no verifiable references?"

The agent's face went gray. "You think Helms is a terrorist?"

"We don't know what he is," Devereaux returned, his voice disgusted. "Just give me a copy of the rental agreement."

Cleo departed the Charleston police headquarters a little after three. Devereaux would have to subpoena the phone records for the calls made to and from Frank Helms's condo. Until they came through, he had to work the other cases stacked up on his desk.

"I'll let you know if I come up with anything," he told Cleo.

"Same here," she promised.

Since police headquarters was only a few miles from Sloan Engineering, she decided to stop in and update Marc on the day's developments. She wheeled into the underground garage, pulled into her reserved space and buzzed for the elevator. It pinged its way up from the lower two parking levels and opened with a full complement already on board.

"'Scuse me, folks."

Wedging inside, Cleo hit the button for the seventh floor. As the glass cage worked its way upward, she collected her thoughts. She had confirmation Trish was pregnant. A phone call to a pricey condo. A rental agreement signed by a man who didn't pop in any police or civilian databases. Not much to report, but the case was certainly starting to take on some interesting hues.

Slowly, the elevator emptied. Two smartly dressed women got off on floor three. A clerk on five. Three men in business suits on six. The doors swished shut. The elevator started for seven.

Suddenly, an arm reached past Cleo. A blunt finger stabbed the red emergency stop button. In the next heartbeat, the hand had snaked around her waist and yanked her back against a hard slab of a chest.

6

Caught against an unknown assailant, Cleo kicked instantly into fight mode. Before she could execute any of her more lethal moves, however, the arm banding her waist shifted and a warm breath tickled her ear.

"Feels like you've shed a few pounds, Cleopatra Aphrodite."

The deep, laughing drawl checked her initial instinct to inflict bodily harm. The use of her much-despised middle name had her rethinking that check. Disgusted, she shook free and swung around.

"Dammit, Donovan! Do you have any idea how close you just came to singing soprano?"

Major Jack Donovan, chief of the Criminal Operations Division at headquarters, Air Force Office of Special Investigations, grinned down at her.

"Yeah, I do. I've tangled with you before, remember?"

She remembered. She most definitely remembered. But Donovan must have decided she needed a refresher course. Planting a hand against the elevator panel behind her, he swooped in for a kiss.

Okay. All right. Cleo could admit it. A mere glimpse of Donovan's sun-streaked tawny hair and those squinty little laugh lines at the corners of his blue eyes was enough to get her hot. But the feel of his mouth on hers did things to her female organs she wasn't about to acknowledge—particularly considering the weeks that had elapsed since the bastard had rung her bells like this.

It took a moment or two for her to realize that the clanging in her ears came from without, not within. The elevator was sending out distress signals loud enough to wake the dead. Or at least the security guard at the other end of the camera mounted high in the glass cage.

The clanging cut off. A gruff, disembodied voice floated through a hidden speaker. "This is Sloan Security. Is there a problem?"

"No problem," Donovan replied, his mouth still playing with Cleo's. "The elevator just stopped."

"Hold on. I'll hit Restart."

The glass cage gave another little jolt and resumed its upward glide. When the doors whooshed open a second or two later, Cleo had herself mostly together.

"What the heck are you doing in Charleston?" she demanded as she and Donovan stepped into the hallway of the executive suite.

"I just flew in. I'm here to see your pal, Sloan. What are *you* doing here?"

She suspected he wouldn't be real thrilled with the answer. Jack had witnessed the moves Sloan had made on her in Santa Fe. He hadn't liked them then. He wouldn't like them now.

Tough noogies.

"I'm working a case for Marc."

She'd guessed right. There was a definite cooling in Donovan's attitude. "What kind of case?"

"One of his employees is missing. He brought me in to find her."

"That so?"

He hitched his thumbs in the pockets of his black slacks. He'd dressed in one of his more sophisticated special agent uniforms for this meeting, Cleo noted. Black loafers to match the trousers. Gray gabardine sport coat. Sunshine-yellow, button-down oxford shirt. He'd even knotted on a tie.

Cleo carried a different set of images of this man around in her head. The most vivid sprang from their days in Honduras. Donovan's face smeared with jungle paint. His assault rifle spitting rounds at the dopers who'd opened fire on them. His jaw locked as Cleo dug a bullet out of his right shoulder.

His belly muscles rippling as she straddled his thighs two days later.

That particular memory caused her own stomach muscles to do some serious rippling. Gulping, she covered the sensation with a grin. "Interesting that we both turn up in Charleston at the same time."

"You know what the Old Man says about coincidence. It just don't…"

"…happen in our line of work," she chorused.

That was one of the OSI commander's favorites, she remembered. Along with several others that didn't bear repeating in public.

Cleo had heard 'em all, though. General Barnes, commander of the Air Force Office of Special Investigations, hadn't minced words the various times he'd ordered Lieutenant North to headquarters. She still wasn't sure who'd been more relieved when she decided to turn in her badge, Barnes or her immediate supervisor at the time, who swore she'd turned his hair gray with her unorthodox investigative techniques.

Then again, those same unorthodox techniques had broken some tough cases. They'd also busted a billion-dollar procurement fraud that went back years and put the squeeze on two former secretaries of Defense. That little exercise had earned Special Agent Cleo North a Meritorious Service Medal. The expression on General Barnes's face when he'd pinned on the medal constituted one of Cleo's favorite moments from her years in uniform.

Smiling at the memory, she turned and pushed at the etched-glass door to the executive suite. The workers in the outer office recognized her and merely nodded as she led the way into the inner suite of offices.

Diane Walker glanced up at their entrance. Her gaze slid from Cleo to Jack and back again. "Is Marc expecting you, Ms. North?"

"No, he isn't."

Cleo tipped the man beside her a curious glance. A favorite technique among investigators was to show up unannounced, catch a suspect off guard and get him talking before he gathered his wits enough to lawyer up.

"How about you, Jack? Is Marc expecting you?"

Eyes glinting, he acknowledged the unsubtle probe. "Yes, he is."

He slid a hand into his coat pocket, produced the black leather case containing his credentials and introduced himself to Sloan's executive assistant. "I'm Special Agent Jack Donovan, with the Air Force Office of Special Investigations. My secretary called earlier this morning to arrange a meeting for me with your boss."

His gold OSI shield gave Cleo a funny little twinge. She'd carried one just like it for years. She didn't miss the paperwork and bureaucratic hassle that came with being an air force investigative agent. She did miss the authority packed into those few ounces of metal, though.

Diane Walker responded to that authority with her characteristic efficiency. "Oh, yes, Mr. Donovan. Mr. Sloan is expecting you. Unfortunately, he had to attend a city council planning meeting that ran late. He's on his way back to the office and should be here shortly. Would you like something to drink while you wait?"

"Coffee would be great. Black, three sugars."

"Ms. North?"

"I'll have coffee, too. Black, no sugars."

With a flick of an intercom button, Walker relayed the order. The bright young subordinate on the other end in turn relayed the information that Dubai was holding for her on line two.

"I'm sorry. I need to take this call. Would you care to wait in the conference room? I'll have your coffee brought there."

The vista from the seventh floor had already worked its magic on Cleo. Settling into one of the chairs lined up around the massive conference table, she waited while Jack shoved his hands in his pockets and drank in the stunning view of the harbor and the Atlantic beyond.

She drank in his posterior view. She couldn't help but note the way his sport coat molded a set of linebacker's shoulders. And the way the back vent parted to display his nice, tight butt. Recalling how many weeks had passed since she'd skimmed her nails over those iron buns, she cleared her throat.

"So how's the debrief going?"

The question brought him around. His gaze locked with hers across the acre or so of mahogany.

"We finished the debrief three weeks ago."

She was damned if she was going to ask why he hadn't bothered to call her. The question hung between them, though, like a hot-air balloon hovering right over the conference table.

"I was going to hop a plane to Dallas," Jack said slowly.

She lifted a polite brow. "But?"

"But my ex-wife called. From the Cincinnati PD drunk tank."

The little knot of irritation Cleo had toted around for the past several weeks eased. She didn't know much about Jack's ex. He'd never talked about the former Mrs. Donovan.

The OSI was like one big frat house, though. Good news worked its way slowly through the ranks of agents, but dirt got passed around at the speed of light. Well before Cleo and Jack had worked their first op together, she'd heard that his marriage was on ice.

Rumor had it the bust-up had been painful and long in coming. Ditto the reconciliation that had lasted less than a year. From the sound of it, Donovan's ex was still reaching out to him.

"Bad scene, huh?"

"Yeah, bad scene."

Both the tone and the shrug said "end of discussion." Cleo took the hint and didn't probe. The timely arrival of a fresh-faced assistant with their coffee gave them both the chance to fall back and regroup.

"So what's up with you and Marc Sloan?" she

asked, reaching for the sleek stainless-steel carafe. "Or can you tell me?"

"I'm here to talk to Sloan about the ocean-going cargo vessels he retrofitted for the air force."

"Huh?" The carafe stopped in midair. "Since when does the air force have ocean-going cargo vessels?"

"Since it got heavy into the APP. The Afloat Prepositioning Program," he added at her blank look.

Cleo vaguely recalled hearing about the program during her air force years. She knew it involved supersize cargo ships packed with military equipment and placed on station in the Atlantic, Pacific and Mediterranean. That was about it, though.

"I thought the navy ran the APP."

"The navy's Military Sealift Command acts as executive agent. But we manage the three ships dedicated to air force use. They're handled by the Ogden Air Logistics Center."

Hooting, she thumped the carafe back onto the tray.

"That's what I *loved* about the military. Nothing like designating a logistics center smack in the middle of landlocked Utah to manage a fleet of ocean-going cargo vessels."

The rigid set to Jack's shoulders relaxed. An answering grin tugged at his lips. But before he could issue a defense of military logic, the door to the conference room opened again and Sloan strolled in.

With a single assessing glance, Marc took in the sight of Cleo tipped back in her chair, laughing up at the man she'd tumbled into bed with in Santa Fe.

Marc didn't slow his stride. His smile remained easy. But Cleo suspected that the primitive instincts of a male on the hunt were razoring through his gut.

"Hello, Donovan. Sorry I kept you waiting."

After shaking hands with Jack, he gave Cleo a slow smile.

"Hello, Brown Eyes. How did your meeting go? The one you told me about at breakfast?"

It didn't take a Dr. Phil to interpret Jack's reaction to the cozy shared-breakfast bit. His facial muscles didn't so much as twitch, but the air in the conference room suddenly got heavy.

"The meeting produced some unexpected results," Cleo replied into the charged silence. "I'll brief you after you finish your business with Jack."

"Whatever that business is." Sloan turned to Donovan with a look of cool inquiry. "I assume it has to do with whatever information you've managed to extract from Alex's assailant."

"Actually, it has to do with the Afloat Prepositioning Program. I need to verify when you last accessed the APP database."

The engineer's eyes narrowed. Cleo could see he was trying to make the leap from the person who'd put a bullet into his brother's skull to an ocean-going resupply system managed by an air logistics center in Utah.

"Are you conducting an official inquiry concerning the APP?"

"It's still just a preliminary verification of facts at this point."

The distinction didn't appear to reassure Sloan. He was a former naval officer. He knew how the military investigative services worked. Preliminary fact-finding was only a step away from the real thing.

With so much of his company's work defense-related, Sloan had to cooperate or risk becoming the subject of a formal investigation—*not* a good move if he hoped to pull down other lucrative government contracts.

"I'll have to check my computer log," he said, all business now. "As best I can recall, the last time I accessed the APP was a month or so ago, when the Navy Sealift Command requested an updated set of schematics for one of the cargo ships we retrofitted for them. May I ask why you need this information?"

"Because the DNA signature on file for you was used recently to gain access to a highly classified portion of the database."

Sloan's brows snapped together. "How recently?"

"Yesterday."

"That's impossible. I didn't go into the APP yesterday."

"Someone did, and they used your DNA signature to get in."

"You'll have to give me a little more to go on," the executive bit out. "What portion of the database was accessed, and at what specific time?"

Donovan countered with a question. Another standard investigative technique. Find out what the suspect knows, but tell him as little as possible.

"How familiar are you with the APP operation at the Ogden Air Logistics Center?"

"I know it manages the three cargo ships dedicated to the air force. Their computers track every weapon—five-hundred-pound bombs, air-to-surface missiles, cluster bombs—shipped to the loading facility just north of here."

Surprise had Cleo popping out a question. "The ships are loaded here in Charleston?"

"About a hundred miles north, in North Carolina. At the Sunny Point Military Ocean Terminal."

Sloan's mind was obviously racing ahead of his words. Frowning, he drummed his fingers on the conference table.

"The exact breakdown of the munitions packages loaded onto each ship is classified. As you might expect, the military doesn't particularly want outsiders to know what mix of armaments they have floating around on the high seas."

Particularly, Cleo thought on a swift breath, if that mix had been specially packaged to support an upcoming operation or incursion.

She began to appreciate the scope of the problem. She also understood why the air force had dispatched one of its top agents to investigate a possible breach of the APP database.

"Was that what was accessed?" Sloan asked. "The current air force packaging?"

"Possibly."

The noncommittal response tightened Sloan's jaw. "When, specifically, did this unauthorized incursion take place?"

That Jack answered. "Last night, at 6:12 Ogden time."

"Which would be 8:12 eastern time. It wasn't me, Donovan. I was otherwise occupied at the time."

"You have a witness who can confirm that?"

"Yes, I do."

"And that would be?"

Uh-oh. Cleo braced herself. She suspected Donovan wouldn't appreciate the candlelight-and-shrimp scenario any more than he had the cozy breakfast bit.

To her surprise, Sloan didn't jump on the opportunity to score more points. Instead, he took control of the interview. Or tried to.

"I'll supply the witness if and when it becomes necessary. At the moment, I'm more concerned with how someone obtained the DNA signature I filed for access to the APP."

"Right," Jack drawled. "Let's talk about that. You and your brother are identical twins, which means your DNA profile is also identical. Therefore you couldn't use your own DNA when you applied for access to the APP. The system requires a strand that can't be matched or duplicated by another living human."

"You've done your homework."

"Yes, I have. What I couldn't determine from the records, though, is exactly whose DNA you supplied when you established your signature."

"I used the general's. General Sloan's."

"Let me make sure I have this right. The DNA you supplied Ogden in your initial request for access to the Afloat Prepositioning database belonged to your dead father?"

"It belonged to the man who adopted Alex and me," Marc corrected. "Neither of us has any idea who our real father was."

Donovan pulled out a pen and notebook. "What was the exact sample source? Hair? Teeth? Fingernail clippings?"

"In accordance with the general's express wish, his remains were cremated immediately after his death. Neither Alex nor I saved any body parts as personal mementos."

"You saved something." The pen clicked. Once. Twice. "What was it?"

When the silence stretched, the trained investigator in Cleo zoomed into high gear. There had to be a reason for Sloan's reluctance to admit to the source of the DNA. Her first thought was he'd collected a vial of his father's blood, voluntarily or otherwise. Her second, that he'd preserved a urine sample. Or possibly excrement.

She could think of a dozen reasons why he would save a DNA sample, besides the one presently under discussion. Maybe the Sloan brothers had anticipated a legal battle over the general's estate, if he'd left one. Maybe they thought the volumes he'd published on ancient warfare would put him in the same category as Thucydides or Machiavelli one of these days, thereby making his DNA a scholarly treasure.

Or maybe Sloan's reasons were more macabre. His few references to his father had suggested anything but a loving relationship.

Cleo's fertile mind was conjuring up all kinds of potential uses for a dead father's DNA, not excluding high-tech voodoo dolls designed to keep a soul writhing in hell for all eternity, when Sloan abruptly invited them into his office.

"I keep the DNA source in my safe."

Ugh! The mere *possibility* he might store fifteen-year-old excrement in his office safe put the suave executive in a whole different light.

7

Since Donovan didn't invite her to butt out, Cleo tagged along when the two men adjourned to the inner sanctum. Her pupils took a moment to adjust to the dazzling afternoon sunlight streaming through the angled glass panels.

Her mind took a moment longer to make sense of Sloan's actions when he crossed his office and slapped a palm against one of the floor-to-ceiling panels. To Cleo's astonishment, the window retracted to reveal another room beyond.

"What the heck…?"

"I had the windows in this inner office specially manufactured to refract the light," Sloan explained. "They were also placed at angles to produce a one-way, mirror-type effect. Essentially, this room is invisible from both the interior of my office and the outside of the building."

He had that right. Squinting through one of the other windows, Cleo saw nothing but sunlight and glass reflected back at her.

"What is it?" she asked. "Some sort of corporate safe room?"

"Exactly."

Cautiously, she slid a foot over the threshold. With glass on either side of her, she couldn't shake the eerie sensation of stepping into a chamber suspended in midair. The boats chugging along in the harbor directly below only added to the sensation.

When two well-muscled males followed her into the room, Cleo fought the impulse to throw out both palms and brace herself against the glass wall. Her rational mind told her an engineer of Sloan's obvious abilities wouldn't design a safe room that would plunge earthward with the addition of another four hundred or so pounds. Her not-so-rational mind screamed for a parachute.

"There's an elevator behind that panel," Sloan indicated with a nod to a side wall.

"Let me guess," Jack said. "The shaft doesn't appear on any architectural plans or building specs."

"Correct."

Considering the number of disgruntled employees who brought Uzis to work these days, Cleo figured an escape hatch was probably smart of Sloan.

Then again, a hidey-hole like this would come in

handy if a man wanted to dally with the hired help. Or slip out of the building unseen by said help.

"How many folks know about this safe room?" she asked.

"Only a handful of my top security personnel. And Diane, of course. Her infrared-heat signature will also activate the release. It won't, however, get her into the safe. Excuse me a moment."

Another palm slap, another panel, another hidden room. This one was a mere closet and lined floor to ceiling with steel-encased strongboxes. The second glass panel slid shut behind Sloan.

He reappeared some moments later with a small, pod-shaped case. To Cleo's relief, he carried it onto terra firma. Donovan followed, and she sort of crabbed her way out. With a silent glide, the glass slid into place behind her.

"I gave this to the general for Christmas one year," Sloan said. "It's the only possession of his I retained after his death."

Sloan's voice was even and his expression flat. He flicked the small brass latch on the leather case, revealing a pipe with an ivory bowl carved to resemble the head of some Greek god.

"He fired it up twice, but it didn't draw as well as his old Briar. So he gave it back to me and told me to return it and try to recoup my money."

Cleo wondered how old Marc had been when his father had been so callous.

"The DNA came from the saliva residue in the stem," he informed Donovan. "I'm sure you'll find plenty left to run it against the signature used to access the database."

Cleo's mind sped off in another direction. "Just out of curiosity, how long does old saliva hang around in a pipe stem?"

"Forever, I would assume."

Her glance zinged to Jack. He responded with a wry grin that told her he was thinking the same thing she was. His current boss—the same general who had strongly suggested Cleo turn in her OSI shield years ago—collected pipes. Some of them were centuries old. The Old Man smoked 'em, too.

Lord, she'd love to be a fly on the wall when Jack told General Barnes he might be sucking in DNA from some scurvy-ridden eighteenth-century sailor or pox-ridden London merchant!

To her delight, it turned out she *would* be there, in print if not in person. Before Jack took possession of the pipe nestled in the felt-lined case, he produced a plastic evidence bag, a property receipt and a chain-of-custody log.

"I'll need you to sign a receipt for the property," he informed Sloan. "Cleo, you can sign as witness."

Well, now she knew why he'd allowed her to remain present while he conducted his preliminary inquiry. Not because they went way back. Not because she was a former OSI agent and therefore fairly reliable. Not even because they'd mixed a little spit themselves once or twice. But because Major Jack Donovan was a rules kind of guy.

The paperwork attended to, he sealed the pipe in the bag and attached the tamper-proof plastic lock before signing and dating it. Cleo added her signature and the date just under his.

"I'll take the pipe to a lab here in Charleston and have them extract a sample," Donovan informed Sloan. "I'll see it gets returned to you."

The evidence bag went into his jacket pocket. As he dug out a business card and left it with Sloan, a dozen questions tumbled through Cleo's head. She wanted to know more about this DNA-signature business. She also itched to hear a few specifics on the APP breach.

Even more compelling was the goosey feeling she got from watching Donovan walk out the door. The way things worked between them, she might not see or hear from the man for another three or four or God knew how many months.

"Hang on a sec," she said to Sloan. "I'll be right back."

She caught Jack in the outer office. Under the politely curious eyes of Sloan's staff, she tugged him to a private corner.

"How long are you going to be in Charleston?"

"Just today. I only flew in to talk to Sloan and collect a DNA sample."

"Oh. Right."

"There's a lot of high-level interest in this APP incident. More than I can talk to you about, Cleo."

"I get it, Donovan."

He blew out a breath. "I didn't know you were in Charleston. If I had…"

"Yes?"

"I might have scheduled a later flight back to D.C."

Cleo knew the kind of pressure he operated under. She'd also sensed the possible global ramifications of the case he was now working. Still, something more than a few hours squeezed in before the man jumped a flight back to D.C. would have been nice.

"I have to brief my client on his missing employee," she replied, hiding her disappointment. "See you around, Donovan."

Jack mentally kicked ass all the way down to the parking garage. His own. Sloan's. A certain former air force special agent's.

He knew damned well his reaction to watching Sloan put his hand on Cleo had been pure Neanderthal. It had also been completely irrational. Jack was the one who'd let the weeks slip by without calling her.

So bailing his ex out of another drunk tank had tied him in guilty knots? So Kate still blamed him for the pit she'd fallen into? Cleo wasn't Kate. She was *nothing* like Kate. She couldn't do clingy and helpless and tortured if her life depended on it. Nor would she give up her career for his. Jack wouldn't ask it of her.

He hadn't asked it of Kate, either, he remembered with a kink in his stomach. But every move to a different state required her recertification as a teacher. Every new school system had its backlog of applicants. Boredom and loneliness and increasing resentment of the weeks and months Jack's job took him away from home had taken their toll on his wife.

He knew it would be different with Cleo. Despite the guilt that still gnawed at his insides, he told himself they'd handle things differently. If and when they ever got a chance to put the matter to the test, that is.

Given last night's security breach, that didn't appear likely to happen anytime soon. Jack would be on a plane back to Washington as soon as he delivered the DNA sample to the lab. God knew he'd barely had time to draw a breath since the Old Man's call had jerked him awake at three that morning.

Barnes had wanted Donovan to handle this one personally. The rationale was that Jack had met Sloan in Santa Fe and could formulate a gut feeling for whether or not they were dealing with a deliberate breach of national security. Unfortunately, his gut feel had been somewhat tainted by the fierce urge to plant his fist in Sloan's face.

He'd get past it. He had no choice. The implications of this security breach were too serious to let personal considerations weigh in.

Despite the stern lecture Jack made to himself,

Sloan's deliberate reference to breakfast with Cleo kept the acid churning in his belly all the way across town.

The navy was the largest employer in the Charleston area. Jack had contacted the commander of the local Naval Criminal Investigative Command detachment to find out which lab they used to process DNA samples to support their investigations.

Marshall Labs was located on the south side of town, not far from the Charleston Naval Support Facility. The lab director turned a little green around the gills at Jack's request for a priority run but promised to have the results within twenty-four hours. Nodding, Jack retreated to a private office and flipped open the new video-imaging cell phone General Barnes had procured for his key personnel.

The device was state-of-the-art. Secure, encrypted audio not even the CIA could intercept. Clear-streaming video. Instantaneous satellite transmissions from anywhere on the globe. A techie's wet dream.

Jack hated the damned thing. He didn't mind going face-to-face with his boss. He just didn't like having it out via a two-inch screen.

Before tackling the Old Man, though, he placed a call to the rehab center where Alexander Sloan was currently undergoing treatment. That call made, he punched speed dial for the commander of the Air Force Office of Special Investigations.

"I need to talk to the boss," he informed the haggard-looking captain currently serving as Barnes's exec.

"Hold on. I'll see if he's available."

Jack felt the tendons in his neck cord as he put himself into a mental brace. Even then he wasn't prepared for the craggy face that suddenly glared at him from the miniature screen.

A single glance told him that Brigadier General Sam Barnes wasn't happy. His bushy, salt-and-pepper eyebrows formed straight lines above his beak of a nose. The stem of the pipe he kept clamped between his teeth 24/7 hung like a black fishhook from the corner of his mouth.

"Where the hell are you, Donovan?"

"Still in Charleston."

"Can you talk?"

"Yes, sir."

"Then what's the problem? Why aren't you on your way back to D.C.? Couldn't you get the sample?"

"I got it. It took some prodding, though."

Barnes jumped on that like a hound on a badger. "Why? You think it was Sloan himself who breached the classified portion of the APP database?"

Jack hesitated. He wanted to be sure it was the investigator talking and not the Neanderthal.

"I can't say with any certainty at this point. By the way, I verified the source of the DNA Sloan provided for APP access. He used his father's."

The thick brows beetled. "Major General

Sloan's been dead for fifteen, twenty years. His son saved a sample of his DNA?"

"Yes, sir."

The pipe made a shift from left to right. Jack toyed briefly with the idea of telling his boss the source of the sample, but decided discretion was the better part of valor.

The general didn't have much of a sense of humor to begin with and none at all when it came to his collection of antique pipes. Barnes hadn't been able to fire one up at work since the air force offices went smokeless almost a decade ago. He was still pissed about that.

"That opens new possibilities," Barnes growled. "If one twin saved some of his father's DNA, the other probably did, too."

"If he did, he didn't use it to access the APP last night. I just checked with his rehab center. Both the physician overseeing his treatment and the physical therapist assigned to his case confirm Alex Sloan has regained only limited mobility and dexterity. Barely enough to drag his legs. They also confirm he hasn't had access to a computer since he arrived at the rehab center."

"So we're back to Marc Sloan."

"Yes, sir."

Jack hesitated. He'd been dreading this moment.

"There's something else you should know, sir. Cleo's here."

"Cleo *North?*"

The general's teeth locked on the black stem.

His lips curled back. Not a pretty sight, coming from two square inches of screen.

"What is she doing in Charleston?"

"She's handling a case for Sloan. One of his employees is missing. A woman who works in his administrative section."

Plastic crackled like gunfire as the pipe stem shot to the left again. "Any chance this missing woman is connected to the APP breach last night?"

"I don't know, sir. Maybe. Maybe not. I'm thinking I should stay over in Charleston for a day or two and check it out, though."

Jesus! Where had that come from? Scrambling, Jack searched for a plausible rationale for delaying his return to Washington.

"It might also be useful to drive up to the Military Ocean Terminal at Sunny Point and talk to our people there. I need to know more about this operation."

Jack was reaching. He knew it. Might as well go for broke.

"I'll take Cleo with me. She doesn't know what's driving this query, but I trust her instincts."

The pipe came out of the general's mouth. The stem jabbed at the camera. "Her instincts may be sound, but that woman's as bullheaded as they come."

Jack managed to keep a straight face. Barely. Cleo didn't have the patent on bullheaded. The crash and thunder of antlers butting had resounded through OSI corridors whenever she and Barnes had come within spitting distance.

"She was also one of the best, sir."

The OSI commander leaned into the camera, until only one eyeball glared from the screen. "Just keep her in line."

Yeah, right. Like that was going to happen. Barnes hadn't been able to accomplish that while he had Cleo in uniform. How the hell did he figure Jack could do it?

"I'll keep you posted, sir."

"You do that."

The eyeball receded. The general's whole face filled the screen once more. Some of the ruddy color left his cheeks as he imparted his own bit of news.

"The lieutenant-colonel promotion-board results just hit the Pentagon. They won't be released for another couple of weeks yet, but I got the word from a friend in the Chief of Staff's office. You're on the list. Two years early."

"Well, damn."

"Congratulations."

Barnes let him savor the news for all of three or four seconds.

"Don't screw up on this case, Major. Figuratively *or* literally. You do, and you'll kiss those silver oak leaves goodbye."

Jack signed off. The Old Man's parting shot didn't worry him. Barnes knew he'd give the case everything he had. Despite his grumbling, the general also trusted Cleo.

Her unexpected appearance on the scene added a new twist to matters, though. The woman complicated Jack's life every time their paths crossed. She also tied him in knots Houdini would have had a hard time slipping out of.

And now she was in Charleston, working for the same defense contractor he had been sent to check out. The same smooth operator who'd put the moves on her in Santa Fe and was obviously trying to pick up where he'd left off there.

Jack had to walk a fine line here. Too fine to give in to the urge to call Cleo and pick up where *they'd* left off. Resigning himself to a long night with only his laptop for company, he called for a reservation at the airport Marriott.

8

For the second morning in a row, the phone jerked Cleo from sleep. Not even the prospect of steaming croissants could soothe the beast this time. Thumping around on the bedside table, she fumbled for the phone.

"Go away," she croaked into the receiver.

It took a moment for the steady dial tone at the other end to penetrate. Another few seconds before she realized a different phone was ringing. Mumbling a curse, she downed the house phone and snatched up her cell.

"This better be good."

"Christ, I forgot about you and mornings."

"Donovan?"

"I'm driving up to the Sunny Point Military Ocean Terminal," he said with exaggerated patience. "At Southport. In North Carolina. To get a better feel for how this APP system works. You want to come with me?"

She glanced at the digital clock and groaned. God! Six-ten—a.m., yet. Dragging her tongue over teeth that seemed to have grown moss overnight, she tried to force her sluggish brain cells into gear.

"Where are you?"

"In Charleston."

"I thought you were heading back to D.C. last night."

"I was. I decided to delay my return and drive up to Sunny Point first."

So why hadn't he called her last night? Cleo was still trying to fuzz that one out when he reissued his invitation.

"Do you want to tag along?"

With some effort, she sorted through her options. She remembered Sloan saying the Military Ocean Terminal was a hundred or so miles north of Charleston. She and Donovan could drive up there and back by early afternoon.

That would give Detective Devereaux time to subpoena the phone records on this Helms character. Cleo couldn't really proceed with her own investigation until they came through. The delay more than justified her time away from Charleston in her mind.

"Why do you need me?" she asked. She'd already decided to go but wanted to understand his motives for including her.

"I could use a second set of eyes. Are you in or not?"

"Yeah. Okay. I guess."

"Meet me at the airport Marriott in an hour. Come prepared to walk through a few acres of sand and pine needles."

Grunting an acknowledgement, Cleo flipped the cell shut. She needed caffeine. Preferably via IV.

Her sleep shirt hugging her thighs, she padded downstairs, got the coffeemaker chugging and held a mug directly under the drip. When a thin layer of brown coated the bottom of the cup, she made a lightning switch, pot for cup.

A tantalizing sniff.

A first, greedy sip.

Thank you, Lord.

By the second cup she was feeling almost human again. Carrying the mug with her, she went back upstairs, wiggled into jeans and pulled on a hot-pink tank top. Her hair went into a ponytail that poked through the back opening of a ball cap. The Gucci boots remained in the closet. Sand and pine needles called for the comfortable, air-cushioned Oakleys.

After a brief inner debate, Cleo locked her handgun in her suitcase. They would be visiting a military installation. For a civilian, carrying a weapon onto a military post these days required prior approval by just about everyone, up to and including God.

Charleston at 6:50 a.m. presented no traffic challenges to a driver with her kamikaze skills. She zipped out to the airport and pulled into the Marriott parking lot just a little past the allotted hour.

The knowledge Donovan had spent the night in Charleston, just a few miles away, apparently alone, hadn't exactly put Cleo in a chipper mood. It soon became apparent Jack's wasn't any better. He responded to her comments in monosyllables and shielded his eyes behind mirrored sunglasses.

Cleo had a pretty good idea what was bugging him. She let the sleeping dog lie for about seventy miles. When they passed the turnoff for Myrtle Beach, though, she decided to poke it with a stick. Plunking her foam cup into a holder, she thrust up a hand and ticked off the topics they'd covered so far.

"Okay, we've talked about Trish Jackson. We've discussed how they establish a DNA signature for access to the APP. We've also discussed the Old Man's less-than-enthusiastic response to my presence in Charleston, the Orioles' chances in the play-offs and the construction clogging the Woodrow Wilson Bridge."

Frowning, she waggled the fingers of her other hand.

"Let's see. What haven't we kicked around? Oh! Hey! How about whether or not I've hopped in the sack with Sloan?"

Donovan didn't take his gaze from the road. "That's your business."

"You're right. It is. And how you feel about the possibility is yours."

She waited. Threw an idle look at the skinny pines whizzing by. Searched the dunes on the other side of Route 17 for a glimpse of the ocean. Turned a questioning face back to the man at the wheel.

He'd shed the sport coat he'd worn yesterday and rolled up the cuffs of his shirt. The gold-tipped hairs on his forearms glinted in the morning sun. Thinking about how those arms had *not* reached for her last night made Cleo feel downright peevish.

"C'mon, Donovan. We both know you got tight-assed when Sloan dropped that bit about us having breakfast together. Your cheeks still haven't unclenched. Why don't you just ask what's going on between him and me?"

Jack wanted to. He'd picked up the phone a half dozen times last night, itching for an answer to that exact question. The same restraint that had stopped him then put an edge in his voice now. "We're both working cases here, Cleo. Important cases. How I feel about you jumping in the sack with Sloan doesn't play in either of them."

"Bullshit."

"Is it?" He ripped his gaze from the road. "Then what about the little speech you made the last time *we* jumped in the sack?"

"The one about keeping the door open?"

"That's it."

Her chin jutted. She looked like she was spoiling

for a fight, but Jack suspected he'd struck a nerve. "You're right," she conceded with something less than graciousness. "The best we seem to be able to manage is once in a while."

Yeah, Jack thought. And that was the problem. "Periodic" and "infrequent" just didn't hack it over the long term. He had the scars to prove it. The truth came hard, but he forced it out.

"'Once in a while' doesn't afford me much basis to come on strong about Sloan, does it?"

The steam went out of the woman beside him. Sighing, she folded her arms and slumped in the bucket seat.

"No, it doesn't."

He kept his eyes on the road. He didn't have to look at Cleo to know she was chewing on the inside of her lower lip. She did that when she needed to think through things. One of her personal quirks.

He could make a list. There was the lip business. The surly temper when dragged from sleep. The absolute loathing of anything that resembled paperwork. The descriptive—and often libelous—private labels she assigned witnesses and suspects to keep them straight in her mind.

The snuffling little snorts she made in her sleep.

The way water pearled on her long, sleek thighs when she came out of the shower.

The groan that ripped from the back of her throat when she climaxed.

Sweat pooled on Jack's palms. The fists he'd

forced himself to relax just moments ago went white at the knuckles again.

They stayed white as the last few miles sped by. Sunlight shot dizzying patterns through the tall pines crowding the two-lane road. Coastal dunes gave brief glimpses of the green, rolling Atlantic. The quaint fishing village of Southport, North Carolina, fell behind them.

A few miles past Southport, Jack turned off onto NC 133. The two-lane road followed the Cape Fear River to where it emptied into the sea. It also led through mile after mile of marshy, undeveloped coastal backwater to the largest munitions depot in the United States.

Mountainous sand berms surrounded the entire 18,000-acre site—to protect unsuspecting passersby from a catastrophic explosion, Jack guessed. That wasn't a completely improbable event, as he'd learned in the research he'd conducted last night.

One of the links he'd followed had referenced the 1917 explosion in the harbor of Halifax, Nova Scotia. A ship packed with munitions to support the war in Europe had collided with another cargo ship. The resulting explosion leveled the entire north end of the city, killed almost two thousand residents and injured nine thousand more. That horrific accident remained the single most devastating loss of life due to man-made weaponry until Hiroshima.

The details of that incident were vivid in Jack's mind as he pulled up at the south entrance to the Sunny Point Military Ocean Terminal. The civilian guard at the gate scrutinized his ID and called to verify his appointment with the noncommissioned officer in charge of the air force contingent on site. The guard also had Jack sign Cleo in, thereby delegating to him full responsibility for her conduct on post.

First Barnes, he thought wryly. Now this guy. The whole world seemed to think he could accomplish the impossible.

"Here." He passed her a plastic-coated visitor's badge. "Clip this on, stay close to me once we get to the port and don't go looking for trouble."

"You wound me, Donovan. I never look for trouble."

"You never seem to avoid it, either." He thought of the Halifax explosion again and shuddered. "We're going to be around bombs, Cleo. Big bombs. Lots of 'em. Just stay cool."

She whipped up a knife-edged salute. "Yes, *sir!* Whatever you say, *sir!*"

Once they were inside the gate, it was another five miles to the main complex. Cleo eyeballed the sign welcoming her to the home of the 597th Transportation Group, United States Army, and shook her head.

"This is an army post? Silly me. For some reason, I thought the navy would run a port facility."

"Actually, it's a joint-use facility. The army's Transportation Command acts as executive agent for the overall movement of military supplies and equipment to a transshipment point. That can be either an aerial terminal or, as in this case, a deep-water port. If it's a port, the navy contracts for cargo ships. Handlers from each of the services then oversee loading of their own cargo packages. Merchant-marine crews man the ships at sea."

She slanted him a considering look. "You've done some research."

"I don't like going into a case blind."

"Or into a potentially hostile situation. You always had an escape route mapped out before the bullets started flying. Saved our butts down in Honduras," she remembered with a small smile. "We made a good team on that op, Donovan."

He dragged his gaze from the road cutting as straight as a spear through the mounded sand berms.

"Yeah, we did."

USAF Master Sergeant Harry Stevens waited for them at the small building that housed the on-site air force contingent. A tall, tanned Californian in battle-dress uniform, Stevens was more than a little curious why an air force OSI agent had requested a tour of his operation.

Jack hadn't advised him of the possible APP database breach when he'd called for this appointment. That information would come from

Stevens's superiors when and if they determined he had a need to know. For now, all he could do was feed him the standard line.

"I'm working a preliminary inquiry concerning one of the cargo ships retrofitted for the air force."

"Which ship?" the NCO asked as he escorted his guests into his one-room operations center.

"The *Pitsenbarger*."

"The *Pits*? She was just in for replenishment four months ago."

Cleo's ears perked up. This was her first indication Jack was interested in a specific vessel.

"The *Pits*," she commented. "Interesting name for a ship."

"It's named for Airman First Class William H. Pitsenbarger."

Stevens led her to a wall featuring three framed photos and thumped one of a young troop in helmet and flack vest standing beside the hatch of a chopper.

"Pits was a PJ."

He looked like a pararescueman, Cleo thought. Cocky. Self-assured. Tough as boot leather. Her few encounters with PJs during her years in uniform had engendered a profound respect for the breed—and a sincere hope she never had to make use of their combat rescue skills.

"Pitsenbarger flew almost three hundred missions in Vietnam," Stevens was saying. "On his last mission, his crew responded to an army squad under intense fire from the Viet Cong. He went down on the hoist and treated six wounded. While the chopper ferried the first load back to base, Pits stayed on the ground to administer to more."

Cleo's stomach began to twist. She guessed what was coming. The air force honored dead heroes by naming bases after them. It was beginning to sound as though they did the same for their small fleet of ocean-going cargo vessels.

"When the helo returned for a second load," Stevens continued, "it took a hit and had to leave the scene. Instead of climbing into the basket and leaving with his crew, Pits stayed with the ground troops. He treated the wounded, gathered ammunition clips from the dead when the defenders ran low, and grabbed a rifle himself to help hold off the Cong. When they recovered his body the next day, he was still clutching the rifle in one hand and a medical kit in the other."

Cleo's throat went tight as she stared at the grinning young PJ. "How old was he?"

"Twenty-one. He was awarded a posthumous Air Force Cross for that action. It was upgraded to a Medal of Honor after a special review in December 2000. The award came through just in time for the navy to name one of the new cargo vessels they dedicated to air force use after him."

He nodded to the framed photos flanking the young airman's. "Our other two ships are the *Major Bernard F. Fisher* and the *Captain Steven L. Bennett*. All three are named for men I'd be proud to go into combat with."

Cleo never missed the military—except at moments like this. During her years in uniform she'd balked at doing things by the book and bent more rules than she'd followed. But she'd never found anything in the civilian world that came close to the camaraderie she'd experienced in the air force. There was a fraternity, a brotherhood of arms that came with the absolute certainty you could trust the troop next to you to do his or her job even under intense enemy fire.

With a last look at the young PJ, she accompanied Stevens to meet his crew. The four NCOs who came forward to shake hands possessed a combined total of more than sixty years' experience in munitions, transportation and logistics planning.

"This is only a small slice of our team," Stevens advised. "Since it takes up to a year to prepare for a replenishment operation, most of my troops are at Ogden, working the logistics for the next round. They'll load the requirements in the database, source the weapons packages, then make the buys."

Jack didn't comment. Cleo, too, kept her mouth shut.

"The entire APP team will assemble here on-site a few months before the ship is due in port," Stevens explained. "I'll have fifty, sixty people counting pallets and working cranes as the munitions arrive by truck or train. We'll get everything sorted and packaged before the ship docks, then work round the clock until it's loaded and ready to go back on station."

"How long does the ship stay on station?" Cleo asked.

"They're contracted for five years, but they can come in whenever the air force directs."

The NCO then proceeded to give his visitors a crash course in the three-tiered munitions-supply system. Cleo pretty much grasped the concept of starter, swing and replenishment stock. Stevens lost her, though, when he described the three air force munitions ships as rapid swing stock.

He tried again, using terms she could understand. "Our ships bridge the gap between the munitions we can get to a location immediately via airlift and what's needed to sustain a long conflict. Given their dispersed locations, they can pull into just about any port and off-load their cargo within hours."

His chest puffed out. "That's what happened in Afghanistan. One of our ships went in with the first strike and kept our planes supplied with bombs and missiles throughout the attack."

Cleo remembered the TV clips of bombs burrowing into caves and blasting terrorist strongholds. She also remembered how she'd cheered every bunker-busting blast. Master Sergeant Stevens and his crew deserved to puff out their chests.

"There's an army ship in port," he told them. "I can't take you aboard, but I can drive you down to the dock. You'll get a better feel for what we do if you see it for yourself."

Jack didn't need a second invitation. "Let's go."

* * *

Cleo began to get a sense of how big this operation truly was during the trip to the dock.

Stevens drove them past acre after acre of crated weaponry and equipment. Forklifts rumbled back and forth as crews opened the crates, sorted the material and repacked it in shipping containers about half the size of train boxcars.

"Every item you see is bar-coded," Stevens explained. "And each of those shipping containers is tagged with an electronic identifier. We track which items go into which container and where that box is stored in the ship's hold. We can even follow the container's movement by radio signal as the ship crosses the ocean. If necessary, we can off-load different packages at different locations."

"Pretty impressive," Cleo had to admit, eyeing the endless strings of mini-boxcars.

"It is when you consider a vessel like the *Pits* can haul more than nine hundred of those containers—seven hundred twenty below deck, the rest above deck in air-conditioned, dehumidified pods to protect the ammunition. That equates to about twelve thousand short tons of cargo, or about five million pounds of explosive weight."

"Five million, huh?"

She was still trying to wrap her mind around the notion of sailing across an ocean sitting atop millions of pounds of explosives when Stevens drove into the port complex.

"The ship you'll see in a few minutes is an

army-provisioning ship. It's smaller than the *Pits* but still carries a pretty good tonnage."

When their vehicle rounded the end of a mile-long warehouse a few moments later, Cleo discovered "smaller" was in the eye of the beholder. Craning her neck, she looked up. And up. And up.

"Ho-ly *shit!*"

It was the biggest, blackest hull she'd ever seen: twelve or fifteen stories of steel plate, topped by five super size cranes swinging stacked containers from dock to deck as if they were Lego blocks.

9

When Cleo and Jack departed Sunny Point almost an hour later, her respect for logisticians had taken several quantum leaps and her neck had developed a severe crick.

As Jack's rental car ate up the miles back to Charleston, she also developed a decided reluctance to end that little excursion. Despite their rocky start that morning, it felt good to be working with him. Damned good.

Apparently he was experiencing some degree of reluctance, too. That became evident when he pulled up alongside the Escalade and hooked his wrists over the steering wheel.

"What's next on your agenda?"

"I've got to meet with the detective working my missing-persons case. Hopefully, by now he'll have subpoenaed the phone records of this mysterious man Trish Jackson called from her doctor's office. How about you?"

"I still have a few matters to check out here in Charleston."

She waited, wondering if he was going to spend another night alone in his hotel room, with her bunked down just a few miles away.

Evidently not. The invitation came slowly, but it came.

"Do you want to get together later? We could have dinner. Compare case notes."

The casual suggestion didn't necessarily include a night of lewd and lascivious activity. The potential was there, though. Most definitely there.

Still, Cleo stepped cautiously. "If I know the Old Man, he probably singed off a few of your eyelashes when you told him I was in Charleston. Sure you want to risk his wrath by, uh, comparing case notes?"

"He did, and I am."

He gave the grin then. The Jack Donovan Special. Slow, lazy and all sex.

"You're worth a few singed eyelashes, Cleopatra Aphrodite. I'll pick you up at six. Where are you staying?"

"Why don't I get a recommendation for a good seafood place and call you? We can meet there."

No sense spoiling the moment by letting him know she was bedding down just a hop, skip and a jump from Sloan's back door.

"Good enough. You've got my cell number?"

"I've got it. Later, Donovan."

She climbed out of his vehicle and into the Escalade. The key went into the ignition. The motor turned over with a well-bred hum. Cleo shifted into Drive and sat with her foot on the brake, engaged in a fierce, silent debate.

What the hell.

A jab at the side button sent the window whirring down.

"Hey, Donovan!"

His window lowered. Sunlight glinted on his tawny hair as he poked his head out. "What?"

"Just for the record, I'm not getting it on with Marc Sloan."

With a waggle of her fingers, she drove off.

When her cell phone pinged a few moments later, she figured it was Donovan following up on her announcement. Lafayette Devereaux's smoky bass rumbled out instead.

"Thought you might want to know I'm lookin' at a record of all calls made by our boy, Helms."

"Any interesting ones on there?"

"I haven't checked them all out yet, but these five calls to Malta caught my attention."

"Malta, where?"

She was thinking some small town in South Carolina or Kentucky or Ohio. She *wasn't* thinking a tiny speck of an island in the Mediterranean. After Devereaux set her straight, she made the connection.

"Red-Spandex Gal said Helms spoke with a British accent. Isn't Malta a former British colony?"

"Beats me."

"Did you try the numbers?"

"I did. No one answered. I forgot about the time difference, though. It's after business hours over there."

Wherever "there" was. Scrunching her forehead, Cleo tried to construct a mental map of the Mediterranean. She was pretty sure Malta lay just south of the Italian boot, somewhere close to Sicily.

"This case is starting to take on a stink," Devereaux commented, breaking into her mental cartography. "I'm thinking I'd better call in the feds."

Cleo swallowed a groan. Her encounters with various government security agencies since going into business for herself had almost—*almost*—made her regret leaving the air force. At least then, she'd been considered one of the good guys.

Belatedly, she recalled she was having dinner with one of those government agents in a few hours. "Listen, Lafayette, I just got back from Sunny Point Military Ocean Terminal. I drove up there with a friend of mine. Jack Donovan. Air Force OSI."

Devereaux was former Special Ops. She didn't have to explain the initials.

"If you want, I could ask Jack to run these Malta calls through his networks, see if they link to anything hot."

As she'd anticipated, he leapt on the chance to cut through the organizational maze that constituted the United States government.

"Are you someplace where I can fax this list?"

"Not at the moment. Tell you what. Zap it to me at Sloan Engineering. Ask Sloan's assistant to have it waiting for me in the lobby. I'll swing by and pick it up."

"It's on its way."

The man was right, Cleo thought as she cut across two lanes of traffic, ignoring the idiot who leaned on his horn. This case was starting to take on a stink.

She didn't realize how much of a stink, though, until she pulled up in front of Sloan Engineering's corporate headquarters. Leaving the Escalade idling in a red zone, she flashed her ID at the receptionist manning the lobby desk.

"Do you have a fax for me?"

"Yes, Ms. North." She handed over a sealed envelope. "Ms. Walker sent it down a few minutes ago."

With a word of thanks, Cleo folded the envelope and stuffed it in her back pocket. She started out of the lobby, then spun back to eye the huge globe dotted with little red lights.

The *Forbes* article she'd digested while flying into Charleston indicated Sloan Engineering had cornered the market on this emission-control retrofit business. Given Jack's interest in the *Pitsenbarger*—and the unauthorized access to the

Afloat Prepositioning database—Cleo would bet one of those little red lights represented the *Pits*.

"How do you know which ship is which dot?" she asked the receptionist.

Smiling, the young woman pointed to a marble panel set amid the lush greenery on the far side of the lobby. Five rows of buttons marched down the marble slab, aligned as precisely as Prussian soldiers.

"Those buttons represent an alphabetical list of all our ships at sea. You just look up a particular ship, push the button beside its name, and its dot will glow a bright, steady red. Push the button twice, and you'll see the route of its current voyage."

"Thanks."

Sure enough, Sloan Engineering claimed the U.S. Motor Vessel *A1C William H. Pitsenbarger* as one of its own. Cleo pushed the button beside the ship's name and searched for a bright, steady glow. She found it in the eastern Mediterranean. The *Pits* was probably standing by to resupply U.S. aircraft operating from Turkish bases. Curious, Cleo pushed the button a second time.

A line of amber dots appeared, cutting a long trail that led from what she guessed was Sunny Point Military Ocean Terminal. The stream crossed the Atlantic. Made a blip of a stop in the Azores. Passed through the Strait of Gibraltar. Cruised by Sardinia. Made another stop at...

Cleo's chest squeezed. Ice spread from her neck

to her toes. Stone cold, she stared at the small island group just off the southeastern tip of Sicily.

The larger of those islands was Malta. She was sure of it.

Every investigative instinct she'd honed over the years sat up and started screeching. Her gut told her there had to be a connection between Sloan's missing employee, the unauthorized intrusion into the APP database and that ship on station in the eastern Med.

Eyes locked on that steady red glow, she dug out her cell phone. Donovan answered on the second ring.

"It's Cleo, Jack."

"You decided on a restaurant already?"

"Forget the restaurant. Meet me at Sloan Engineering."

"What's up?"

"I'll brief you when you get here. Look for me in the lobby."

While she waited for Jack to arrive, Cleo debated the ethics of the situation. Sloan was her client. He'd hired her to find a missing employee. The fact that the employee could be linked to a possible breach of a classified database put Cleo in an awkward position.

If she assisted Jack with his investigation, she might uncover evidence that involved or affected her client. Then again, she reasoned, she might not. At this point, there were a whole lot more questions than there were answers.

And she couldn't shake the growing conviction that at least some of the answers would lead back to that little red dot in the eastern Mediterranean.

If so, she'd protect her client's interests. Professional ethics required her to. But she'd back off the Trish Jackson case immediately.

Jack wheeled into the underground garage some fifteen minutes after the call from Cleo. He jabbed the elevator button, his mouth twisting when he remembered how, yesterday, the elevator had stopped one floor up, the doors had whooshed open and Trouble had wedged her way aboard.

She was waiting for him in the lobby this time. Her brown eyes held no trace of their usual irreverent gleam when she spotted Jack and waved him over.

"I want to show you something." She punched one of the buttons set into a gray-green marble panel. "See that bright red light in the eastern Med?"

He searched the freestanding globe that dominated the lobby until he spotted the bright pin-prick of red.

"I see it."

"That's the *Pitsenbarger*. And this is the route it followed on its current voyage." She hit the button again. "Note the stops."

Jack tracked the dots. "I see two. The Azores and…" He squinted at the small island group in mid-ocean between Sicily and the African coast. "What are those? The Maltese Islands?"

"You got it."

She slid a white envelope out of her pocket and extracted a folded sheet of paper.

"And this is a record of phone calls made from the condo rented by the man Trish Jackson—Sloan's missing office assistant—called from her doctor's office. Detective Devereaux of the Charleston PD just faxed me a copy."

The paper crackled as she unfolded it, a tiny sound almost lost amid the splash of the waterfall across the lobby. Her face grim, she passed it to Donovan.

"The five calls you see circled were made to a number in Malta."

It took Jack less than a heartbeat to make the connection. Suddenly the investigation that had brought him to Charleston took on a new scope and urgency.

"Well, hell."

"I figured that would be your reaction. Mine was pretty much the same."

Jack's gaze whipped back to the globe. The bright red dot burned into his mind as his thoughts charged down a dozen different alleys. All of them dark and suddenly dangerous. And all circling back to Marc Sloan.

"Let's go upstairs. I think it's time I turned this informal inquiry official."

Diane's intercom rang. Once. Twice. A third time. She ignored the chime. Fingers laced in a bone-crushing grip, she stared unseeing at the hazy afternoon sky beyond the wall of windows. Fury boiled inside her, hot and thick. It had since yesterday, when Cleo North had dropped the bombshell about Trish being pregnant.

Marc was the father. Diane didn't want to believe it, but couldn't deny the awful certainty that buzzed around in her head like a swarm of angry wasps.

Why else would Trish have avoided sharing any details about the man she was seeing? She knew—everyone who worked here in the executive suite did—how Diane felt about office romances. Particularly with the handsome, charismatic boss. Diane had made that clear enough after that incident on Marc's yacht.

Had Trish sensed that Diane's rigid prohibition against office affairs stemmed from the fact that she herself lusted after Marc? Had Trish sat there, with her cheerful smiles and respectful "Yes, Ms. Walker's," all the while laughing at the middle-aged fool so hopelessly in love with her boyfriend?

God! Boyfriend. What an absurd, asinine, *ridiculous* label for a man like Marc Sloan.

She was making a mental list of a few more appropriate labels when the door to Marc's office flew open. Shirtsleeves rolled up, Marc clutched a set of schematics in one hand.

"Isn't that your intercom?"

As if in answer, the instrument rang again.

"Aren't you going to answer it?"

"No."

The annoyance on his face rearranged itself into irritation. "What's the problem here, Diane? You've been acting like a robot with a short circuit all day."

"Robot?" Her head snapped up. *"Robot?"*

That's all she was to him. All she'd ever been. A machine! A damned machine!

The emotions she'd kept locked inside her for so long screamed for release. She tried to swallow them, tasted only bile. She couldn't choke them back. Not again. Never again.

Shoving out of her chair, she slapped both palms on her desk. "You want to know what the problem is? I'll tell you what the problem is."

The rage erupted, white hot and scorching.

"The problem," she hurled across the room, "is the oversexed, overaged *prick* I work for!"

He couldn't have looked more astonished if one of the welders at the shipyard had lit an acetylene torch under his bare ass. Diane tasted a single, searing instant of triumph before his glance sliced to the left.

Her head whipped around. One of her assistants stood frozen in the open door to her office, his hand on the knob, his mouth agape. Two other people were partly visible behind him. All three, obviously, had had a ringside seat for the main event.

"Uh…er…" Her assistant was almost incoherent. "We have, um, visitors, Ms. Walker. For Mr. Sloan."

"Show them in and get out!"

"Yes, ma'am."

He jumped aside, waved the other two in and scuttled off like a crab poked with a sharp stick.

Diane didn't try to rein in her fury. She'd kept her thoughts in check for so long, it felt glorious to finally release them.

"Ms. North and Special Agent Donovan are here to see you, Marc." Yanking open her desk drawer, she snatched out her purse. "I'll have someone bring in coffee."

"Wait just a minute!" Jaw working, he crossed the office in two strides and planted himself between her and the door. "You think I'm going to let you waltz out after the display you just put on?"

"Yes, I do."

"Diane, for God's sake! What's going on here?"

Her lip curled. "You idiot! If you can't figure it out for yourself, I'm sure as hell not going to enlighten you. Get out of my way."

He didn't appreciate being labeled an idiot any more than he had liked *prick*. His eyes went harder than she'd ever seen them.

"You go through that door and you're fired, Walker."

"I'll save you the trouble. I quit, Sloan. Now…get…out…of…my…way."

Stiff-shouldered, he moved aside, but the promise in those slate-gray eyes told Diane this wasn't the end of it. He'd track her down, wring the truth from her, add to the humiliation that now fueled her rage.

Plotting an immediate escape to some remote resort in Arizona or Montana or New Zealand, she lifted her chin and marched to the door. This time it was Special Agent Donovan who moved to block her exit.

"I need to talk to you, Ms. Walker."

"Some other time. I'll call you and arrange a—"

"Now, Ms. Walker."

Brought up short, Diane blinked in surprise. No one ever used a tone like that with her. Not even Marc. He wouldn't dare.

"I can get a warrant if I need to."

The breath slid out of her, leaving a sudden hollow feeling in the pit of her stomach. She'd worked for defense contractors for more than twenty years. Military investigative agents didn't threaten to procure a warrant unless they had grounds for one.

"Is there some place we can talk privately?"

"I…uh…"

Her hand went to her throat, an instinctive attempt to hide her suddenly wild pulse. Was she in trouble? What did this man know? What *could* he know?

"A private office, Ms. Walker? Or a conference room, perhaps?"

Before she could force out a response, Marc strode forward. "You're not interviewing one of my employees without a corporate attorney in attendance, Donovan."

Gray eyes clashed with blue.

"Ms. Walker is no longer your employee. If she desires to have an attorney present during the interview, it's her call, not yours."

He was right, Diane realized. Her runaway pulse stopped dead for a second before taking off again. She didn't answer to Marc anymore. She didn't answer to anyone.

"There's a small conference room across the hall. We can use that. And no, I don't want a lawyer."

Marc caught her elbow. "Listen to me, Diane. You could be in over your head here."

"Are you worried about me? Or what secrets I might reveal about Sloan Engineering?"

His breath hissed out. His fingers went tight and bruising on her elbow. "I can't believe you'd say that to me after all our years together."

Diane didn't quite believe it, either. Now that the words were out, though, she couldn't bring herself to take them back. Chin high, she shook off his hold.

"This way, Mr. Donovan."

"Cleo, I'd like you to act as witness during this interview. Sloan…"

Jack shot a hard glance over his shoulder. "I want to talk to you after I finish with Ms. Walker."

10

Cleo hunched her elbows on the small conference table while Jack produced a palm-size tape recorder and went through the ritual she remembered all too well from her days in uniform.

After obtaining Walker's permission to tape the interview, he stated his name for the record. The date. The time and place. He also identified the interviewee by name and former position at Sloan Engineering, Cleo by name and current occupation. The mundane details attended to, he sliced right to the bone.

"Ms. Walker, I've been informed you have access to a hidden safe room in Mr. Sloan's office. Is that correct?"

She blinked, taken aback by the direction of the question. Whatever she was expecting, it wasn't that.

"Yes," she replied carefully, "that's correct."

"Can you tell me what Mr. Sloan keeps in that room?"

Her brow furrowed. "Disks containing corporate financial records. Engineering schematics. Proprietary designs. Some personal items."

"Such as?"

"Mostly papers. His prenuptial agreements. Divorce decrees. His father's death certificate, I think. Things like that."

"You think? Don't you know?"

"He stores the personal items in a separate, sealed area. I don't have access to that area."

"Who does?"

"No one except Marc."

Jack wanted it spelled out for the record. "By Marc, do you mean Mr. Marcus Sloan?"

"Yes. Mr. Sloan. My employer. Excuse me, former employer."

Frowning, she smoothed the wrinkles from her skirt. It was starting to sink in, Cleo thought. The woman had just chucked her job, her security and the man she'd obviously lusted after for some years.

"You're certain no one else in your office has access to the sealed area?" Jack asked.

"I'm certain. Marc—Mr. Sloan—programmed the sensor that reads the infrared signature himself."

"Could someone have altered the program?"

Cleo saw where he was going. Whoever hacked into the APP might also have the smarts to bypass

Sloan's sophisticated security system. Her pulse kicked up a beat.

"I suppose so," Diane conceded. "It's not likely, though."

"What about your missing assistant? Is there any way she could have gained access?"

"Trish?" Astonishment blanked Walker's face. "Absolutely not. She's bright, but not bright enough to work around a system Marc designed."

"How about an authorized access, then? Could Sloan have programmed her heat signature into the system?"

"No, he would never…"

She stopped, and sudden doubt flooded her face.

"Sloan would never what, Ms. Walker?"

The blonde squeezed her eyes shut. When her lids lifted, the misery in their green depths was sharp and slicing and almost too painful to witness. Cleo felt the first stirrings of sympathy for the woman.

"I don't *think* Marc—Mr. Sloan—would give Trish access to his private papers. I can't say for certain, though. You'll have to ask him."

"I will." Jack shifted gears. "Let's talk about the Afloat Prepositioning database. Do you have access to that, Ms. Walker?"

"Certain unclassified portions of it. I often feed in or retrieve schematics, as do our engineers and construction supervisors."

"Are you aware of what's required to get into the classified portions?"

"A verifiable DNA profile. As far as I know,

Marc is the only person at Sloan Engineering who's gone through the verification process."

"Do you know the source of the DNA Mr. Sloan provided for his profile?"

She looked confused. "Do you mean did it come from his hair or blood? I really don't have any idea."

Jack nodded and slipped in the blade, calmly, casually.

"Did you ever use Mr. Sloan's DNA profile to access classified portions of the APP database, Ms. Walker?"

Shock zeroed out the confusion.

"No!"

"Never?"

Her chin snapped up. *"Never."*

The questions went on awhile longer. By the time Donovan finished, Cleo had formed a number of distinct impressions.

One, Walker didn't know Sloan had used his father's DNA to establish his access profile. Two, she didn't have a clue who this Frank Helms character was. Three, she hadn't been aware of her subordinate's pregnancy until yesterday. Four, she harbored a sick suspicion Marc Sloan had fathered Trish's baby.

Jack terminated the interview with a promise to have the statement typed out and hand-delivered to Walker for her review and signature.

"Is there an address I can send it to?"

Gulping, she rattled off her home address and phone number.

"Thank you, Ms. Walker. I'll get back to you if I have any further questions."

Looking slightly dazed, the blonde picked up her purse and left. Cleo kept her in view through the glass inset beside the door and saw her hesitate in the corridor.

She tried to guess what the woman would do now. Go back into Sloan Engineering's corporate offices and collect her personal belongings? Maybe confront Marc about the paternity of Trish's baby? Or swallow her pride and beg for her job back?

Walker did none of the above. Squaring her shoulders under her jewel-toned Versace blouse, she marched to the elevator.

Marc Sloan didn't provide any more useful information than his assistant had.

He denied granting anyone, including Trish, access to his dead father's DNA. He also denied fathering her child. Nor could he shed a glimmer of light on Frank Helms or the phone calls to Malta.

Sloan left the small conference room tight-lipped. Cleo had the idea he was more pissed about his executive assistant's sudden defection than about becoming the subject of an official OSI investigation.

Thinking about that, she had to assess how this recent turn of events affected *her* investigation. Since Donovan had more or less co-opted her into his inquiry, she'd reached a definite conflict-of-interest situation with Sloan.

It wasn't until Donovan had tucked the recorder back into his pocket that it occurred to Cleo to wonder if that might have been his intent, consciously or otherwise. Curious as to his motives, she hitched a hip on a corner of the conference table.

"Let's review the bidding here, Jack. You've now opened an official investigation with my client as the subject. That puts me in an awkward position regarding the case I'm working for him."

"I know."

The prospect that she might be out of a fat fee didn't appear to concern him unduly. What did worry him, though, was the Malta connection.

"I need you to stay on the Jackson case, Cleo. Sloan trusts you, or he has to this point. Any information you can get out of him regarding his missing employee and her link to the man who made those calls—"

"Whoa! Hold it right there, Donovan."

The camaraderie they'd shared, the sense of being on the same team again, went up in a puff of smoke.

"I'm on retainer. I'm working for Sloan until one of us terminates the agreement. I won't reveal anything he tells me in confidence."

"I'm not asking you to violate your professional ethics."

"Really? Sure sounded like it to me."

His shoulders stiffened under the cotton shirt. "How many cases have we worked together, North?"

"Exactly two," she shot back, "if you count Santa Fe and our little foray into Honduras a few years ago."

"Did either of those cases involve deliberate violation of established procedures?"

"Deliberate? No. The rulebook got tossed out the window, though, when the bullets started flying."

He moved closer, until his thigh pressed into her bent knee. "You hear any shots popping here?"

"Not so far."

But they might start at any minute. Cleo could feel the muscle corded hard and tight in his thigh. Feel, too, the anger working its way through his system. Donovan's temper came slow, but when it did, blood usually flowed.

Hers, on the other hand, came fast and hot. It was close to boiling at the moment.

"Let me ask you this, Special Agent Donovan. Did your invitation for me to join you on the drive to Sunny Point this morning stem from a desire for my company, or were you merely using me to assist you with your case."

"Both."

Well, that answered that. Totally pissed now, she angled her chin.

"How much was me? Give me a percentage. Fifty-fifty? Seventy-thirty?"

"I'm not walking into that one."

He started to turn away. Snagging his arm, Cleo yanked him back. "I want to know. Give me a number."

His hand shot out. Before she could blink, he'd wrapped a fist around her ponytail.

"You want to know how much was you, North?" A swift tug jerked her head back. "This much."

The crush of his mouth on hers was in no way, shape or form similar to his kiss in the elevator yesterday. That one had been lazy and slow and thorough.

This one was rough. And hard. And greedy. Luckily for him, Cleo recognized the hunger behind it while still trying to decide whether or not to bring up her knee and tenderize a certain portion of his anatomy.

She was still pissed enough to jerk her head away before his tongue started playing tag with her tonsils, though.

"All right. I've got the equation."

"Do you?" Jack's eyes were a hot electric blue. "I wish to hell I did."

With that disgusted mutter, he gave her ponytail another yank and released her.

"I'll see you later, North. Call me when you decide on a restaurant."

Restaurant. Dinner. Seafood.

Cleo had forgotten about that small matter in all the excitement. She hadn't forgotten her promise to Lafayette, though.

"Hey, Donovan."

Hopping off the conference table, she tugged at the hem of her tank top. Somehow it had worked its way out of the waistband of her jeans and halfway up her ribs.

"I told Detective Devereaux one of us would get back to him after you run those calls to Malta through the system."

"I should have something by dinner."

And by then, she might have a feel for her status vis-à-vis her client. For that, she needed to talk to Sloan.

The executive wasn't in his office when she went across the hall, though. According to the still-shell-shocked assistant, Mr. Sloan had stormed out some time ago.

"He, uh, said we weren't to contact him unless the building was on fire. And then only if the fire department's ladders couldn't reach this floor."

"Oooo-kay."

Diane was swimming in misery.

With a hiccupping sob, she clunked the neck of the crème de menthe bottle against a water glass.

A nondrinker, she'd had to search through every cabinet in the kitchen to find the liqueur she'd bought years ago to make a grasshopper pie for a party at a friend's house. It tasted like old toothpaste, but she filled the glass and chugged down half the contents, anyway.

"What do you think, cat? Is Sloan a bastard, or what?"

Trish's feline declined to answer. Crouched on the seat of an upholstered chair, he flicked his tail back and forth. Diane detested cats, particularly nasty-tempered ones who hissed at her approach and clawed her drapes. She hadn't had the heart to dump Trish's pet in a kennel, though. The animal had been locked in an empty apartment for days, without food and only the toilet bowl for water.

Another hiccup hit Diane, this one so full of mint she sneezed. Blinking away the tears that came with the sneeze, she transferred her glare to the framed photo on the mantel above her fireplace insert.

Two smiling faces. One pair of giant scissors.

Marc had been between wives at the dedication of Sloan Engineering's new corporate headquarters, so he'd asked his executive assistant to help him cut the ribbon.

Diane's lip curled back in a sneer. How pathetic was *that?* The only photograph in her living room, the only human being accorded a place of honor in her home, was the bastard who'd broken her heart.

Over and over again.

Why in God's name had she stayed with him all these years? Why had she managed his schedule, rewritten his pedantic speeches, juggled calls from his girlfriends and wives? Why had she sat there, just *sat* there, and let him devour her soul inch by inch?

Green liqueur sloshing, she toasted the photo.

"Here's to you, Sloan. I hope they pin whatever

it is they're investigating on you and hang you by your balls. And here's to me."

Head back, she took another slug. Then she wound up and let fly.

To her surprise and considerable delight, her aim was dead on. The framed photo crashed off the mantel and onto the terrazzo tile floor. Glass shattered. Green liqueur spewed across photo and floor. Trish's cat jumped straight up, leapt from the chair and streaked into the bedroom.

"God, that felt good!"

Wrapping her fist around the bottle's neck, Diane searched for another target. She found it in the blood-red Baccarat bowl Marc had given her for her last birthday.

Her fortieth birthday.

The bottle went flying. The bowl toppled off its corner pedestal.

"Bam! Another direct hit."

Cackling gleefully, she lurched to her feet. Moments later the sleek laptop engraved with Sloan Engineering's blue-and-gold logo departed her desk and sailed through the sliding patio door to smash against the flagstones.

She was looking around for another missile when someone leaned on her doorbell. The hard, angry jabs gave her a good idea as to the identity of the lean-ee.

Blood up and battle-ready, Diane snapped the dead bolt Marc had insisted she have installed on all her doors because single women needed security. That memory gave her the impetus to send the door slamming back against the iris wallpaper decorating her hall.

"Surprise, surprise. It's my late, unlamented employer."

He looked furious enough to bite through a steel-hull plate. "I want an explanation, Walker."

Smiling sweetly, she flipped the back of her hand under her chin in a gesture straight from *The Sopranos.* "Go screw yourself, Sloan. And while you're at it, you might as well screw the rest of the office."

"What the hell does that mean?"

"It means I'm out of ammunition. Hang on a sec, I need to reload."

"What?"

She took a couple of steps back, got a grip on the dainty asparagus fern perched on the hall étagère and arrowed it straight at his head. His arm came up in time to block the shot, but dirt and moss showered onto his head and shoulders.

"Are you out of your mind?" he roared, shaking off the debris.

"Actually, I'm just coming into it."

Another step backward. Another missile. This one the Ming temple dog Marc had bought her during a trip to Beijing some years back.

Cursing, her intended target leapt forward and caught her wrist. A hard twist sent the ceramic dog to the floor. Another twist brought her arm up behind her back.

The brutal hold wiped out Diane's glee and

fired her rage all over again. The sophisticated shell she'd cultivated layer by layer over the years cracked and fell away. All that was left was flaming, furious female.

"I've kept quiet all these years. I've watched you make a fool of yourself over and over again with those...those simpering twits who draped themselves all over you. But I won't keep quiet any longer."

Struggling, twisting, raging, she fought his hold. He took a kick to the shins, cursed again and slammed her against his chest.

"If you seduced Trish, you bastard... If you got her pregnant..."

He needed both hands to hold her now. Both arms. He banded her against him, muscles bunching, his fury every bit as fierce but far more controlled than hers.

She fought him, hating that he could contain her, hating him for being so stupid, so damned blind.

"Trish isn't in your league! She isn't anywhere close to your league! You might just understand that if you'd stop jumping into bed with women half your age and...and..."

The band tightened, cutting into her ribs.

"And what, Diane?"

She couldn't breathe, couldn't wiggle. Gritting her teeth, she choked back the thick, clogging mint that threatened to come up her throat.

"I told...you earlier, Sloan. You have to...figure it out...for yourself."

"Oh, I've figured it out."

The pressure eased an infinitesimal degree, just enough for Diane to gulp in air.

"Are you ready to listen to me now?"

"That depends on what you…" The warning flex of his muscles had her grinding her teeth. "Yes!"

"Then listen carefully. I'm only going to say this once. I didn't sleep with Trish. If she's pregnant, I'm not the father. You got that, Walker?"

She looked into his eyes. She'd worked with this man too many years, had loved him too long, to believe he was lying to her now.

"Yes."

"Good. Then we need to clear up another apparent misunderstanding. The reason I *haven't* tried to jump into the sack with you is because I didn't want to ruin either our partnership or our friendship. The former is what keeps Sloan Engineering humming. The latter happens to be infinitely more precious to me than getting you into bed."

Ignoring her derisive hoot, he altered his stance in a move so smooth and swift it left her blinking. One moment, Diane was locked against his chest. The next, she was off her feet and in his arms.

"Not that I haven't wanted to," he said, as casually as if they were discussing the weather. "You wouldn't believe the number of occasions I've had you naked and on your back in my head."

"What?"

Glass crunched under his feet as he stalked across the room. "Is that the ruby Baccarat bowl I gave you for your birthday?"

"It…it was," she stuttered, still stunned by the bomb he'd just detonated.

It must be the crème de menthe, she thought wildly. It *had* to be the crème de menthe.

"Damn. I liked that bowl."

Shaking his head, he dropped her on the sofa. His knee came down between her thighs, trapping her skirt and Diane with it. Still stunned and decidedly woozy now, she watched him pop the buttons on his shirt.

This wasn't the first time she'd seen him shirtless. She couldn't count the pool parties, the cruises around the harbor with friends and business associates, the sweaty workouts on the Universal tucked away in a corner of his office suite when he couldn't get out for his morning run.

But this was the first time Marc had stripped off his shirt in front of her. The first time he'd tossed it aside and reached down to rid her of hers. The first time he'd hauled her against him again for a kiss that started the room spinning.

She pulled back after a dizzying moment, her insides roiling. "It's…it's the crème de menthe," she gasped.

"Mmm." His mouth moved over hers. "I can taste it."

She'd dreamed of this moment, had fantasized about his touch, his scent, his kiss. But never, ever, in any of those sensual fantasies, had she started to gag.

"It's the liqueur," she cried, shoving at his shoulders. "Marc! I'm going to throw up."

It was a rare moment for Sloan.

Not holding a woman's head while she puked into a toilet. God knew he'd done that often enough. No, what shook him was seeing his cool, unflappable executive assistant flushed and embarrassed and curled into a tight ball of misery.

The sight generated all kinds of unfamiliar sensations, not the least of which was the fierce need to care for her the way she'd cared for him all these years. The urge speared from his chest to his groin, where it produced a hard-on of gigantic and painful proportions.

"Come on," he said when she'd finished emptying her stomach. "Let's get you cleaned up."

Moaning, she put her hands over her face. "Go away."

He wasn't going anywhere. Not tonight. Maybe not tomorrow. He understood her need for a few moments of privacy, though. Pushing to his feet, he closed the bathroom door behind him.

He was at the bed, yanking down the duvet, when a warning hiss made him snatch back his hand. A gray blur shot out from behind the braid-trimmed sham and streaked into the living room.

Marc paid no attention to the cat. His entire body was one taut cable, thrumming with anticipation for the woman who'd taken the animal in despite her professed dislike of all things feline.

She came out of the bathroom mortally embarrassed. Marc didn't give her a chance to utter a word. Striding across the room, he covered her mouth with his.

She tasted of toothpaste this time. And eager, glorious woman. All this time, he thought. All these years. What a waste.

He wasn't blind. Or stupid. He knew what they had went deeper than friendship, involved more than business.

Nor had he lied about wanting her. But respect and an awareness of his dismal record when it came to long-term relationships had always held him in check. He couldn't imagine Sloan Engineering without Diane any more than he could believe she'd walked out on him this afternoon. Incensed that she'd even consider leaving him, Marc deepened the kiss.

Five minutes after getting her into bed, he was quivering like a prize bull at stud. Five minutes more, and he was fighting desperately to fish his wallet out of his pants pocket.

"Wait. Diane. Let me get some protection for you."

He was so eager he hurt. So anxious, he shredded the foil and ripped the condom.

"Dammit!"

She lifted her head, saw him toss aside the

package. Her face took on a look of near panic. "*Please* tell me you always carry a spare."

"I always carry a spare."

He snatched up his wallet again, dug out an extra and attacked the wrapping with more care. When the rubber snapped into place, Diane wet her lips. The glimpse of her tongue moving over the smooth, slick flesh almost pushed Marc over the edge again.

He was surprised to find himself sweating and as nervous as a pimply faced teenager his first time out of the gate. Deliberately, he focused on her needs instead of the ache just about bending him double. Slicking his hands over her hips and rear. Using his tongue and his teeth on her nipples. Employing every skill he'd mastered over the years to bring her to a writhing, moaning climax.

Only after she'd exploded under him did he allow himself to ram home.

11

Cleo drummed her fingertips against the tall, dew-streaked beer glass. It was well past six. She'd give Donovan another ten minutes. Max.

The sizzle of fish and shrimp in hot grease had been tantalizing her for a good half hour. Her stomach had been making obnoxious feed-me noises just as long.

True, she'd arrived well before the time she and Jack had agreed to when she'd called him with the name of the restaurant. It hadn't taken her long to shower, pin her hair up in a twist and wiggle into the splashy, jungle-print dress she'd thrown in her bag at the last minute.

The little designer number was ninety-eight-percent cotton and two percent spandex, cool enough for comfort and stretchy enough to hug her curves. The fact that its hem rode a good five inches above her knees and showed off her newly trim thighs was only a secondary consideration.

Her primary consideration was the tingle in her breasts and her belly whenever she thought about the kiss Donovan had laid on her this afternoon. If he didn't piss her off by keeping her waiting much longer, he might just get lucky tonight.

She'd reasoned through it. Calmly. Logically. There wasn't any rule that said sex had to be accompanied by pledges of lifelong devotion. If all she and Jack could manage was once in a while, why not make the most of those whiles? Every so often wasn't bad when you thought about it, and Cleo had been thinking about it pretty much continuously for the past few hours.

It was in her head now, getting mixed with her belly-rumbling hunger. The mental image of Jack naked, his muscles slick with perspiration and his eyes a hot, liquid blue as he thrust into her, had Cleo squirming.

Grabbing her condensation-coated glass, she downed a long swallow. The ping of her cell phone caught her in mid-gulp. A glance at the number on the screen had her swallowing a sigh along with the beer. Anticipating the inevitable, she hit Receive.

"Okay, Donovan, where are you?"

"At the airport."

The sigh was harder to swallow this time. "Where are you off to now?"

"Salt Lake City."

"Salt Lake, as in the Ogden Air Logistics Center?"

"You got it. The Old Man wants me to brief the center commander."

"So you're going to let a three-star general beat you out of dinner with a lowly former captain?"

"Looks that way. Sorry about standing you up."

There was genuine regret in the apology. Fat lot of good regret would do either of them tonight.

Cleo was tempted to make him suffer. Drop just an itty-bitty hint of what he was missing out on. Like ice-cold beer. Hot fried fish. Wet, squirming female.

On second thought...

"Did you run those phone calls?" she asked, deciding not to go into detail on her present condition. No sense letting the man get too full of himself.

"I did."

"Anything to tell me?"

"Not over a cell phone."

Tilting to one side, she peered around the high-backed bench. "There's a pay phone just a few feet away. Hang on while I get the number. You can find a phone booth there at the airport and call me back on a land line."

"No time. They're announcing my flight. Later, North."

"Later when? Hey, Donovan! When are you...? Dammit!"

Thoroughly frustrated in more ways than one, Cleo snapped the phone shut and signaled for a waiter.

She ordered the Captain Joe's Combination #1.

The mounds of fried grouper, fried shrimp and fried hush puppies came with french fried sweet potatoes. The platter also contained a ramekin of coleslaw that Cleo ignored. She wasn't in the mood for anything but grease.

It was sloshing around happily in her stomach when she drove back through the warm April night. As chance would have it, Marc pulled into the alley leading to the guesthouse and garage right behind her. Leaving the Escalade parked in the guest-house drive, Cleo crossed the alley and waited while he steered his Porche into the three-car garage attached to his home.

He swung out, unfolding his long, lean frame with an easy grace. Cleo caught a flash of tanned ankle above his polished oxfords and blinked. Had the California mania for going sockless finally reached genteel Charleston?

"I need to talk to you, Marc. Got a minute?"

"Of course."

He ushered her toward the house with his usual courtesy, but Cleo couldn't shake the sense that something was out of whack. She finally pinpointed the problem. His shirttails were tucked neatly in the waistband of his pleated slacks, but he'd missed a couple of buttonholes. And when he reached past her to slide a key card into the security slot, Cleo spotted what looked like a world-class hickey on his neck.

Well, at least *someone* had gotten lucky tonight. Cleo had a pretty good idea who Marc had hitched up with, too.

"How's Diane taking her newly unemployed status?" she asked casually.

Her nonchalance didn't fool Sloan for a minute. He shot her a swift look before his aristocratic features relaxed into a grin she could only describe as goofy.

"Diane's no longer unemployed. I convinced her to return to work."

"Took a lot of convincing, did she?"

The grin got goofier. "Some."

He escorted her down the hall to the music room. The ornate chamber was fast becoming Cleo's favorite. Her fingers itched to pluck a few strings on that monster of a harp.

"Care for a drink?"

"No, thanks. I had my limit with dinner."

Nodding, he poured a generous shot of Tennessee sour mash and knocked it back like a pro. Cleo noted the resulting slump to his shoulders with some interest. The superefficient Ms. Walker had obviously taken the starch out of him.

Splashing in more bourbon, Marc went easier on this shot. "You wanted to talk to me?"

"We need to discuss our relationship."

The look he gave her hovered between chagrin and apology. "I'm sorry, Cleo. This business with

Diane has thrown me off stride. You deserve more of my attention." His gaze slid from her neck to her knees. "Especially in that dress."

Didn't take him long to slide back into his playboy skin, Cleo thought with a dart of genuine sympathy for Diane. The woman would have to shorten Sloan's chain considerably to keep him in line.

"Nice to know my attire has your stamp of approval, but I was talking about our professional relationship."

"What about it?"

"We have a conflict of interest going here."

"Because of the Afloat Prepositioning inquiry?"

"Because the APP inquiry *may* lead back to your missing employee."

The playboy disappeared. The executive sent her a sharp look. "Have you established a link?"

"Not yet."

"Then I don't see the problem. I hired you to find Trish. I still want you to find her."

Giving in to impulse, Cleo twanged one of the harp's strings. Damn. You'd have to have Brillo pads for fingertips to play one of these suckers.

"This isn't the best time to bring this up," she commented as the golden note resonated through the high-ceilinged room, "but have you considered the possibility Diane may not want Trish found?"

Sloan opened his mouth. Snapped it shut.

"Yes, I've considered the possibility. Diane and I discussed it this afternoon, after she all but accused me of seducing the girl."

Ha! Cleo suspected they hadn't gotten around to discussing anything until they were both too limp to do anything else.

"Diane Walker didn't have anything to do with Trish's disappearance," Sloan stated.

"Are you thinking now with your head or with your..."

"My dick?"

"I was going to say heart, but dick works."

"I'm thinking with all parts. And just for the record, I didn't engineer Trish's disappearance as a way to avoid paying child support, either. I would hardly have brought you in to find her if I had."

"Let's talk about that."

Cleo plucked another string, let the note float across the music room.

"Some folks might think hiring a professional to look for Trish would make a good cover."

"They might," he agreed, "unless they knew the professional in question."

She took the compliment with a small nod. She wasn't ready to let go of the love triangle possibility yet. But she had to admit the case had taken on more shades than your standard jealous-lover-eliminates-rival scenario.

It had also piqued her interest, big time. She hated to back out of it now, particularly since Donovan had appeared on the scene.

She was skirting the line here, though—mixing personal and professional, her client's interests with the government's. She needed to make sure Sloan agreed to the altered rules of engagement.

"So you want me to keep looking for Trish?"

"I do."

"You understand I'm going give Donovan any information I turn up relating to the Afloat Prepositioning Program?"

"So am I." Sloan polished off the rest of his drink and set the glass down with a clatter. "My reputation is at stake here, as are my company's future government contracts. If my DNA signature was used to access a classified portion of the APP database, I damn well want to know who used it and why."

That was good enough for Cleo. Her professional conscience folded and went down without a whimper.

"Okay, we're agreed. I continue the hunt for Trish, you work the DNA problem from your end, and we both read Donovan in when appropriate."

That "appropriate" qualifier left her a little wiggle room. She'd been in the business too long to spill *all* her guts, even to Donovan.

Besides, she knew damned well he would play his cards close to the chest. He had to follow the rules, work through the bureaucratic maze. What was worse, he had the Old Man to contend with.

Profoundly grateful she didn't have that black thundercloud hovering over her head, Cleo left Marc contemplating his altered relationship with his assistant and headed back to the guest house to plot her next moves.

There weren't many that offered real promise at this point. She needed to follow up with Donovan on those calls to Malta. That topped her list of to-dos. She also needed to pick up the trail of Frank Helms. She'd get Devereaux to run an airlines check, she decided. There was an off chance Helms departed Charleston after making those phone calls. How many folks would jet directly from South Carolina to a miniscule speck of an island in the Mediterranean?

Only after she'd started to call it a night did she remember the digital photos she'd taken at Trish's apartment. There was that one of the footprints in the sand she'd wanted to play with. Retrieving her camera, she hooked it to her laptop via a fire-wire cable and hit a button to transfer the images. She then logged onto the Internet and linked into the Geophysical Satellite Imaging Database Doreen had insisted was the best of its kind.

"Okay, Beany Doreeny, let's see if this topograpical data you keep touting can tell a shoreline from a shopping center."

The program opened innocuously enough. But when Cleo dragged the image of the beach into the search box, she had the feeling she'd stepped into a *Matrix* movie.

The image lifted. Rotated. Became a three-dimensional graphic. The graphic zoomed in, then out. Numbers flashed across the top of the screen, so swiftly Cleo couldn't tell what the heck they were supposed to represent. Good thing, as she and numbers had a real hate-hate relationship.

And they kept flashing. Long, incomprehensible strings of them. They were still flashing when she left the computer to do its thing and went to bed.

Cleo waltzed into Devereaux's office the next morning, a green and white Krispy Kreme box held high on one palm.

"I have raspberry-filled. I have cinnamon twists. I have four, count 'em, four glazed crullers, two of which are tagged as mine. Please tell me you have fresh coffee."

"I have fresh coffee."

Lafayette rolled back his chair, departed his cubbyhole and returned with a chipped mug. Cleo downed a hearty swallow while he dived into the doughnuts.

"I also have to say your man works fast," he got out between bites.

"My man?"

"Special Agent Donovan. He called earlier this morning. Said those phone calls traced to a phone in a pub—a taverna, I think he called it—in Valletta, the capital of Malta. He also indicated the CIA had the place on their watch list some months back."

Cleo gave a nonchalant nod, acting as if this was old news. Privately, she was more than a little ticked. Donovan could have passed her the info directly instead of letting her get it secondhand.

"I've been thinking about those calls," she said. "Also about our mysterious Mr. Helms. We should run an airlines check and—"

"It's done. Your man took care of that, too."

Her *man* was going to be chopped liver before very long.

"Donovan cut through the bureaucracy faster than grease through a goose," Devereaux informed her. "Got the FAA to do a check of all passengers departing the East Coast in the past two weeks with connecting flights to Malta. He also had State screen visas, then got the Transportation Security Agency to match names to faces on their airport-surveillance tapes."

Downing the rest of his cinnamon twist in one gulp, the detective dusted his hands and used a forefinger to slide a grainy faxed image across his desk.

"Here's our boy. Frank Helms, aka Adrian Mustafa Moore."

"Aka, huh? That doesn't sound good."

"It isn't."

While Cleo studied the thin face in the photo, Devereaux reeled off some details.

"Born Riyadh, Saudi Arabia. Mother Saudi, father a British businessman. Educated at Chilton Academy, outside London. Philosophy degree from Oxford. Hired to teach at King Abdul Aziz University six years ago. Quit after being questioned in regard to his participation in protest against the royal family. Entered the United States a little more than three months ago. Dropped out of sight until he departed Charleston four days before Patricia Jackson's parents reported her missing. Deplaned in Valletta. Present whereabouts unknown."

Cleo sucked in a swift breath. "I'd say that's an uh-oh, Lafayette."

"A big, fat uh-oh," he agreed, pursing his lips. "The question now is how a twenty-two-year-old office worker from South Carolina hooked up with a former philosophy professor from Riyadh."

"Tell you what. You work the how. I'll work a little more on the where."

"Come again?"

"I found a picture in Trish's apartment showing two sets of footprints in the sand. Looked to me as if she might have been strolling along a beach with someone bigger and heavier."

"Yeah, I saw that photo. I thought maybe I could get a tag on the location of the beach, but no luck. South Carolina has almost two hundred miles of coast. With all the islands, inlets and coves, that adds up to nearly three thousand miles of shoreline."

"I found that out when I digitized the picture and ran it through a special program that uses NASA satellite imagery. It took a while, but the program came up with two possibilities in the Charleston area."

"No shit?"

"No shit."

Tossing the uneaten half of her second cruller

in the wastebasket, Cleo produced the maps she'd printed out based on the computed coordinates.

"One is right here in Charleston harbor. The other is about fifteen miles south of the city. I thought I might hire a boat and do a little exploring."

"No need to hire out. The Charleston PD Harbor Patrol is a little busy these days, but I can pull a few strings."

Two phone calls later, Devereaux handed Cleo a scrap of paper with directions to the marina where the Harbor Patrol moored its craft and the name of the officer who'd be waiting for her.

12

The Escalade's OnStar system took Cleo right to the marina, where a uniformed patrol officer met her at the gate. Sergeant Alicia Thornton wasn't more than five-two or three, but she radiated a don't-mess-with-me confidence that won Cleo's instant approval.

"Detective Devereaux said you wanted to check out Duck Island, then head down to Sand Creek State Park."

"That's right."

"Might be a bumpy ride," she warned, leading the way to the slips. "The wind's whipping up the water this morning."

"You've already been out?"

Laughing, the auburn-haired patrol officer lifted a life vest from a locker at the end of the slip. "I've been on patrol since 6:00 a.m. I've crisscrossed the harbor three times already, taking inspectors out to transients. Here, put this on."

"Transients?" Cleo asked, poking her head through the dun-colored vest.

"Ships, not people. Charleston's one of the busiest ports on the East Coast. More than eighty-five thousand ships enter our waters every year. Only a few are registered in South Carolina. The rest are transients that include everything from thirty-foot sailboats to supersize cargo vessels."

This was obviously Cleo's week to get educated on things nautical.

"I saw one of those supersize jobbies up at Sunny Point yesterday," she commented as she followed Thornton aboard a sleek white speedboat with prominent police markings on its hull.

"Then you can imagine what fun it is for our inspectors to crawl through them to check for contraband or illegal immigrants."

"I wouldn't have thought inspecting commercial cargo ships fell under the purview of the Charleston PD."

"It didn't, before 9/11."

After untying the stern line, Thornton nudged the throttle into Reverse.

"Used to be our job was mostly crisis response. Handling distress calls, performing search and rescue, recovering bodies. Stuff like that. Now we're part of a joint task force that includes Customs, the Coast Guard and the Charleston County Sheriff's Office Marine Patrol."

Peering over her shoulder, she backed the speedboat out of the slip before continuing.

"Our focus has shifted to homeland security. We escort ships into the harbor, perform inspections and provide protection for high-profile targets like bridges and military vessels. In addition to handling distress calls, performing search and rescue, and recovering bodies," she added dryly as she brought the bow around. "Makes for long and interesting days."

Cleo could imagine. Much as she herself had disliked being a cog in the bureaucracy, she felt a real appreciation for those who were still turning the wheel. Particularly with the increased terrorist threat these days.

"You'd better grab a strut and hang on," Thornton warned. "Once we clear the marina, I'll open her up."

With her passenger in a brace and the marina behind them, the harbor patrol officer shoved the throttle forward. The engine revved to an ear-busting roar, and the speedboat leapt ahead like a sprinter coming off the chocks.

"It's only about three nautical miles to Duck Island," she shouted over the engine's thunder. "Won't take us long to get there."

Not at this speed! Legs spread, body angled forward against thrust, Cleo kept one fist wrapped around the metal pole supporting the fold-back canopy, the other clamped on the bill of her ball cap. Wind whipped tears out of her eyes as the speedboat wove past the pleasure craft and commercial vessels navigating Charleston's busy harbor.

Within minutes they were approaching Duck Island. According to Thornton, it had once been home to a lighthouse keeper. Electronic beacons and navigational aids had long since replaced both keeper and lighthouse. The pilings of the pier where the beacon tender had once tied his skiff was still there, though, as was the small curve of sandy beach stretching out from the pier.

"Can we go ashore?" Cleo shouted.

"Sure. As long as you don't mind getting wet."

Throttling back, Thornton brought the speedboat in on a sweeping arc that got them within wading distance of the shore. Thankful that she'd opted for her rubber-soled Oakleys this morning instead of the Gucci ankle boots, Cleo rolled up her pants legs and hopped over the side. The harborpatrol officer threw out an anchor and joined her.

It didn't take them long to make a circuit of the island. They spotted the usual effluvia washed up by the harbor tide—kelp, clam shells, plastic sixpack holders, a child's sneaker. No starfish, though, and nothing that linked Duck Island to Trish Jackson or the mysterious Frank Helms, aka Adrian Mustafa Moore.

Cleo wasn't sure what she'd been hoping to find. Shell collectors shuffling through the shallow waves, maybe. Or bird-watchers studying the resident gull population. Some fishermen hunkered over their poles. Anyone who might have spotted

Trish and a friend strolling this stretch of beach within the past few weeks.

"I don't see anything here," she admitted. "Let's try beach number two."

The wind picked up during the trip south to Sand Creek State Park. Whitecaps skittered across the gray-green water. With every plunge of the bow against the waves, Cleo's stomach performed a corresponding lurch. A sigh of relief feathered through her lips when Alicia throttled back once more and aimed the speedboat toward an isolated stretch of beach.

Sand Creek Park lay outside Charleston proper but still within the sheltering arms of the harbor. Unlike Duck Island, the park showed signs of human habitation. Cleo spotted a boat launch, several dozen day-use sites tucked among the spindly pines and scrub oak, campsites with hookups and what looked like trailer dumping facilities.

At the near end of the beach, a weathered cypress pier jutted out into the bay. A solitary fisherman lazed in a folding lawn chair at the end of the dock, tending the three rods that sprouted up at his feet.

"Let's start with him," Cleo suggested, eyeing the cross ties nailed to one of the pylons. "Can you boogie up next to that ladder?"

"Does a red-ear have a snout?"

"Beats me. Does it?"

"It does."

Demonstrating the same skill she'd displayed

off Duck Island, Thornton danced the speedboat right up to the pier. Cleo dug the black-and-white of Trish and the grainy fax of Frank Helms out of her purse and slid them into her waistband at the small of her back. She was reaching for the cross ties when Thornton waved a pair of heavy canvas work gloves.

"Better put these on. With the tide going out, the barnacles on the bottom rungs of that ladder could do a serious number on your palms."

She hadn't exaggerated the case. The lower struts were encrusted with a thick coat of slippery, spiny crustaceans. Cleo managed to make the pier without slicing palms, elbows or knees. Thornton tied her craft to a low rung and followed. Together the two women made their way down the weathered boards to the solitary fisherman.

He looked to be in his mid to late sixties. The caked perspiration riming his ball cap and the three poles anchored to the boards suggested he spent a lot of time out here on the pier.

"Good morning."

The fisherman eyed Thornton's uniform curiously and bobbed his head. "Mornin'."

"Are they biting?"

"Now and again."

"I'm Officer Alicia Thornton with the Charleston Harbor Patrol. This is Ms. Cleo North, a private investigator. Okay if we ask you a few questions?"

"Yes'm, I s'pose so."

Tugging the folded photo from her waistband, Cleo passed it into a hand leopard-spotted by sun and age.

"We're looking for this woman. She may have come out to Sand Creek Park sometime in the past few weeks to collect shells."

"We get a lot shell-hunters out here," the fisherman mused, squinting down at the photo with rheumy eyes. "'Specially after a storm. The shells pile up like old bones then. Something about the tidal currents where the creek empties into the bay." He tipped his lawn chair, peering at the two women from under the brim of his hat. "Why are you looking for this one? She in trouble?"

"Possibly," Cleo replied. "She's gone missing, and her friends and family are worried about her."

"Hmmm."

His narrow-eyed squint when he perused the photo again killed any hope he might provide a lead. With those clouded corneas, Cleo doubted he could see to the end of the pier. So she didn't immediately leap for joy when he bobbed his head.

"I've seen her."

"Are you sure?"

"Yes'm."

"When?"

"More'n once. She's a regular. Comes out every so often, splashes along the shore, puts her bits and pieces in a pink plastic bucket."

Cleo's pulse skittered and jumped. She'd spotted that toy bucket in Trish's cupboards.

"What about this man?" She passed him the surveillance photo. "Did you ever see this guy with her?"

"Well…"

She held her breath while he frowned over the copy.

"I'm not saying for certain, you understand, but this fella *looks* like the one she was holdin' hands with the weekend before last."

Cleo could have kissed him. She might have done just that if one of his fishing poles hadn't bent almost in half at that instant. Thrusting the photocopy into her hands, he dived for the rod.

He lost the battle with whatever was on the other end of his line. Since he couldn't supply any additional information, the two women left him grumbling to himself while he rebaited his hook. As they retraced their steps along the pier, that tingle of excitement that came when a case took unexpected twists and turns crawled up Cleo's spine.

The link between Frank Helms and Trish was tenuous, but it was there. Cleo had the phone call from the doctor's office and now a relatively positive ID placing him with Trish at Sand Creek. She also had a link between Helms and a taverna in Malta that was on the CIA watch list. What she didn't have was Trish Jackson.

She'd find her. The certainty was growing in Cleo's gut. So was the certainty that she wouldn't find her alive.

"Do you have a chart that shows the tidal currents for this area?" she asked Alicia as they got ready to climb back down the wooden ladder.

"You caught that comment about shells piling up around here like old bones, did you?"

"I did. I'm thinking we may want to check out that shell graveyard after we talk to the campers set up on shore."

None of the campers recognized Trish or Frank Helms from their pictures. Nor did Cleo and Alicia find anything sinister poking through the shells piled up at the mouth of the creek.

They decided to split up at the creek. Cleo walked the shore for some distance to the south. Alicia headed north. Mangrove and live oak grew right down to the water's edge, their roots snaking together like Medusa's locks. Gulls whirled and squawked overhead. With the sand sucking at her boot soles, Cleo scanned the tangled undergrowth.

She wasn't sure what she was looking for. Even when she spotted the weathered shack housing the camp's water pump, she didn't attach any particular significance to it. The pump house sat back from the beach, almost hidden among the palmettos and scrub oak. A neatly lettered sign on the side facing the beach warned that the building was state property and off limits to campers.

When Cleo wandered in for a closer look, the first thing she noted was the padlock on the pump-house door. It was shiny and new, much newer than the rusty hasp it secured. She studied that lock for long moments before making a slow circuit of the building.

There was only one window, small and high and coated with salt spray. Cleo had to stretch up on her toes to peer inside. At first all she saw was a small generator and an eight-inch pipe that humped up, then down to disappear beneath the floorboards of the shack. The boards themselves were coated with a thin layer of sand that had likely seeped or blown in under the door.

Cleo dropped onto her heels, got the kink out of her left arch and went back up on her toes again. She squinted through the salt spray, studying the patch of flooring at the near side of the pump house. Someone or something had disturbed the sand pattern. It sure looked to her as though that same someone or something had pried up at least two of the floorboards.

Returning to the front of the building, Cleo eyed the lock and hasp again. One good kick would separate the rusty hasp from the jamb. If she hadn't spent those years as an air force investigator, she might have put her boot to the door. Instead, she took the sandy path back to the beach and shouted for Alicia Thornton. If they found what Cleo's gut was telling her they might find under those floorboards, they'd need at least two pairs of eyes to record the details of the scene.

It took Alicia fifteen minutes to work her way by phone through several levels of the state parks and recreation department's bureaucracy. Whoever she talked to on the third call gave her permission to pry open the pump-house door.

When the door swung open, the stench exploded into the hot air. Alicia jumped back, her hand over her mouth and nose.

"Jesus!"

Cleo's stomach took a dive. She recognized the stink of rotting flesh. Dragging up a shirttail, she breathed through its salty tang.

"See those two boards there, right behind the pump. Looks to me as if they've been pried up recently."

Nodding grimly, Alicia tied a handkerchief around the lower half of her face and pulled on her gloves. Luckily, she'd brought a long-handled tool with her from the boat. It was designed for tightening cleats and repairing engine ring snaps, but worked fine on the uneven floorboards.

The first board came up with a groan. The second resisted until Cleo locked her fingers under the edge and added her weight to the effort. The board popped up, sending her back a step or two.

One glance at the shallow hole beneath the boards told her they'd found Trish Jackson. Cleo recognized that short, pixie haircut from the photograph. That was all she recognized, though. Trish was lying facedown, half buried in the soft, sandy soil. The sand crabs had already begun to feast on her flesh. What little Cleo could see of her had been eaten down to the bone.

Pity knifed through Cleo, followed swiftly by

rage. Such a young, vibrant woman, pregnant, in love. Murdered and left here to rot. The vicious waste pierced the professional detachment all trained investigators had to use as a shield.

The Crime-Scene Unit responded first.

Giving the CSU room to work, Cleo waited outside the pump house while they photographed and analyzed the scene. They held off bagging the remains until Devereaux arrived, accompanied by the homicide detective who'd just inherited the case.

"Is it Jackson?" Lafayette asked Cleo.

"What's left of her. You'll need something to cover your nose. It's pretty grim inside."

Cleo used her shirttail again and wedged back inside the small pump house with the two detectives. Hunkering down on his haunches, the homicide cop studied the remains.

"Any guess on the cause of death?" he asked the senior CSU investigator.

"My guess is drowning. We didn't find any wounds, ligature marks or visible signs of trauma. These look interesting, though."

Using a gloved finger, he lifted the short hair to expose the victim's nape. The flesh was pasty white where the crabs hadn't gotten to it. Gulping, Cleo leaned forward to squint at the faint bluish marks.

"Could be bruises," the investigator muttered, "made by the fingers of one hand. The other side of her neck is pretty much eaten away, so there's no corresponding thumbprint."

"Made by a hand, huh? You think someone held her underwater?"

"That's my guess. We won't know for sure until the M.E. gets her on the table. Oh, we found something else, too."

He sorted through a small assortment of plastic evidence bags filled with the samples they'd collected from the scene.

"This was in her mouth. So far down she must have choked on the damned thing."

Cleo's stomach did a quick roll. The same sadistic bastard who'd held a pregnant woman's head underwater had also stuffed a perfect, five-point starfish down her throat.

13

A cold fury had settled in Cleo's chest by the time she returned to the marina. Thanking Alicia for ferrying her around the harbor, she climbed behind the wheel of the Escalade and headed downtown. The police might need to wait for the medical examiner to do his thing before making the official ID. She didn't.

Until now, the twists and turns in this case had roused her professional interest. That starfish had made it personal. There was something so vicious, so obscene about that. It was as if Trish's murderer had wanted to drown her joy and her dreams along with her.

Cleo intended to stay on the case, either on retainer or off. She also intended to follow the one real lead they now had. It was looking more and more like the last person to see Trish Jackson alive was a man who'd departed Charleston for Malta shortly before she was reported missing.

She broke the news to Marc and his executive assistant in his office.

He went rigid with the kind of helpless rage most men of action experience when confronted with something they can't control. Diane Walker sank onto the leather sofa. Ashen-faced, the blonde put a hand to her mouth and stared in shocked dismay at the scene outside the windows.

"I want to go after him," Cleo said into the stunned silence. "To Malta."

Marc nodded, his eyes as flat and hard as polished steel. "I'm going with you."

"That's not necessary at this point. Or particularly smart. I can go into Malta as a tourist, with nothing connecting me to Trish or Sloan Engineering. You can't."

He looked as though he intended to argue the matter. Cleo cut him off with a promise to provide regular progress reports and to call in the cavalry if and when she deemed necessary. He acceded with something less than his usual smooth charm.

"When do you intend to leave?"

"Not until tomorrow. I'll have to get my office to overnight my passport."

And a few other essentials, Cleo thought grimly. There was no way she could obtain the necessary clearances to bring her Glock into the country on such short notice, but she wasn't going in unarmed.

Diane shook herself out of her white-faced trance. "I can have your passport and whatever else you need couriered in from Dallas within a few hours."

"That'll work," Cleo said, composing a quick mental list. "I'll call my office and have them get a few things together for me."

"Tell them a courier will contact them for pickup within the next thirty minutes. In the meantime, I'll check on flights to Malta. Since you don't want to display any overt connection to Sloan Engineering, I assume you won't want to use the corporate jet."

With a twinge of real regret, Cleo declined the use of all that leather-and-burled-wood luxury.

Diane surged to her feet. She looked relieved to have something to do. "I'll get to work on airline and hotel reservations."

With a new appreciation for the woman's efficiency, Cleo dialed her office. Four rings and a forwarding click later, her part-time office manager answered.

"North, Incorporated."

"Mae, it's me."

"Hush!"

Cleo assumed the stern command was directed at the yapping schnauzer she heard in the background.

"I need you to pack a few items for me," she said when Baby subsided. "A special courier will come by to pick them up within the next half hour."

"As long as it's not later than that. I have an appointment at the gym."

"What gym?"

"The same one you use. I've requested private instruction in self-defense."

An ugly suspicion wormed its way into Cleo's head. "Is your appointment with Goose, by any chance?"

"It is. He doesn't know that, of course. He'd be headed back to Mexico if he did."

Mae had that right. She terrified the hulking, ex-Special Forces trainer. She was also determined to get him into the sack. Shuddering, Cleo forced that image from her mind.

"What do you need, dear?"

"My passport. It's in the strongbox. You know the combination, don't you?"

"I do. Anything else?"

"The T-26, my tool kit, a dozen of the mil spec sensors, and my *ebu*."

The African *ebu* was carved from a single piece of ironwood, one of the hardest natural substances on earth. The wooden blade had been honed to stiletto sharpness. The grip was also of wood and contained no material detectable by X ray or chemical agents.

"Passport, T-26, tool kit, sensors, *ebu*," Mae reeled off. "I'll have them ready for the courier. Where are you going, if I might ask?"

"Malta, to start with."

After that, wherever the case took her.

Her next call was to Donovan, but all she got was his voice mail. He was probably still briefing the commander of the air-logistics center.

Cleo left a terse message advising him that they'd located the body of Sloan's missing employee. She also informed him she was following the trail of the last person known to have seen Trish Jackson alive.

After Cleo left for New York to catch a transatlantic flight, Diane lingered at the office. The staff was gone for the day. The outer office was deserted. All that remained was for her to empty Trish's desk of her personal possessions and hold them for the police.

Her hand shaking, Diane deposited an empty box on the desk. One by one, Diane emptied the desk drawers. The secret stash of candy tucked away at the back of the bottom left drawer made her bite her lip. But it was the shellacked starfish sitting on the blotter that had her fighting a wave of grief and guilt.

Neither she nor Marc had mentioned the object found in Trish's mouth to her co-workers or her parents—Marc because he didn't think her parents needed to deal with that right now, Diane because she couldn't. The thought that someone would do something so vicious made her feel sick.

"Are you okay?"

She glanced up and saw that Marc had come into the reception area.

"I was until I found this."

Her hand shaking, Diane lifted Trish's star-shaped souvenir. Marc muttered a curse and crossed the room. White lines bracketed his mouth as he took Trish's prized paperweight and turned it over and over in his palm.

"Someone's going to pay," he said softly, almost to himself. "Someone will most definitely pay."

Watching him, Diane felt her stomach lurch again. The medical examiner would autopsy Trish's body. He'd run the DNA on her baby, too. If Marc *was* the father, if he'd…

No!

Furious at herself for doubting him again, she surged to her feet. She might have private reservations about Marc's ability to remain faithful to one woman, but she knew with every fiber of her being he wouldn't have committed that grotesque desecration of her body.

She also knew she'd wasted half her life waiting for the man to work his way through his string of wives and mistresses. If nothing else, Trish's death had brought home the absurdity of wasting another hour. Reaching up, Diane cupped a hand over his cheek.

"This isn't the right time to say this, but I think you should know I love you."

He stared at her, his thoughts still dark and private. She died a little inside until the murderous glint faded from his eyes.

"I figured that out," he said. "Finally."

Her hand flattened against his cheek. His skin was warm, and the bristles he always sprouted after a long day tickled her palm.

"You don't have to worry, Marc. I just needed to say it aloud this once. I won't let my feelings for you get in the way."

"Of what?"

"Of Sloan Engineering."

He gave an un-Marc-like snort. "Now who's being the idiot? Sloan Engineering wouldn't be what it is today if the two of us hadn't worked so hard and so well together all these years."

He caught her hand and brought her palm to his lips.

"Maybe we should think about formalizing the partnership," he suggested.

It was what she'd ached to hear. She'd imagined this moment so many times, had scripted a dozen different responses. The one that came to her lips surprised them both.

"Maybe we should. After we've had time to figure out what that new partnership might entail."

14

Cleo flew out of JFK first class and waited three hours in London for a connecting flight. She used most of the wait time to do research.

She lost six hours due to the time change, so it was midafternoon local time when Cleo stepped off the plane into sunlight so dazzling she had to take instant refuge behind sunglasses. She passed through Customs with the *ebu* strapped to her ankle and undetected. Exiting the airport, she hailed a taxi.

The driver's prominently displayed license tagged him as Salvatore Sayed. Whipping into a stream of traffic, he aimed his cab down a palm-lined road, hooked an arm over the passenger seat and twisted around to converse with his passenger.

"This is your first time to Malta, yes?"

Cleo kept one eye on Salvatore, another on

the donkey cart they were hurtling toward at warp speed.

"First time."

"I will tell you our history."

She started to inform him she'd Googled up most of Malta's colorful past, but he'd already launched into full tour-guide mode.

"We are Phoenician. We are Carthaginian. We are Greek and Roman and…"

"We are dead," Cleo interjected, jerking her chin at the obstacle now just yards ahead.

Her driver threw a careless glance over his shoulder, gave the steering wheel a yank and careened around the donkey cart on two wheels.

"The Arabs come after the Romans," he continued without missing a beat. "The Normans invade and drive out the Arabs."

He punctuated his recital with extravagant gestures that necessitated taking one or both hands off the wheel at different points. Cleo had to admire his technique even as she darted wary glances at the road ahead.

"After the Normans come the Sicilians. Then the pope makes a plea to Catholic nations to send knights to hold Malta against the Turks, who want our harbor for their Mediterranean fleet. Knights come from all across Europe, yes? Castile. Portugal. Provence. They fight a great battle. Eight thousand Turks against nine hundred knights."

Not unlike the battle fought hundreds of years later, Cleo had discovered in her research, when the Germans conducted a determined air campaign to gain Malta's deepwater harbor as a staging base for their invasion of Africa. The native Maltese and a handful of British defenders had held out against two years of continual bombing and strafing.

"You will visit the cathedral built by our knights, yes? The Co-Cathedral of St. John?"

"If I have time."

"But you must, *signora!* It is of all the most magnificent."

Since he took both hands off the wheel to slap his palms together in a passionate appeal, Cleo hastily promised to visit his cathedral.

Reassured, he resumed his narrative. By the time he'd detailed Napoléon's invasion, Britain's subsequent rout of the French and Malta's eventual transition from crown colony to independent nation, Cleo was awed by both his grasp of history and his blithe disregard for everything around him.

And people accused her of kamikaze road tactics! This guy beat her out in every category. Breakneck speed. Screeching, two-wheeled turns. Evel Knievel-style leaps over every bump. All conducted on the wrong side of the road.

Between the history lesson and the daredevil driving, she caught only fleeting glimpses of the passing scenery. Most of it seemed to consist of colorful fishing boats, red tile roofs and whitewashed buildings that glowed a pale gold in the afternoon sun.

But as they approached the city perched atop a distant hill, she leaned over the front seat to drink in the spectacle of massive, crenellated walls complete with sally ports and watchtowers. Inside the walls was a maze of buildings constructed centuries ago, all crowned by the cathedral built by those industrious knights.

"Your hotel, it is inside the walls. No taxis can go into the old city, you understand. You take a horse, yes?"

"Uh, I guess."

To her relief, the horses lined up at the gate to the inner city came equipped with carriage and driver. Her only luggage was her leather carryall, but Taxi Man insisted on transferring both it and her from vehicle to vehicle with Old World gallantry. Moments later, she was clip-clopping through streets so narrow the balconies of one building almost kissed those on the opposite side of the street.

The Auberge St. Georges sported a narrow facade, a set of ancient wooden doors and a doorman attired in an embroidered surcoat and a square velvet hat dripping gold tassels at each corner. When he handed her down from the carriage and escorted her into the lobby, Cleo's jaw sagged.

She could have sworn she'd just stepped into the Middle Ages. Tapestries embroidered in rich, glowing jewel tones adorned the walls. Flambeaux flickered in iron holders. Medieval suits of armor stood at attention on either side of a stone fireplace large enough to roast a mastodon.

Dangerously close to being a gawk, Cleo approached the front desk. The attendant was too well trained to give her jeans and wrinkled linen blazer more than a cursory glance, but his polite smile turned positively effusive when she provided her name and passport.

"Ah, yes, Madame North. We have you booked into the King's Suite."

"Which king?" she couldn't resist asking.

"Actually, three monarchs have occupied those rooms. Also two prime ministers and four presidents. You'll find information regarding their visits in the suite."

Ooooh-kay.

Somehow, she managed to keep her cool when he slid the registration form toward her and she saw the daily room rate. Good thing Sloan Engineering was covering her expenses. Signing the form with a flourish, she accepted an iron key that weighed at least a pound.

"Can you give me directions to the Café Corinthia?"

Visiting the taverna Frank Helms had called topped her list of priorities—right after she'd showered away the effects of her long flight.

"The café is just a block away, *madame*. In the square directly behind the cathedral. You cannot miss it."

"Thanks."

"Phillipe!" A snap of his fingers summoned the doorman. "Escort Madame North to her rooms."

The lobby had pretty well prepared her for the suite's baronial opulence. *Nothing* could have prepared her for the view.

"Oh, man!"

She stepped out onto the balcony that ran the length of the sitting room, awed by the panoramic vista of stone battlements, swaying palms and a row of glistening white cruise ships docked just below her in the Grand Harbor. And to the right, almost close enough to touch, were the square towers of the cathedral.

"Do you desire anything else, *madame?*"

"What? Oh, no thanks."

Fumbling in her purse, Cleo dug out the roll of Maltese lira she'd purchased at the airport.

Numbers weren't her strong suit. In fact, she'd expended considerable energy trying to convince her high school math teachers she lacked the necessary gene for geometry. After the long flight from the States, she was too ragged to even *attempt* the exchange rate, but the porter's beaming smile told her she had erred on the right side of the equation.

She closed the door behind him, longing to get at that opulent shower with its twenty-four-karat-gold fixtures. Years of training and an inbred caution exerted an inexorable pull, though. Before stripping off and leaving herself vulnerable, she set the deadlock and attached one of the military spec sensors to the assembly. That done, she dug the T-26 out of her carryall.

The unit consisted of off-the-shelf electronics considerably enhanced by the inventive Doreen. In transmit mode, the palm-size box emitted silent signals designed to trigger any listening device. In record mode, it could pluck the vibrations caused by those same listening devices right out of the air.

Cleo didn't really expect to find any bugs. Given the high-profile guests who'd occupied these rooms, she figured security teams from just about every nation on the planet had swept the suite at one time or another. So when the T-26 burped, she blinked in surprise.

Frowning, she tracked the signal to the fridge in the well-stocked minibar. No device of Doreen's making would react to vibrations caused by the champagne bottles squeezed into the racks or even the hum from the copper tubing that fed the ice-maker. There had to be something else.

She found it behind the fridge, wedged into a crack in the baseboard. The metal collar was corroded with rust, but the glass diode was intact…and right out of the fifties.

"Well, damn!"

Cleo had seen a bug just like this one in the Spy Museum, otherwise known as the Air Force Office of Special Investigations Historical Devices Display. It had been invented by a Russian by the name of Lev Termen back in the dark ages of electronic spookery.

A Lev Termen bug had found its way into the Great Seal of the United States that had hung for years behind the desk of Henry Cabot Lodge, America's ambassador to the Soviet Union. This particular copy looked to have been planted about the same time. Cleo could only imagine the conversations it must have transmitted before more sophisticated devices made it obsolete. Dropping the rusty diode into her bag, she completed her sweep and headed for the shower.

After tugging on her jeans and a clean, cream-colored rib-knit shell, she caught her still-damp hair up under a ball cap. She strapped the sheathed *ebu* to her right ankle, then placed the faxed surveillance photo of Frank Helms into her shoulder bag.

A short walk through streets frozen in time brought her to a square surrounded on three sides by the palatial medieval residences of former knights. Café Corinthia occupied one corner of the square. The lively taverna was wedged between two similar establishments, all apparently popular with locals and tourists alike.

Red-and-white-striped umbrellas shaded the outdoor tables, where sweaty soccer players sat elbow to elbow with businessmen in suits, students hunched over laptops and visitors in T-shirts decorated with cruise ship logos. As Cleo wove through the tables, she picked up a smattering of French, German, Italian and Japanese. Crisp British accents dominated, although the delegation from one of the cruise ships was definitely American.

Inside the café, blue cigarette smoke mingled

with the heavy scent of garlic. The waiter who approached pinpointed Cleo's nationality in a single glance.

"Are you only one?" he asked in perfect English.

"Only one."

"This way, please."

"I need to make a call first. Is there a phone in the café?"

"Yes, *madame*. There, by the bar."

Obtaining the appropriate Maltese coins from the waiter, she dialed the Auberge St. Georges to make reservations for dinner. It was a feeble excuse for a call with the hotel just a block away, but it served her purpose. The number printed on the phone's placard was the one Frank/Adrian had called from Charleston.

When she hung up, the waiter appeared at her side. "This way, *madame*."

Cleo squeezed through the crowded bar and into the chair the waiter held out for her. She ordered tea, which she sipped while nonchalantly scrutinizing the restaurant's patrons. None of them resembled the man in the airport-surveillance photo.

Just as casually, she downed a late lunch consisting of the house specialty, a spicy, boat-shaped pastry stuffed with ricotta cheese, egg and peas. When she asked for the check and peeled off a wad of lira, the waiter fought a brief, heroic battle with his baser self.

"It is too much, *madame*."

"Maybe. Maybe not." She unfolded the surveillance photo and nudged it across the table. "I'm looking for this man. Do you know him?"

He flicked the printout a quick glance. "No, *madame,* I do not."

"Are you sure?"

Cleo tapped the lira with a fingernail. The waiter took another look.

"This is not a very good photocopy."

"I know. The man's name is Adrian Mustafa Moore. In the States, he went by Frank Helms."

"He is American?"

"British and Saudi."

"And he lives here in Malta?"

"He has friends here."

"I'm sorry, *madame,* I do not recognize him. But I will ask at the bar, yes? Perhaps one of them knows this man."

The photocopy made the rounds of the locals at the counter. Cleo picked up a lot of muttering and head shaking, but nothing that registered as recognition. She hadn't really expected it to be that easy.

Pocketing the faxed image, she passed the waiter the lira.

"Here's my business card. I'm staying at the Auberge St. Georges. Call me if anyone recalls seeing or speaking to this man."

Her next stop was the Pulizija ta' Malta.

Cleo's research had confirmed that Malta's police force was one of the oldest in Europe. Her worry that it might have gotten stuck in some past century vanished when Inspector Renaldo Aruzzo introduced himself.

The man only came up to Cleo's shoulder, but the shrewd intelligence in his dark eyes was as reassuring as the sleek laptop on his desk. Dapper in his Italian-cut suit and neatly trimmed Vandyke beard, he invited Cleo to take a seat.

"I have received a fax from the Charleston Police Department, Ms. North. They wish information on the same individual you are inquiring about. I understand they desire to question him in regard to a missing woman."

"She's no longer missing. Her body was found yesterday."

"Ah. How unfortunate. Perhaps you will tell me your connection to this woman?"

"I was hired by her employer to find her. Now I want to find her killer."

"You have evidence she was murdered?"

"The autopsy was still pending when I left the States, but there's little doubt in anyone's mind."

"I see."

Crossing his arms, the inspector stroked his pointed beard. His gaze was thoughtful as he regarded Cleo. She suspected he'd received recent inquiries about Frank Helms from several other sources besides the Charleston Police Department. Donovan had to be working his channels, too.

"So do you have anything on Mr. Helms-slash-Moore?"

"Only that he flew in last week, cleared through Customs with a British passport and has since dropped from sight."

"Why am I not surprised?"

"Nor am I, *madame*, given the sudden flurry of interest in this man. My people are looking for him. As yet, we've had no success, which is why I should very much like you to keep me apprised of your findings, if any," he added on a polite note that suggested he didn't expect her to do any better at tracking down Mr. Moore than his people had.

"Certainly," Cleo returned. "And hopefully you'll notify me of whatever information you turn up. If any."

The inspector's mouth twitched, but he merely noted that she was staying at the Auberge St. Georges and gave her his card for future reference.

Cleo spent the rest of the afternoon familiarizing herself with Valletta. She had no idea how long she'd remain in the city, nor did she anticipate requiring an escape route out of it. Old habits died hard, though.

Map in hand, she roamed the streets. She soon discovered no map could capture either the character or the complexity of the capital city.

The layout was simple enough. Valletta was crowded onto a narrow spear of land that jutted into Malta's great natural harbor, dividing it into two deepwater basins. At the tip of the spear sat the medieval fortress built by the knights of St.

John to protect the entrance to the two harbors. Behind the fortress were the *auberges*—or sectors—assigned to the various Catholic nations that had responded to the pope's plea to hold the island against the invaders.

Knights from each of these nations had constructed residences—some austere, some magnificent—in their assigned sectors. They'd also built hotels, armories, granaries and stables for the armies they'd brought with them. Many of those medieval structures now housed government offices. One contained Malta's House of Parliament and was guarded by men in colorful uniforms from a bygone era.

Cleo brushed past tourists snapping pictures of the rigid, unsmiling guards, fixed the location of the American consulate and wandered through an open-air market crammed with stalls offering everything from fresh squid to Beyoncé CDs. Noting the bullet holes still scarring many of the facades from the fierce World War Two strafing, she worked her way down to the fortress at the tip of the spear.

She'd intended to walk back via the battlements and make a complete circuit of the old city, but jet lag caught up with her after the first couple of sally ports. Abandoning the wall, she cut through cobbled side streets on her way back to the hotel.

"Madame!"

The call was low and urgent and came at her from a narrow alley a few yards from the entrance

YOUR PARTICIPATION IS REQUESTED!

Dear Reader,

Since you are a lover of fiction – we would like to get to know you!

Inside you will find a short Reader's Survey. Sharing your answers with us will help our editorial staff understand who you are and what activities you enjoy.

To thank you for your participation, we would like to send you 2 books and a gift – **ABSOLUTELY FREE!**

Enjoy your gifts with our appreciation,

Pam Powers

SEE INSIDE FOR READER'S SURVEY

What's Your Reading Pleasure...
ROMANCE? <u>OR</u> SUSPENSE?

Do you prefer spine-tingling page turners OR heart-stirring stories about love and relationships? Tell us which books you enjoy – and you'll get 2 FREE "ROMANCE" BOOKS or 2 FREE "SUSPENSE" BOOKS with no obligation to purchase anything.

Choose "ROMANCE" and get **2 FREE BOOKS** that will fuel your imagination with intensely moving stories about life, love and relationships.

Choose "SUSPENSE" and you'll get **2 FREE BOOKS** that will thrill you with a spine-tingling blend of suspense and mystery.

Whichever category you select, your 2 free books have a combined cover price of $11.98 or more in the U.S. and $13.98 or more in Canada.

And remember. . . just for accepting the Editor's Free Gift Offer, we'll send you 2 books and a gift, ABSOLUTELY FREE!

YOURS FREE! We'll send you a fabulous surprise gift absolutely FREE, just for trying "Romance" or "Suspense"!

® and ™ are trademarks owned and used by the trademark owner and/or its licensee.

Visit us online at
www.FreeBooksandGift.com

YOUR READER'S SURVEY
"THANK YOU" FREE GIFTS INCLUDE:

▶ 2 Romance OR 2 Suspense books

▶ A lovely surprise gift

PLEASE FILL IN THE CIRCLES COMPLETELY TO RESPOND

1) What type of fiction books do you enjoy reading? (Check all that apply)
○ Suspense/Thrillers ○ Action/Adventure ○ Modern-day Romances
○ Historical Romance ○ Humour ○ Science fiction

2) What attracted you most to the last fiction book you purchased on impulse?
○ The Title ○ The Cover ○ The Author ○ The Story

3) What is usually the greatest influencer when you <u>plan</u> to buy a book?
○ Advertising ○ Referral from a friend
○ Book Review ○ Like the author

4) Approximately how many fiction books do you read in a year?
○ 1 to 6 ○ 7 to 19 ○ 20 or more

5) How often do you access the internet?
○ Daily ○ Weekly ○ Monthly ○ Rarely or never

6) To which of the following age groups do you belong?
○ Under 18 ○ 18 to 34 ○ 35 to 64 ○ over 65

YES! I have completed the Reader's Survey. Please send me the 2 FREE books and gift for which I qualify. I understand that I am under no obligation to purchase any books, as explained on the back and on the opposite page.

Check one:

ROMANCE
193 MDL D37C 393 MDL D37D

SUSPENSE
192 MDL D37E 392 MDL D37F

FIRST NAME

LAST NAME

ADDRESS

APT.#

CITY

STATE/PROV.

ZIP/POSTAL CODE

▶ DETACH AND MAIL CARD TODAY! ▶

(SUR-MI-05) © 1998 MIRA BOOKS

The Reader Service — Here's How It Works:

Accepting your 2 free books and gift places you under no obligation to buy anything. You may keep the books and gift and return the shipping statement marked "cancel." If you do not cancel, about a month later we'll send you 3 additional books and bill you just $4.99 each in the U.S., or $5.49 each in Canada, plus 25¢ shipping & handling per book and applicable taxes if any.* That's the complete price and — compared to cover prices starting from $5.99 each in the U.S. and $6.99 each in Canada — it's quite a bargain! You may cancel at any time, but if you choose to continue, every month we'll send you 3 more books, which you may either purchase at the discount price or return to us and cancel your subscription.

*Terms and prices subject to change without notice. Sales tax applicable in N.Y. Canadian residents will be charged applicable provincial taxes and GST.

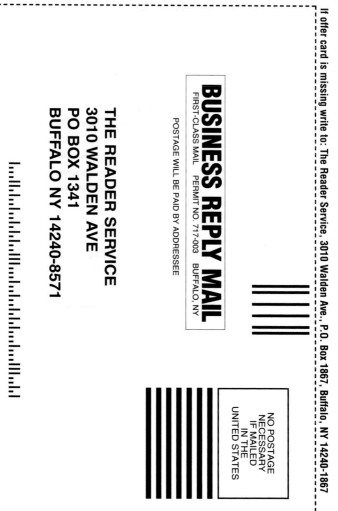

If offer card is missing write to: The Reader Service, 3010 Walden Ave., P.O. Box 1867, Buffalo, NY 14240-1867

BUSINESS REPLY MAIL

FIRST-CLASS MAIL   PERMIT NO. 717-003   BUFFALO, NY

POSTAGE WILL BE PAID BY ADDRESSEE

THE READER SERVICE
3010 WALDEN AVE
PO BOX 1341
BUFFALO NY 14240-8571

NO POSTAGE
NECESSARY
IF MAILED
IN THE
UNITED STATES

to the Auberge St. Georges. Cleo peered into the alley, her breath catching when she spotted the waiter from the Café Corinthia.

He shot a glance in either direction before emerging from the shadows. "I have been waiting for you."

He started toward her, took two steps and stumbled. His head jerked back. His eyes went wide.

"Madame!"

The strangled cry was both a plea and a groan. Cursing, Cleo sprang forward just as the man's knees began to buckle. In one flying leap, she jerked him away from the alley and dove for cover, taking him with her.

She knew before they hit the cobblestones it was too late. Still, she flattened herself on top of him, squirming frantically to get at the *ebu* strapped to her ankle, straining to hear over the pulse jackhammering in her ears.

There were no shouts, no running footsteps, no soft pops from a silencer. Nothing but city noises and the clip-clop of a carriage coming up the hill.

Her heart slamming against her ribs, Cleo lowered the needle-sharp *ebu* and wiggled off the waiter. His eyes were already glazed.

Cursing again, she rolled him over. The bullet hole was small and neat and centered squarely between his shoulder blades.

15

"A lucky shot, or the work of a true professional?"

Cleo shrugged, recognizing that Inspector Aruzzo's question was purely rhetorical. The small, clean entry wound aligned between the shoulder blades with almost surgical precision spoke for itself.

Folding one arm across his chest, Aruzzo fingered his beard while his crime-scene unit measured and photographed the body. A good-size crowd had clustered just outside the taped-off area. Gawking tourists. Curious locals. Shop owners drawn by the commotion.

Was the shooter there, too? Taking clever, malicious pride in his work? Cleo swept the crowd again, searching faces, scrutinizing features. She didn't recognize any patrons from the Café Corinthia.

"Do you have anything to add to your statement, Madame North?"

The inspector's air of polite courtesy had worn a little thin. Cleo could tell he wasn't pleased that a murder had been committed in the heart of Valletta's historic area. Bad for the tourist industry.

"No, nothing to add."

"Very well. I will be in touch."

Summarily dismissed, she left him attending to his business and headed for her hotel. Adrenaline still spiked through her veins. Too antsy for her planned catnap, she dialed the hotel restaurant, canceled her dinner reservations and ordered a room service meal.

The waiter set the table on the balcony of her suite. Her mind churning, Cleo forked down garlicky risotto and squid while the sun sank into the now-purple sea and the cruise ships pulled away from the docks below.

She thought about going back to the Café Corinthia, but nixed the idea. Word had gotten around. They—whoever *they* were—knew where she was staying. She'd sit tight tonight and see if they came to her. If they did…

Her teeth ground a rubbery morsel of squid to a pulp. Having a man die in her arms tended to make Cleo just a tad annoyed. Anyone who showed up uninvited at her hotel room in the foreseeable future had better come prepared.

She might not have access to her full bag of tricks, but she hadn't gained a reputation in the security-consulting business for no reason. Although she'd only brought limited equipment with her, anyone trying to get into her room would meet with a surprise or two.

He'd kill her!

Jack stood at rigid attention before his boss's desk, plotting the imminent demise of one Cleopatra North while General Barnes peeled long strips from his hide.

Barnes had both fists planted on his blotter. His face was brick red. The pipe that rarely left his mouth lay abandoned. The general had tossed it aside so as not to interfere with the blistering speech he'd been delivering for almost fifteen minutes now. Jack had taken the blasts with little outward show of emotion. That seemed to set the Old Man off even more.

"Dammit, Donovan, I don't like having my chain yanked by the CIA."

"No, sir."

Barnes leaned forward, his bushy eyebrows bristling. "I like even less being informed that the intelligence community's most reliable source on the island of Malta just died in the arms of one of my former agents."

Jack suspected that "former" rankled more than anything else. Barnes still hadn't gotten past the fact that he'd given up on Cleo. But this wasn't the time to remind him that Lieutenant North's stubbornness had pissed him off as often as her persistence and thoroughness in working an investigation had won his grudging praise.

"I've had my exec call Base Ops," Barnes huffed. "They're diverting a C-17 in to pick you up. It'll be on the ground in an hour. I want you on that plane, I want you in Malta, and…"

He thrust himself forward so far Jack half expected he would wind up facedown on the blotter.

"I want you *to get that woman on a leash!*"

He'd do better than get her on a leash, Jack vowed as he stalked out of OSI headquarters. He'd put her in a permanent straitjacket.

Whizzing across the Woodrow Wilson Bridge to his Alexandria apartment, he picked up his passport, a change of underwear and certain tools of the trade he couldn't have carried aboard a commercial flight. Forty minutes later, he boarded the C-17 Globemaster that had swooped into Andrews Air Force Base to pick him up.

The transport was loaded with cargo destined for Iraq. The C-17's four Pratt and Whitney engines revved to a thundering roar as Jack strapped himself in, his knees mere inches from the stacked cargo pallets. The transport began its takeoff roll, then lifted into the air. With the metal struts rattling against his backbone, Jack closed eyes that felt as gritty as sandpaper.

He hadn't slept more than a few hours in the past three days. In that time, he'd briefed the Ogden Air Logistics Center commander, delved into the guts of the Afloat Prepositioning Program, gone several rounds with his counterparts in the FBI and CIA, and had the shit scared out of him by what he'd been able to piece together so far.

This was bigger than he'd feared, much bigger. What had begun as a potential breach of a classified database was now starting to look like an intrigue of global proportions—one that pitted billions of dollars in stolen armaments against the fragile world order.

And Cleo had landed smack in the middle of it!

"Coffee, Major?"

The transport's loadmaster squeezed between the pallets, a cardboard cup in hand. Jack wrapped a fist around it gratefully.

"Thanks."

"Sorry we don't have room to let down another rack so you could unfold and grab some sleep," the staff sergeant apologized, pitching his voice to a near shout to be heard over the roar of the engines. "We're maxed out on this run."

"No problem."

The loadmaster had a seat up front, just behind the two pilots, but curiosity kept him lingering in the transport's cavernous belly. Jack guessed it wasn't often the air force diverted a plane crammed with supplies for the troops to pick up a plainclothes OSI agent.

"It'll take us six hours to make the Azores," the staff sergeant said. "If your legs get too cramped, you could climb atop one of the pallets and stretch out. That's usually what I do on these long hauls."

"I'll keep that in mind."

Six hours to the Azores. Another three or four from there to Malta aboard the navy P-3 he was told would be waiting for him. Wedging his shoulders between the C-17's metal ribs, Jack did the calculations. It was only a little after 7:00 p.m. by his watch, which made it the middle of the night in Malta. Given the time difference, he should arrive at Cleo's hotel by 11:00 a.m. or so.

And then he'd kill her, he swore.

Assuming the consortium of renegade arms dealers she was sniffing around hadn't gotten to her first.

16

The phone rang as Cleo stumbled toward the bathroom. Jet lag had caught up to her with a vengeance. Despite a solid night's sleep, she was fuzzy headed and desperate for her first injection of caffeine. She snatched up the receiver, praying it wasn't room service advising her of a delay in the order she'd just placed.

"Yes?"

"Ten o'clock. The Co-Cathedral of St. John."

The line went dead before she registered much more than the message and the fact it was delivered in a throaty female voice. Her brain belatedly clicking into gear, Cleo jabbed the button for the front desk.

"Yes, *madame*?"

"Someone just called my room. Can your switchboard trace the number?"

"Unfortunately, we are not so equipped. Er, is there a problem?"

The query contained more than a hint of nervousness. Evidently yesterday's shooting had made management wary of the guest presently camped out in their King's Suite.

"No, no problem."

Cleo shot a glance at her watch. She'd forgotten to reset it to local time yesterday and she wasn't up to the calculations required to make the switch.

"What's the time?"

"It is now twenty minutes to ten, *madame*."

Crap! Canceling her room service order, Cleo slammed down the phone and charged for the bathroom.

She hit the lobby ten minutes later and snatched a to-go cup from the service set out on a table supported by rampant stone lions.

Gulping down the bitter Mediterranean brew, Cleo threaded through streets crowded with tourists fresh off the three giant ships now docked in the harbor. The ship funnels showed different markings from the ones she'd spied from her balcony yesterday. They must have pulled in while she was still dead to the world. Busy place, Malta.

"'Scuse me. Pardon me."

The camera-snapping herds outside the cathedral parted enough to allow her up the steps. From the outside, the structure looked more like a fortress than a cathedral. That was probably the architect's intent, Cleo guessed, given Malta's turbulent past. Ignoring several nasty looks from the crowd lined up at the entrance, she wedged through the narrow front doors and plunged into a canyon of gloom.

Yesterday's incident was still fresh in her mind—so fresh that she planted her shoulder blades against the interior wall and gave a little flick of her wrist. The familiar smoothness of the *ebu*'s wooden handle slid into her palm. She'd strapped it to her arm this time for faster access. Just in case…

Gradually, her pupils made the transition from the dazzling outside light. The shadows inside the church lightened enough for Cleo to make out the ocean of marble tombstones under her feet. Laid out end to end, the embellished slabs stretched all the way to the massive Baroque altar at least two football fields away.

Some of the slabs were inlaid with gold heraldic devices. Others contained religious motifs in mosaics that glowed like gemstones. All, she heard a tour guide inform his group in precise English, memorialized the aristocratic knights belonging to the Order of St. John.

"In addition, each knight was required to give a *gioja*, or gift, upon admission to the order," the guide intoned. "The masterpiece you see on the ceiling, painted on stone by Mattia Preti between 1662 and 1667, was the gift of two such knights.

The painting depicts the life of John the Baptist, patron saint of the order."

Cleo darted a quick peek at the ceiling some hundred or so feet above her head. The cathedral's barrel-vault design required no inside support pillars, so there was nothing to obstruct her view of the gilded panels.

And nothing for her mysterious caller to hide behind, either.

Pulling her gaze back to the milling crowds, Cleo watched for a glance aimed her way, a face turned in her direction, a shuttered look. Five minutes slipped by. Ten.

When no one approached or appeared to take any particular interest in her, she edged away from the wall and infiltrated the tour group now trailing their guide toward one of the side altars.

Three side chapels and several dozen masterpieces later, Cleo was beginning to wonder if her caller's intent had been merely to lure her out of her hotel room so someone could slip in and go through her things. If so, that someone was in for a surprise. She'd give the Co-Cathedral of St. John ten more minutes, she decided, then head back to the hotel.

Still mingling with the tourist group, she dutifully gawked at altars inset with gold and lapis lazuli, admired the Grand Master's throne, and touched a fingertip to one of the exquisite silver gates guarding a side chapel.

"These are the famous Napoléon Gates," the guide informed his group. "Weighing close to one ton each and made of solid silver, they are among the few movable treasures the emperor did not send back to France after capturing Malta in 1798. Does anyone know why he left them?"

A few desultory murmurs rose from the cruise-ship crowd. They were getting restless, Cleo noted. More than one husband looked as if he was about to OD on marble slabs and medieval masterpieces.

Valiantly, the guide forged on. "The Grand Master of the order, known by then as the Knights of Malta, devised a scheme to outwit Monsieur Bonaparte. He ordered the gates coated with lead paint, and thus they escaped the looting that cost the island so much of its heritage. The gates remained painted for quite some time, incidentally, long after British troops retook Malta. The Grand Master wasn't sure he could trust the British any more than the French."

The sally raised a polite titter among the predominantly American group. Cleo began edging toward the exit.

"Take a lesson from the gates, Ms. North."

The soft remark stopped her with one foot on the tombstone of a knight of Castile. Angling her head, Cleo took an instant mental snapshot of the woman who eased out of the shadows beyond the chapel. Mid to late forties. Dark hair arrowing to a dramatic widow's peak. Pleated gray slacks, a cream-colored silk blouse, and eyes hidden behind chic rimless sunglasses.

"Matters here aren't what they seem," the brunette murmured as the group around Cleo shuffled off to the next tour point. "You'd be wise to have a care."

The accent was British, the tone educated. The woman looked oddly familiar, but Cleo was damned if she could place those high cheekbones or that long, aquiline nose.

"Who are you?"

"My identity needn't concern you. It's quite enough that I know yours. I would advise you to—"

"Omigod!"

The startled shriek came from one of the tourists who'd just ambled by.

Nerves already strung wire-tight, Cleo reacted on pure instinct. Lunging to one side, she whirled. She had the *ebu* out of its sheath before another shrill screech followed the first.

"That man's got a gun!"

Tote bags and pamphlets flew like chaff shot from a dispenser. Screams ricocheted off the cathedral walls. The tourists stampeded.

Only one man remained unmoving. The silenced weapon in his hand bucked at the same instant Cleo sent the *ebu* slicing through the air. A half a heartbeat before the wooden blade buried itself in his throat, a second shot exploded right beside Cleo's ear. A dark rosebud blossomed in the shooter's forehead. He went down with a crash that sent the tourists into mass hysteria.

Cleo spun around in time to see the brunette slide an automatic into the pocket of her pleated slacks. She mouthed something, but her words were lost amid the frenzied screams. She flicked a glance over Cleo's shoulder, stepped back and disappeared behind the massive silver gates.

Before Cleo could follow, several hundred pounds of tourist slammed into her back. She landed hard, nose to nose with the engraved effigy of a long-dead knight.

"I've got her! Someone call the cops!"

She could have dislodged her attacker. A quick twist, a knee to the groin, and he would have been weeping. But a second tourist piled on top of the first, followed in short order by two more. Everyday, average Americans had had enough of being terrorized.

Cleo didn't mind being handcuffed and hustled into the back of a police van. She started to get annoyed, however, when Inspector Aruzzo put her through several rounds of questioning. Perched on the edge of the interrogation-room table, the inspector palmed his beard.

"Describe your accomplice to me once again."

"Five-five or six. Dark hair. Dark eyes. British accent. And I repeat, she was not my accomplice."

"A number of witnesses disagree. They seem to believe the two of you acted in concert."

"They believe wrong. We both *re*acted to shots fired."

"Yes, let us go back to that. You say you aren't sure which of you was the target."

"That's correct."

"You also maintain you've never seen this woman before?"

"Not that I recall."

There was something about her, though. A look. A mannerism. She'd struck a chord. Cleo just couldn't figure out which one. Frustrated, she decided she'd had enough.

"Look, Inspector, your witnesses confirmed the shooter fired first, right?"

"That is correct."

"You've also told me the weapon he was carrying matched the one used to kill that waiter last night."

"We won't be absolutely certain until the tests are completed but, yes, it appears the ballistics match."

"So what's the problem here? Aside from those two corpses, that is. How much longer do you intend to hold me?"

"Two corpses and the fact that you imported a lethal device are sufficient for me to hold you indefinitely, if I was so inclined."

Her eyes narrowed. "Are you so inclined?"

"No, *madame*. I'm merely responding to a request from your government."

"Come again?"

"We've received a satellite communiqué requesting we detain you at police headquarters until a representative from the United States arrives."

"You're kidding!"

"I assure you, *madame*, I am not." Aruzzo permitted himself a small smile. "The communiqué also suggested wrist and leg irons. How fortunate for you we retired our last set to the police museum some years ago."

Cleo's breath left on a hiss. "Donovan!"

"Yes, I believe that was the name of the individual who forwarded the request."

"I'll kill him!"

The inspector looked pained. "Please, Ms. North. Not on my watch."

17

The view through the one-way mirror at Valletta's police station almost made up for the permanent dent the C-17's metal struts had put in Jack's shoulder blades.

Hands shoved into the back pockets of her jeans, Cleo paced the small interrogation room. Anger radiated from her taut body in waves. She wasn't any happier about being detained at police headquarters than Jack was about chasing her across a frigging ocean.

She was about to get a whole lot unhappier.

With a nod to the inspector who'd briefed him on the situation, Jack strolled through the door separating the viewing area from the interrogation room.

"Nice going, North. Two DOAs in two days."

Her slit-eyed stare told him she'd merely been waiting for his arrival to up the body count.

"Took you long enough to get here, Donovan. What the hell did you do? Swim across the pond?"

"You want out of here or not?"

Spots of color jumped into her cheeks. She was primed for blood. Or at the very least, a knock-down, go-for-the-throat tussle.

So was Jack.

"Save it until we get back to your hotel," he warned, his jaw set.

His mood didn't improve when he got an eye-ful of Cleo's opulent suite.

"Sloan paying for this?"

"That's the way it works in the real world, Donovan. The client covers expenses."

Jack dumped his bag on a chair upholstered in striped silk. "Did you conduct a sweep?"

"What do you think?"

"I'll tell you what I think in a minute. Did you conduct a goddamned sweep?"

"Yes."

"And?"

"And I found a Lev Termen."

Frowning, he shook his head. "I rode across the pond on a C-17. My eardrums are still revved up to full throttle. I could have sworn you said you found a Termen."

"I did." She unbent enough to smirk. "The metal collar's all rusted and corroded, but the diode was intact. I'm guessing the KGB proba-bly caught several presidents, ambassadors and/or kings with their pants down in the fifties."

Still shaking his head, Jack shrugged out of his rumpled sport coat. As much as he'd love to see that relic of the Cold War spy days, he had a more current situation to worry about.

"All right, North. You want to tell me why you took off for Malta without waiting for me to get back to you?"

"Where is it written that I have to get permission from you to work a case?"

"We had an agreement, dammit!"

"Which you nullified when you managed to squeeze in a call to Detective Devereaux but somehow couldn't find time to zap me so much as an e-mail."

"You couldn't just trust me?"

Her chin jutted. "Like you trusted me?"

"I don't suppose it occurred to you things might have been breaking so fast I didn't have time to brief you."

"Sure they were." Arms folded, she tapped a toe. "You've got time now, Donovan. What the hell's going on?"

He'd give her the basics. He'd already decided that. And he'd take great pleasure in what would follow.

"One, a person or persons unknown tapped into the classified portion of the Afloat Prepositioning database..."

"Tell me something I don't know."

Jack's jaw locked so tight he thought the bones would pop out of their sockets. "Two," he ground out, "the classified area that was breached detailed the exact mix of weapons currently loaded aboard the *Pitsenbarger*."

Cleo's arms dropped. He had her attention now.

"Three, the CIA intercepted a satellite transmission they think came from a British agent in the field. It contains a coded reference to the *Pits*."

"British intelligence is tracking the *Pits*?"

"Evidently. One of the analysts at Langley forwarded the intercept to DIA."

"Uh-oh." Cleo's grimace indicated her opinion of the Defense Intelligence Agency. "How long did it take DIA to tell us about the transmission?"

Jack lifted a sardonic brow, but refrained from pointing out that she was no longer "us." She'd get that message soon enough.

"The Old Man passed me the intercept when I got back from Utah. Along with strict instructions to sit on my investigation until the CIA verifies the source and significance of the transmission."

"Sit on it? You can't be serious!"

"Yes," Jack growled, not liking this any better that she did. "I am. Evidently Washington isn't ready to admit we're spying on one of our staunchest allies. Until the Old Man gets feedback from the CIA, we're on ice."

"*You're* on ice," she began.

Jack cut her off before she could launch into a full-blown protest. "There's more."

The terse comment took some of the belligerence from her stance.

"This may be bigger than the *Pits.* After Barnes told me about the intercept, I spent a solid thirty-six hours with the threat-analysis folks. We searched every intelligence source."

He didn't have to explain the excruciating process of intelligence-gathering to her. She knew the drill, understood the acronyms.

SIGINT, for signals intelligence plucked from electronic and communications sources. IMINT, for imagery intelligence derived from visual photography, radar sensors, lasers and electro-optics. MASINT, for measurements intelligence and signatures specific to the chemical and physical properties of various weapons systems. HUMINT, the human intelligence information collected overtly by diplomats and military attachés, covertly by spies and undercover agents. Then there was everything else, lumped under the broad category of OSINT, or open-source intelligence. The Internet fell into this category. So did TV commercials, newspapers and commercial databases.

U.S. intelligence agencies harvested millions upon millions of bits of information from all these sources daily. Each item had to be verified, analyzed and synthesized to search for trends. Jack had no idea how many supercomputers were employed in the task. All he knew was that it wasn't a job for the faint of heart.

"What did you find?" Cleo asked.

He scrubbed a hand over his chin. Two days' growth bristled under his palm. Collecting his thoughts, he weighed her need to know against the Old Man's terse instructions.

"I found several references to a source identified only as Domino. Seems he—or she—is interested in purchasing massive amounts of firepower."

"How massive?"

"Enough to fill the hold of a supersize cargo ship."

Cleo let out a low whistle. "What are you saying, Jack? That we may be dealing with an agent for a terrorist organization?"

"That's what it felt like at first," he admitted. "But none of the hits tracked to any known terrorist group. My guess at this point is that Domino may be a renegade arms dealer."

"Or part of a consortium of rogue arms dealers," she murmured, following his lead with the unerring instinct that made her so damned good in the field. "Hard to believe one individual could put together enough cash or credit to purchase a whole shipload of armaments without leaving a money trail."

"The CIA is working that trail now."

"What do you want to bet it leads to our friend Frank Helms, aka Adrian Mustafa Moore?"

"It might."

"C'mon, Jack! Moore had to have been sniffing around Trish Jackson and Sloan Engineering for a reason. It's looking more and more like that reason was the *Pits*."

"Yes, it is. But until I get confirmation…"

"Yeah, I know. You're on ice."

"We're on ice."

"I don't think so. You didn't see what Trish's corpse looked like after the sand crabs had been feeding on it for a week. Or what that bastard shoved down her throat. No way I'm going to sit on my ass while Moore is still unaccounted for."

Jack clenched his fists inside his pockets. They were back to square one, and he was here to keep her from jumping right to square two.

"I'm too wiped to argue with you," he warned.

"So don't." She gestured toward the opulent four-poster dominating the other room. "Rack out and grab a few hours' sleep, big guy. I'm going to—"

"Rack out with me," he said flatly.

"In your dreams, Donovan. As pissed as I am at you right now, you can count yourself lucky if I don't strangle you in your sleep."

"That's what I figured."

Sliding his hand out of his pocket, he thumbed up the lid of a small plastic atomizer.

"What's that?"

When he aimed it her way, sudden suspicion leapt into her eyes.

"Jack! You wouldn't dare!"

She flung up an arm, but the violent gesture came too late to block the spray. The clear, color-less puff had already hit her nostrils. One breath later, she staggered back.

Her eyes blazing with fury, she went down on one knee. "You're a...dead man...Donovan."

Jack snagged her arm just in time to keep her from pitching onto her face. Hauling her up over his shoulder, he transported her to the other room and dumped her on the bed.

18

Cleo came awake with none of her usual fuzzy grogginess. Her brain clicking into gear, she registered several instant impressions. The room was smothered in inky darkness. A lightweight cotton sheet covered her. The patter coming through the closed door just off to her left was the shower.

She knew immediately who occupied the glassed-in stall. Her argument with Jack sprang into her head—along with the sudden, vivid image of his hand aiming a nozzle at her face.

"Sonuvabitch!"

With a surge of fury, she lunged for the edge of the bed. She was halfway off the mattress when something cut into her ankle and jerked her to a vicious halt. Yelping, Cleo tumbled onto the carpet.

At that point she discovered she was wearing only her lace-trimmed silk boxers. She also dis-

covered she was tethered to the bed by a thin strip
of plastic. One end was banded around her ankle.
The other end was looped around the bedpost.

Training and reason told Cleo she couldn't
break the bond. Tactical restraints made of plastic
like this tested to more than three hundred and
fifty pounds of tensile strength. Sheer fury had
her kicking and yanking and clawing at the ankle
cuff, anyway.

She soon gave up the struggle and hauled herself back onto the mattress. She was damned if
she'd let Jack find her flopping around on the floor
like a landed trout.

A glance at the clock radio beside the bed
showed it was the middle of the night. She'd been
out for a solid eight hours. Her fury came to a
fresh boil.

Donovan wouldn't live to see the dawn!

Dragging the sheet around her, she punched
the pillows up behind her back and got a grip on
herself. She'd need a clear head and iced emotions
to get the drop on the bastard.

The shower cut off and Jack strolled out of the
bathroom a few minutes later, toweling himself
off. The light spilling through the open door illu-
minated his tanned chest and legs. His belly was
flat and ridged, his sex loose and pliant between his
thighs. Deliberately, Cleo zeroed in on the puck-
ered skin marking the bullet hole in his shoulder.

"I assume you realize I'm going to put another
hole in you to match that one, Donovan."

"Why do you think you're wearing plastic?"

"You'll have to cut the cuff sooner or later."

"I'm going for later."

Carelessly, he tossed the damp towel back into the bathroom and dragged a pair of jersey sweatpants from his bag. With the sweats riding low on his hips, he prowled over to the antique armoire housing the entertainment center and minibar.

"I'm starving. What have you got in here?"

Rattling among the bottles and jars in the well-stocked fridge, he popped the top on a Diet Pepsi but passed up the assortment of snacks.

"Peanuts and candy won't hack it. Let's hope room service operates around the clock." He snagged the thick, embossed menu from the desk and gave a grunt of relief. "It does. I'm going for a steak. You want anything?"

"Your head on a platter."

"Sorry, I don't see *head* on the menu. What's your second choice?"

"Your balls on a skewer."

"No skewered balls, either. You'll have to settle for peppercorn steak with porcini mushrooms." Reaching for the phone, he shot her a quizzical look. "Should I make this call from the other room?"

"I'm not going to scream for help, if that's what you're asking. This is between me and you, Bubba, and only one of us is going to walk away whole."

"That's the way I see it, too."

The tone was amused. The warning buried in the careless reply wasn't.

"By the way," he added as he hit the button for in-room dining, "those boxers are a real turn-on. They kept me awake longer than I would have imagined possible after all those hours on the C-17."

Cleo's eyes narrowed. She and Jack had stripped down to their skivvies before. Several times. She'd been conscious when it had happened, though.

"Speaking of staying awake," she bit out when he'd placed the order, "what did you use on me?"

"It's a new subduing agent developed by the lab at Langley. The spray hasn't been approved yet for use on humans, but the effects on lab rats and attack dogs were so encouraging, I decided to bring a sample with me."

He was baiting her. For all his seeming nonchalance and lazy grin, he was as furious with her as she was with him.

The realization afforded Cleo immense satisfaction. Perversely, it also took some of the edge off her rage.

She knew how the bureaucracy worked. She'd been part of it herself for years. She understood the restraints Jack had to operate with, under and around. Still, he could have found time for one frigging phone call or e-mail. And he sure as hell didn't have to use an experimental agent on her!

"You know," she ground out, "the last I heard we were both on the same side."

"That's what I thought, too, until you jumped a plane to Malta."

Her arms locked over the sheet, she made what she considered a supremely generous offer. "Cut the cuff, and I won't leave you permanently crippled."

"Later. Maybe."

"Now, Donovan. You're not the only one who needs to make a trip to the bathroom."

He strolled over to the bed then, close enough for her to cause harm. The glint in his eyes told her that's exactly what he hoped she'd do. His eight hours of rack time had put the devil back into him, Cleo saw.

"How about this?" he suggested. "I cut the cuff, you hit the bathroom, and we eat before we tussle."

He looked almost disappointed when she agreed. After he dug a disposable cutter out of his bag and sliced through the plastic, though, Cleo was tempted to reneg on the deal. One good kick with her heel and he'd be wearing his face backward for a while. But she'd given her word and she never went back on it. Not when the other guy expected her to, anyway, which was exactly what Donovan's wary stance indicated.

Better to catch him off guard.

And make him suffer.

With that goal in mind, she tossed the sheet aside and strolled into the still-steamy bath.

Jack remained on full alert until the door slammed behind her. Even then, the cords in his neck refused to relax. He trusted Cleo to hold to their truce—more or less. In retrospect, though, he probably should have defined "eat" with more precision. He half expected her to burst out of the bathroom determined to stuff something other than peppercorn steak down his throat.

Christ, he wished she'd try! Now that he'd caught up on his sleep, he was itching for some action. He'd have her out of those crotch-skimming briefs and on her back in five seconds flat. Less if he used the spray, but that wouldn't entail anywhere near as much fun. He'd keep his options open, he decided. Wide open. If Cleo emerged from the bathroom ready to do battle, he'd certainly oblige her.

She reappeared swathed in one of the hotel's terry-cloth robes and apparently prepared to fulfill the terms and conditions of the truce. Room service delivered Jack's order mere moments later.

Smiling at Cleo, the uniformed attendant in a square hat rolled a cart piled with domed dishes into the room. "Shall I set up at the dining table, sir?"

"Just leave it. I'll put the trolley in the hall when we finish."

"Very good. If you'll just sign here, please."

Cleo's sarcastic comment about how things worked in the real world played in Jack's head as he added a hefty tip to the already outrageous room service delivery charge. The waiter tried to be discreet, but his eyes bulged when he got a look at the tab.

"Can I get you anything else, sir?"

"Not right now."

Cleo observed the man's fawning departure with a lift of one brow. "How much did you give him?"

"Enough to make Sloan break out in a cold sweat when he sees your itemized expense account. Let's eat."

Afterward Cleo was never quite sure when her simmering determination to pay Donovan back for the spray and the cuff edged over the line into something more primitive.

She still wanted physical. That didn't change as they worked their way through their middle-of-the-night supper. She'd spent hours confined in a stuffy interrogation room, more hours stretched out on a bed, unconscious. Her body craved motion, exercise, action.

And the anger bubbling just below her surface required a vent before it blew her apart. With each bite of the peppercorn steak, though, her fiercely banked emotions took on a different hue, almost like a landscape sent back by one of the Mars rovers. One minute she was red and hot and plotting ways to bounce Jack on his butt. The next, she was envisioning what she'd do with him once she had him there.

The possibilities were endless…and included a few variations so carnal that Cleo's belly tightened. Before she knew quite how it happened, her need for revenge had gotten all mixed up with another kind of desire. Both were churning inside her when she dropped her fork onto the gold-rimmed service plate.

"Do you want to see the Termen?"

The curt question elicited a considering look from Jack. He chewed his mouthful of steak, swallowed and lounged back in his chair. The careless sprawl didn't fool Cleo for a moment. She'd gone into action with this man.

"I've already seen it," he replied. "When I went through your carryall."

So he'd searched the suite and her personal effects while she was out cold. She would have done the same if their positions had been reversed.

"Find anything else of interest?"

"Well, that laser-beam flashlight is pretty awesome. Where did you get that?"

Cleo had forgotten all about the high-intensity super beam Doreen had squeezed into the $1.99 penlight. The last time she'd seen the gadget was when she'd dumped her key ring in the bottom of her purse after parking her vehicle at Love Field.

She wasn't in any mood to enlighten Jack about the source of her equipment, though. Particularly when that source was a stepcousin-in-law with a hyena laugh who spent more hours on her back in front of the TV than she did searching for gainful employment.

"You don't need to know where I found it, but you'd damned well better return it. Along with any other items you purloined."

"There wasn't much to purloin. You traveled light on this trip."

"Unlike you, Donovan, I flew commercial. I

didn't have time to work the necessary documentation to get a firearm through Customs."

"Inspector Aruzzo showed me the wooden lance you put into your shooter's throat. Apparently you didn't work the necessary documentation for that, either."

"There are rules, and then there are rules."

Stretching out his legs, he laced his fingers over his bare middle. Someone else might have mistaken the look he slanted her through sun-tipped gold lashes for amusement. Cleo knew better.

"Wasn't that the attitude that got you crosswise of the United States Air Force?"

"That," she answered with a shrug, "and an intense aversion to having my investigations reviewed and critiqued at six different levels of command."

His smile mocking, he fed her back her own line. "That's how it works in the real word, North."

"Not in my world. Not now."

Cleo toyed with one end of the tie belting her terry-cloth robe. "Are you finished with your steak?"

"I'm finished."

His mocking smile deepened. He knew what was coming. Or thought he did.

"Will this be jungle style?" he asked in a drawl. "Or do you want to set some parameters?"

"We'll keep it simple. No blood, no bruises, no broken bones."

"How do we decide the winner?"

"We go three rounds. The winner is the one who walks away."

He hooked a brow. "You're serious about this?"

"As a heart attack."

Casually, she tugged on the end of the tie. The knot gave, her robe parted.

"Just how brave are you, Donovan?"

"You want to wrestle naked? Oh, sweetheart! Tell me I'm not dreaming."

The fervent plea worked on Cleo in a way she hadn't anticipated. The white-hot edge to her anger cooled even as the almost comical joy on the jerk's face sent heat coiling into her belly.

Her determination to make sure Jack remembered this night for a long, long time didn't waver. She still intended to make him weep. But there wasn't anything that said she couldn't enjoy herself in the process.

"You're not dreaming, big guy."

Shrugging, she sent the robe sliding down to her elbows. From there it made a quick trip to the floor. Her thumb hooked in the waistband of the lace-trimmed Brazilian Boxers. Cleo had no idea how the packagers had come up with that label, as the bits of silk and lace were manufactured in China and anything but boxy.

The label didn't matter, however. What mattered was the little hiss of Jack's indrawn breath.

"Like these briefs, do you?"

"*Like* doesn't begin to describe how I feel about them."

Deciding to let him suffer a little more, she kept the briefs on and pushed the trolley out of the way.

Jack didn't alter his slouch when she hooked a knee over his. Or when she settled her weight on his thighs. But his stomach muscles went rigid the instant she reached for the string tie of his sweats.

In a short, fierce battle, his instinct for self-preservation gained temporary mastery over the hunger that was already raising a sweat. Locking his hands over hers, he stilled her busy fingers.

Her smile was a scorching brand. "Scared, Donovan?"

"Should I be?"

"Oh, yeah."

Jack's stomach muscles gave another involuntary roll. He figured he had exactly two options at this point. He could take Cleo to the floor and engage in the physical tussle she was obviously aching for or let her do her worst.

From this vantage point, he had to admit her worst looked pretty damned good. Those lacy briefs were just loose enough to give him a tantalizing glimpse of dark pubic hair…whenever he could drag his greedy gaze from her breasts.

What the hell. A guy could only die once. Releasing her hands, he dropped his arms to either side of the chair and assumed an air of noble martyrdom.

"All right. I admit that subduing agent might have been a little extreme. You're entitled to your revenge, North. Go for it."

The blank look on Cleo's face was worth whatever pain would follow. She hadn't expected him to cave this easily. And, Jack realized with a jolt of wicked delight, she didn't quite know what to do with him now that he had.

His glee took a dive when she set her jaw and yanked on the strings of his sweats, but he maintained his sacrificial pose. There would be no blood, he reminded himself. No bruises. No broken bones.

The mantra replayed in his head as Cleo dragged his sweats down a few inches, and gained considerable urgency when her fist closed around him. He was already semi-erect, no small feat considering the circumstances. But when her hand began to slide and squeeze, he zinged straight to full and hard and aching.

His condition didn't go unnoticed. A feline smile curving her lips, Cleo scooted forward on his thighs and got a better grip.

Sweat popped out on the back of Jack's neck. His mouth went bone-dry. Curling his hands into fists, he managed to keep from reaching for the nipples only a few inches from his chest. All the while Cleo squeezed and stroked and stretched him on the rack.

He could do this, dammit! He could let her have her revenge.

Jesus, who was he kidding? He *wanted* her to have at him. He would let himself be staked out on an anthill before he admitted it, but the woman's combination of pigheaded stubborness and prickly independence roused a hunger in him that wouldn't quit.

It always had.

He'd felt the stirrings years ago, when some jerk had flashed a lingerie ad featuring the OSI's newest recruit around the office's Net. He hadn't really appreciated the mind behind the face and the body, though, until that botched mission in Honduras.

Cleo's flat refusal to leave him after he'd taken that bullet had infuriated him at the time. It had also saved Jack's ass. He figured that was worth a little suffering now.

Besides which, there was no way Cleo was departing this hotel suite until Jack heard from the Old Man. It was either submit to this torture or zap her with another puff from the spray he'd concealed within easy reach.

Cleo almost naked and awake beat Cleo almost naked and out cold any day. Or so he thought until she scooted up another inch. Her hand was squeezed between their bellies now, her breasts flattened against his chest.

"Are you hurting, Donovan?"

"What do you think?"

She thumbed the tip of his erection.

"I think you're getting there."

Her thumb made another pass. Jack refused to groan, but he was damned close to it when she gave a disgusted huff.

"Hell," she muttered. "So am I."

"What?"

"Getting there."

His thoughts ricocheted from her hot, tight fist to the crazy hope he'd read her right.

"You want to run that by me one more time?"

"Ever hear the expression 'hoist by his own petard'?"

"Once or twice." A grin slashed across his face. "Feeling the heat, are you?"

"Don't smirk," she warned, tightening her grip.

"I'm trying not to. So what do you want to do about the situation?"

She gnawed on her lip. "Okay, here's the deal. How about you handle the petard, I'll hoist, and we call this round a draw?"

His belly constricted so hard and fast he almost bounced her off his lap. "Works for me."

Okay, Cleo thought as she planted both feet on the floor. All right. So this scheme had backfired. She'd think of another way to make Jack suffer.

Later.

Right now she was more concerned with getting rid of her suddenly inconvenient briefs.

He solved the problem by hooking an arm around her waist and hauling her upward. Two seconds later, the silk boxers hit the carpet. Five seconds after that, Jack rocketed out of the chair, taking her with him, and headed to the bathroom.

"Don't move," he growled, pawing through his shaving kit. *"Do not move!"*

Since Cleo had her legs locked around his

waist and his petard was poking at her belly, she opted not to take issue with the gruff command. Nor did she find any fault with his lightning speed once he'd located the condom he was searching for.

She was wet and ready when he set her down long enough to sheathe himself. Hot and eager when he hitched her up again. And when he thrust into her, she almost climaxed right then and there.

She managed to hold on as Jack pulled out, surged back and rammed home. Cleo's head thumped against the wall tiles. Her chin jerked up, knocking his in the process. A long, low groan ripped from her throat, almost drowning Jack's strangled grunt.

It didn't, however, drown out the thump of his fist against the wall. Her wild sexual pleasure spun into fierce satisfaction, all female, all-consuming, until Jack froze in mid-thrust.

"Aw, shit."

Only after the tortured expletive did she realize his fist wasn't doing the thumping. The pounding came from the door to the suite.

With another curse, Jack whipped his head around. "You expecting anyone?"

"No."

He was out of the bathroom and racing for his gun almost before her feet hit the floor. "Get dressed."

Screw dressed. He needed backup. As Cleo had discovered, these Maltese boys played for keeps.

Since the terry-cloth robe she'd slithered out of earlier still lay in a puddle in the outer room, she scooped it up on the run.

Jack did the same with his abandoned sweats. Dragging them up with his unencumbered hand, he thrust a leg in and hopped toward the door. The sight might have been comical if not for the nine millimeter SIG Sauer and Cleo's all-too-vivid recollections of the times she'd seen him use it.

The person on the other side of the door pounded again. Hard. Long. Loud.

The solid wood panel was thick enough to block a bullet, but Jack approached at a safe angle, anyway.

"Wait!"

Cleo snatched up the remote and jabbed it at the TV. The screen buzzed to life.

"I programmed a signal retriever for the security camera in the hall," she said in a breathless rush. "Unless you deactivated the system when you messed with my gear, it should swing the camera around and give us a clear view of whoever's at the door."

She thought at first Doreen had failed her. A potted palm jumped into view and looked like it would stay there. Cursing, Cleo stabbed the button again. To her relief, the palm drifted to the edge of the screen.

The camera picked up the elevator. A set of medieval armor. The entrance to the suite across from Cleo's. Then the eye panned around and scanned her door.

Jack's mouth twisted. With another aw-shit, he lowered the SIG and unlocked the door. When he threw the heavy panel open, Cleo gaped at the couple in the corridor.

"Marc! What in the world...?"

Sloan took Diane Walker's elbow in a white-knuckled grip and almost dragged her into the suite.

"What's wrong?" Cleo asked, wrapping her robe around her. "Why are you and Diane in Malta?"

The executive speared a look at Jack, noted the semiautomatic gripped in his fist, then swung his gaze back to Cleo.

"Two reasons. First, the medical examiner made the official ID. That was Trish buried in the sand."

The news didn't surprise Cleo, although the official call added a deeper shade of gray to the murky hues surrounding this case.

"Did the M.E. give an estimate of how long she'd been in that pump house?"

"Ten to twelve days. Which brings us to the second reason Diane and I are in Malta. We've just discovered someone used her password to access Sloan Engineering files."

His glance cut to Jack again, sharp as a scalpel and twice as lethal.

"The file this unknown hacker accessed included an unclassified set of schematics for the U.S. Motor Vessel *A1C William H. Pitsenbarger.* I want to know what's going on here, Donovan, and I want to know it now."

Jack had spent almost twenty years in investigations, first as a military cop, then as an OSI agent. He made it a point to go by the book...as long as the book coincided with his gut instincts. Right now his gut was telling him he needed Marc Sloan to fit the pieces of this dangerous puzzle together.

"Sit down. We'll talk."

19

Room service made a second delivery to the King's Suite in the small hours of the morning. Marc and Diane had been served several meals aboard his private jet during the long flight from the States, so the call was only for coffee. Lots of it.

While waiting for the order to arrive, Jack retreated to the bedroom to dress. Cleo used the interval to brief her client on the shooting in the cathedral while Diane confirmed the reservations she'd made somewhere over the Atlantic for the Queen's Apartments. Evidently queens ranked higher on the hotel's VIP scale than kings, as the suite occupied two floors and ran to three bedrooms.

Not that Diane and Marc would occupy more than one, Cleo guessed when the small group reconvened. The fact that Ms. Super Efficiency had accompanied her boss to Malta instead of remaining behind to keep the office machine running spoke volumes. So did the possessive hand Sloan slid under her hair to massage her nape.

When everyone eventually gathered around the parquetry-topped table in the dining salon, the discussion centered on Trish and the increasingly urgent circumstances of her death.

"The medical examiner was still finalizing the autopsy findings when we left," Sloan said. "But he confirmed the marks on her neck were bruises and theorized she was held underwater until she drowned. The M.E. also thinks she went into the water right there at Sand Creek State Park. Evidently the water in her lungs contained plankton that's specific to the freshwater creek that feeds into the bay there."

"What about the pregnancy?" Cleo asked. "Did the M.E. confirm that?"

"Yes."

When Sloan didn't offer any further information, Diane tucked her hand in his and answered the unspoken question.

"They ran the DNA of the fetus. We got the results just before we landed. Marc wasn't the father."

"Charleston PD is running the DNA profile against federal and international law-enforcement databases," Sloan informed them. "They seemed to think it might be a while before they receive a response."

"I'll take care of that," Jack promised. "Tell me about this business of Trish's password."

"I deactivated it after I went over to her apartment and discovered she was missing," Diane said, her hand still locked in Marc's. "I probably should have done it the first day she didn't show for work, but I assumed... We all thought..."

"We hoped she was just off partying," Marc finished.

"You said someone had accessed your files using Trish's password. Were your people able to trace the query to a specific computer or server?"

"No. Whoever went into the file knew what he was doing. He covered his tracks. My folks only discovered the query when they went in to permanently close Trish's account."

"The OSI is executive agent for the Defense Cyber Crime Center," Jack said. "The specialists at the Center have a little more expertise than most at ferreting out hackers. I'll put them on it. You're sure the only file the intruder hit was the one containing the schematics for the *Pitsenbarger?*"

"I'm sure." His hand still wrapped around Diane's, Sloan leaned forward. "Your turn, Donovan. What the hell's going on?"

Jack rasped a hand across his chin, weighing how much to tell the man. Every investigator worth his salt gave out only enough information to get suspects or interviewees talking or, better yet, to let them trip over their own stories. Years as an undercover agent had added survival to Jack's personal list of reasons for playing his cards close to his chest.

Then there was the slight matter of national security. None of the three people facing him were cleared at the levels needed for specific details. The best he could do was give Sloan and his companion the sanitized version he'd given Cleo earlier.

"It started about a month ago. We picked up some chatter that indicated interest by a friendly government in the *Pitsenbarger*. No one got too excited until person or persons unknown used your DNA profile to access the classified portion of the Afloat Prepositioning database that describes the exact munitions packages loaded aboard the *Pits*."

Cleo gave a little huff. "I imagine the pucker factor shot off the charts when the analysts factored in the connection between Trish Jackson and Adrian Mustafa Moore."

"You got that right. And it's going to reach a new high when I advise the Old Man of this latest hit on Sloan's files."

"I'm betting your cyber-crime folks will track the hit to our friend Adrian," Cleo predicted. "It's beginning to sound as though he romanced Trish with the specific intent of using her as a data source."

Diane glanced around the table, a frown creasing her brow. "I'm having trouble understanding this. If unknown persons could hack into a classified air force database using the DNA profile Marc had on file, why would they want Trish's password? She certainly didn't have access to the sensitive kind of information they could get from the APP."

"Good question," Jack said. "Wish I had an answer for it."

He glanced at the others, once again measuring how much to tell them. Cleo he trusted. Mostly. Her little jaunt across the Atlantic without coordinating with him first had pissed him off royally, but he knew she wouldn't deliberately foul an ongoing op.

Sloan was a different story. Jack recognized that a good part of his animosity toward the man stemmed from his all-out campaign to get Cleo into his bed. Granted, Sloan appeared to have shifted his attentions to his elegant executive assistant. Once a hound, though, always a hound.

Still, this wasn't about whether or not the man could keep his pants zipped. It was about a ship loaded with tons of explosives and an as-yet nameless, faceless presence known only by the code name Domino.

"You've got strong ties to the shipping world, Sloan. Have you heard any references to someone who goes by the handle Domino?"

The executive's breath hissed out. "Christ! So that's what this is about. I was thinking terrorists."

Jack kicked his opinion of the man up a grudging notch. From the sound of it, he'd already made the leap from wondering about the *Pits* to recognizing it as a target.

His assistant hadn't connected the dots yet, though. She glanced from Sloan to Jack to Cleo, saw the grim comprehension on their faces and wanted into the circle.

"Will someone please clue me in? Who is this Domino?"

"He brokers cargos," Sloan said slowly. "The kind that can't be handled through reputable freight or container companies. Contraband products. Illegal immigrants. Stolen artifacts. No one knows his real name or his base of operations, but I've heard rumors about him and his kind for years."

"Good God!" Diane gasped. "You think he's got contraband or stolen artifacts stashed in one of the munitions containers aboard the *Pitsenbarger?*"

"That would be difficult to accomplish," Jack replied, "seeing as the containers were packed, sealed and loaded aboard the vessel when it came in for replenishment at Sunny Point Military Ocean Terminal."

"But not impossible," Cleo countered.

She still had a vivid mental picture of all those acres of crated equipment waiting to be sorted and packed into the seemingly endless strings of shipping containers. She knew firsthand how tight security was at Sunny Point, but *any* perimeter could be breached given time and determination.

Unfortunately.

"I don't think he's interested in brokering contraband stashed away in the munitions containers," Sloan answered. "I think he's interested in the munitions themselves."

"What are you saying?" Her eyes wide with disbelief, Diane slewed around in her chair. "You think this Domino character is planning to steal the entire cargo?"

"Maybe not himself, but he could be putting out the word that he's interested in brokering the deal if someone else takes the initiative."

"Someone like Adrian Mustafa Moore and friends?"

"Exactly."

Cleo played devil's advocate. "But why go through a middleman? Why not just arrange the heist himself?"

"Too risky," Sloan answered with a shake of his head. "Besides which, there would be plenty of profit to go around. From what I recall of the specs, the *Pits* can ship something more than four million short pounds of explosives."

"Closer to five," Cleo murmured.

"You can imagine what five million pounds of the most sophisticated bombs and missiles on earth would bring on the black market."

Actually, Cleo couldn't. She had enough trouble with time differences and currency exchange rates. Estimating the value of all those tons of laser-guided bombs and heat-seeking air-to-air or air-to-surface missiles was so far beyond her capabilities she didn't bother to try.

"What have you heard from the crew of the *Pits?*" Sloan asked Jack. "Have they reported any increased surveillance, either in port or on the seas?"

"Not so far. Just the opposite, in fact. The captain's response to the warnings we sent advising him of the potential threat indicated he'd heightened security aboard the vessel. He also said he hadn't observed any unusual interest or activity in any of the ports they'd pulled into. All this just started to break in the past forty-eight hours, though. We're still fitting the pieces of the puzzle together."

"Now you have another piece," Sloan reminded him. "The entry into my company's files using Trish's password."

"Right." Shoving back his chair, Jack pushed to his feet. "I need to work that. I also want to expedite the DNA run on Trish's baby. Why don't you and Ms. Walker grab some sleep while I set the wheels in motion? You look about as whipped as I felt when I arrived in Malta."

Sloan's jaw set. "Whipped or not, I'm done with sitting on the sidelines. If either you or Cleo get a lead on this Adrian Moore and go after him, I want to go with you. I brought him a present."

Sliding a hand into the pocket of his suit coat, he pulled out a shellacked starfish.

"This is going down the bastard's throat."

The spiny fish Marc had confiscated from Trish's desk went back into his pocket as a bellman escorted them to the Queen's Apartments.

Despite the short notice, the three-thousand-square-foot suite had been readied for the late-night arrivals. Bouquets of fresh flowers perfumed every room. Champagne, caviar and strawberries dipped in white chocolate waited on a marble-topped table inlaid with twenty-four-karat gold. A hand-written note from the mayor of Valletta welcomed Signor Sloan to his city.

Marc saw none of the trappings his wealth and years of hard work had earned him. His thoughts were turned inward, still dark, still murderous. They had been since he'd accompanied Trish's brokenhearted parents to the city morgue to view what remained of their daughter.

Finding her killer had now become a personal quest. The burning need in his gut involved more than wanting justice for a bright, bubbly young woman who should have had long years of life ahead of her. Trish had been his employee, one of the few trusted to work in the inner sanctum of Sloan Engineering's corporate offices. Someone had stalked her, had deliberately seduced her, to gain access to that inner sanctum, and Marc intended to make him pay.

"I will turn down the beds for you and Signora Walker, yes?"

The polite question wrenched him from the dark fury that had brought him across the Atlantic. Shooting a glance across the room at the woman lingering beside a bouquet to sniff a fragrant blossom, Marc wrestled with a different problem.

Matters had moved so fast with Diane. He was still trying to reconcile his sleek assistant with the writhing, gasping woman who'd wrapped her legs around him and blown his world apart.

And he hadn't quite recovered from her suggestion they wait to formalize their partnership.

Arrogant jerk that he was, he'd thought she would jump at the idea. She was the one who'd laid her palm against his cheek. She'd murmured the *L* word.

Marc wasn't sure he'd reached that stage yet. His dismal record when it came to long-term relationships indicated he probably wouldn't recognize it if he had. All he knew at this point was that the admiration and respect he'd always had for her mind were now all mixed up with a fierce craving for her body.

The same body so enticingly bent over the massive display of gladiolas and irises. Just looking at her elegant lines pushed his weariness aside and sent his thoughts in a different, if equally turbulent, direction.

"Yes," he instructed the attendant in a tone that came dangerously close to a growl. "You can turn down the bed. The one in the master bedroom."

Diane lifted her head and snagged his gaze. Marc half expected her to countermand his order. When she didn't, the ache collecting in his groin got serious.

She seemed to sense they both needed relief from the fierce emotions that had gripped them since learning about Trish. At least Marc hoped that was what motivated her to gather her handbag and the crocodile briefcase he'd given her for Christmas a few years ago.

"I'll go up with the bellman," she said quietly. "Come up when you're ready."

He paced downstairs until the hotel attendant returned, his bed-tending mission accomplished. Passing the man a wad of folded lira, Marc flipped the dead bolt and took the stairs two at a time.

There were three bedrooms, each with private bath and sitting area. The master suite was separated from the other two by a set of double doors with ornate latch handles etched in gold. When Marc pushed on the handle and stepped inside, the first thing that grabbed him was the bed. It was a monster, with head- and footboards carved from gilt-trimmed rosewood and yards of shimmering crimson silk draped from an honest-to-God crown.

But it was the woman standing beside the bed that grabbed his heart. Marc felt it squeeze hard and tight inside his chest as she turned to him, her eyes alight.

"Are you feeling royal tonight?"

Marc crossed the room and curled a knuckle under her chin. "I wouldn't describe what I'm feeling right now as royal, exactly."

Her breath hitched. "Oh, I don't know," she replied on a shaky laugh. "I suspect I could find something of princely proportions if I searched for it."

"I suspect you could."

The amusement faded and hesitation took its place. Their altered relationship must still feel as strange to her as it did to him. Then there was the guilt. He'd sensed the regret buried under her grief, seen it in her face when she'd emptied Trish's desk.

Diane had all but accused him of having an affair with Trish. Yet she'd acted as the girl's mentor and assigned her increasing levels of responsibility in the office.

But that was Diane. All cool, calm professionalism on the outside. Inside…

Inside was such a firestorm of passion Marc couldn't imagine how he'd worked with her all these years and not been singed by it.

He fully intended to make up for lost time now, though. No way he was letting these satin-smooth sheets and crown go to waste.

He and Diane made up for so much lost time they were both still sprawled in naked abandon when the phone beside the bed jangled. Grunting, Marc stretched out an arm and fumbled for the old-fashioned ivory-and-gold instrument.

"Sloan."

"You wanted to go along if I developed a lead on Adrian Moore," Donovan said without preamble. "I might have something. Meet me in the lobby in ten minutes."

"I'll be there."

Slamming down the phone, Marc rolled out of bed and scooped up his watch. The dial read nine-twenty, and the bright glow around the edges of the drawn drapes told him that was a.m.

As he pulled on his shorts, a half-awake Diane struggled up on one elbow. "Who was that?"

"Donovan."

"What did he want? What's happening?"

"He might have a lead on Moore." Marc stepped into his slacks and yanked up the zipper. "I'm meeting him downstairs in ten minutes."

"Ten minutes!"

Scrambling onto her knees, she dove under the sheet to search for the various pieces of her clothing she'd lost last night. Marc allowed himself a few seconds to enjoy the view of her bare posterior while he dragged on his shirt and reached into the closet for a navy blazer. When she popped out again, he broke the news.

"Donovan said he wanted *me* to meet him. You weren't invited."

"I'm coming with you."

He didn't have time to argue with her. "No, you're not. This could be dangerous."

The look she gave him underscored more clearly than words their altered relationship. It combined impatience and scorn, flavored with a flash of pure temper.

"I may not possess the same skills as Cleo North, but I'm not entirely helpless. Nor am I stupid. I won't do anything to put myself or you at risk, but I'll be damned if I'm going to sit here twiddling my thumbs while the three of you track down Trish's killer."

"Diane…"

"Do *not* leave these apartments without me!"

When the bathroom door slammed behind her, Marc's own temper flared. He'd always been the one in charge. He was used to issuing orders, not having his executive assistant bark them at him like a drill sergeant. The urge to reassert his authority took him out of the bedroom and into the hall.

The realization that he'd have to learn to give *and* take caught up with him on the stairs. Swearing, he slowed his step.

Eight minutes. He'd give the woman eight minutes.

20

A bellman had delivered the elegantly inscribed invitation. The brief note had sent Jack to the phone to call Sloan and Cleo rushing into the bedroom to slither into her jungle-print dress.

Spandex and spiky sandals weren't exactly what she would have chosen for coffee at the home of one of Malta's foremost patrons of the arts, which is how the bellman had described the author of the note, Lady Marston. Seeing as Cleo's only other option was jeans and a tank top, she figured the thigh-skimming fern-green-and-jungle-red tube would do. Anchoring her hair atop her head with a plastic clip, she dusted on some face powder and grabbed her purse.

Jack was frowning down at the embossed invitation when she emerged from the bedroom. The message was brief—a polite request for Ms.

North to join Lady Marston for coffee at ten, followed by a single line indicating Marston might have information regarding the individual Cleo sought.

That bombshell had prompted Jack to threaten Cleo with another squirt of subduing agent if she even *thought* about slipping out of the suite to meet with this woman alone. It had also prompted his call to Sloan. For reasons Cleo had yet to fully comprehend, Jack had apparently accepted Sloan into their small fraternity.

"I'm ready."

He glanced up then, and the frown blew away. "Damn! And I thought you looked hot in those boxers."

"Eat your heart out, Donovan. I need a weapon."

"You're wearing one, babe."

"Get serious. I didn't bring my Glock and Inspector Aruzzo confiscated my *ebu*. Do you have a backup for your SIG?"

"I might," he said cautiously.

Sighing, Cleo extended the truce they'd negotiated just before crawling all over each other last night. "I won't use it on you."

Unless absolutely necessary.

Donovan debated for several moments before propping a foot on the rung of a spindly antique armchair and hiking up his pant leg.

His wardrobe choices were evidently as limited as Cleo's. He wore the jeans and lightweight sport coat he'd arrived in, paired with a fresh, sky-blue Oxford shirt left open at the throat. He'd brought the necessities with him, though. In addition to the nine millimeter SIG Sauer nested in its underarm holster, he packed a neat, snub-nosed .38 in a Velcro ankle pack.

He passed her the Velcro pack, a glint in his blue eyes. "I can't wait to see where you're going to strap this."

Even with her newly trim silhouette, the ankle band wouldn't fit around her thighs. She was forced to slip the .38 into her purse but kept the zipper partially open for instant access.

"What did you find out on this Marston woman?" she asked as she armed the intrusion-detection devices.

"Not much. The Operations Center is still working her. All they've been able to pull off so far is essentially what we learned from the bellman and the front desk. Her first name is Johanna. She's the widow of a British member of parliament, the owner of a flat in London and a seaside villa in Malta, and a generous contributor to the Opera Fund."

The first image Cleo conjured up was one of Margaret Thatcher in a tiara and long white gloves, on her way to an evening of Mozart or Puccini. The second, a slender, dark-haired woman of about forty-five with a widow's peak holding a small, lethal automatic.

That was the image that stayed with her as she

followed Jack into the hall and punched the button for the elevator.

"Did Ops dig up a picture of this Lady Marston?"

"They did. They sent it to me via my cell."

He retrieved the instrument from his inside coat pocket and flipped up the lid. A quick flick of the call button lit up the screen. Another flick brought up what looked like a society-page color shot of several elegantly clad individuals.

"Lady Marston is the second from the right. Use the bottom left arrow to zoom in on her face."

Cleo was all set to zoom when the picture suddenly dissolved and another image took its place. One glimpse of those bushy brows and bulldog jaw put Cleo in an instinctive, square-shouldered brace.

"Jack!" she whispered. "Please tell me this isn't clear-streaming video!"

The fervent hope that she was viewing a static photo died when those thick brows plunged into a deep V and General Barnes squinted into the screen.

"Is that you, North?"

"Yes, sir."

Damn! All these years, and the Old Man still yanked a "sir" from her.

"Where's Donovan?"

"Right beside me."

"Tell him to go voice only and put the phone to his ear."

"In a minute."

Cleo had recovered from the shock of seeing the

general's craggy face smooshed into two square inches of screen. Batting aside Jack's hand, she retained a firm grasp on the instrument.

"First I'd like to remind you that I'm no longer under your command. I don't answer to you or anyone else for my actions, and I certainly don't appreciate you sending Donovan over here armed with a subduing agent and orders to keep me on ice."

"He used the juice on you?" The V disappeared. Genuine delight appeared on the general's face. "Good man. Put him on."

Thoroughly disgusted, Cleo handed Jack the phone. His smile was sardonic as he switched to voice only and put it to his ear.

"Yes, sir?"

He listened a moment, his gaze on Cleo.

"No, not yet."

The smile stayed in place, but his shoulders shifted under his sport coat. Cleo knew him well enough now to sense his sudden, subtle tension as he checked his watch.

"Twenty-three hundred Zulu. Got it."

The elevator doors slid open. Neither Jack nor Cleo made a move to step inside. Jack listened for a moment longer before terminating the conversation with another glance at Cleo.

"Roger that."

The phone flipped shut and went back into his pocket. Thrusting out an arm to keep the elevator doors from shutting, he motioned Cleo inside.

She knew better than to demand an explanation while they were under the eye of the camera mounted in a corner of the small cage. Once in the lobby, though, she hooked his elbow and tugged him behind a medieval suit of armor complete with conical helmet, shield and battle-ax.

"Okay, Donovan. Re-port."

"The cyber-crimes unit traced the server our hacker went through when he used Trish's password to access Sloan Engineering files. Preliminary indications are the transmission came via satellite from Cyprus."

"Cyprus?"

"It's an island about five hundred miles due east of Malta."

Cleo made an impatient clucking noise. "I know where it is. What's the significance of Cyprus to our op?"

"It happens to be the *Pitsenbarger*'s next scheduled port of call."

"Hooo-boy. Let me guess. The *Pits* pulls into Cyprus at twenty-three hundred tonight."

"Bingo."

"I don't know about you, Donovan, but I think we should probably be on hand to greet it."

"Funny you should say that. The general thinks we should mosey on out and talk to the captain *before* he makes port."

"We?"

His grin slipped out, the one that sent her breath sliding back down her throat.

"Actually, he'd prefer I zap you with another dose of knockout juice, but he agrees it might not hurt to take along some backup. He's sending a chopper from the navy base in Naples to pick us up."

"Before or after we have coffee with Lady Marston?"

"After." He shot another look at his watch. "But we have to move it. Where the hell is Sloan?"

As if in answer, the elevator doors opened again and Marc emerged...with his executive assistant.

The normally well-groomed Diane looked like she'd just rolled out of bed. She was minus makeup, earrings and the narrow leather belt that had wrapped around the waist of her St. John knit jacket last night. Marc looked somewhat better coordinated in gray slacks and a hand-tailored navy blazer, but the bristles still darkening his cheeks and chin suggested he'd just rolled out with her. Of more interest than his wardrobe was the embossed card he gripped in one fist.

"A bellman delivered this just as we were leaving our suite. Who is Lady Marston?"

Jack hooked a brow. "Someone with the resources to know you arrived in the middle of the night, apparently."

"What's her connection to our boy Moore?"

"I expect we'll find out at her villa." His glance slid to the woman at Sloan's side. "Until we do, I don't think it's smart to—"

"Marc and I have already had this discussion," Diane interrupted coolly. "I'm coming with you."

"Short of tying the woman to the bed, there wasn't any way of stopping her."

A wicked glint leapt into Jack's eyes, but Cleo cut him off before he could offer Marc suggestions or advice. "We're wasting time here. Let's talk to the concierge about transportation to this seaside villa."

"It's already arranged," Diane informed her. "I called before we left the suite. They're bringing a carriage around now."

A horse-drawn carriage with the Auberge St. Georges logo etched in gold on its side panels conveyed them to the gate of the walled city. A chauffeur stood at attention beside a limousine just outside the gates. He handed the ladies in and advised the men that the drive would require twenty minutes.

"Lady Marston's villa is in San Pawl il-Bahar— St. Paul by the Sea. It is a small resort on the north side of our island."

"Named for the Apostle Paul," Cleo added as the limo's engine purred to life. "He was shipwrecked here in 60 A.D. while being transported to Rome to answer to the emperor for spreading the doctrines of Christ."

Three surprised faces swung in her direction.

"Hey, I did some research. According to the

record made by his fellow prisoner, St. Luke the Physician, Paul stayed in Malta for three months while recovering his strength. In the process, he converted the Roman governor to Christianity."

"I suspect that didn't win him any points with the authorities in Rome," Marc commented.

"Evidently not, since Nero had him beheaded."

Sincerely hoping the same fate didn't befall any of them, Cleo hit the button to raise the partition between the front seat and back.

"I never did get to see that picture of Lady Marston the Ops Center sent you," she reminded Donovan.

She recognized the thin, elegant face the minute she zoomed in on it. "That's her, Jack! That's the woman from the cathedral."

He squeezed against Cleo's shoulder to take a look. "Interesting that she's such an expert shot."

"Isn't it?"

Firing into a stampeding crowd at a crouched shooter required icy nerves and considerable training—not the kind of training an opera buff and widow of a British member of parliament would normally receive. Frowning, Cleo studied the brunette's features again.

"I know I know her. I just don't know from where."

"Let me see."

Sloan took a turn at the screen. He didn't have any more luck placing Lady Marston than Cleo had. Diane, on the other hand, made an instant connection. She took one look at the screen and gasped.

"Good Lord, Marc! She has your chin and eyes! You could be her brother."

21

The route from Valletta to Lady Marston's villa wound around the harbor basin, through the city of Sliema and out along the north shore. Waves crashed against rocky coastline and flung up tall white spumes. Small, protected coves sheltered brightly painted fishing boats. The villages were tiny gems set alongside a sea that was a palette of turquoise, azure and cobalt.

As they neared the village of St. Paul by the Sea, the limo driver pointed out the fount where the Apostle Paul was reputed to have quenched his thirst after dragging himself out of the sea. He also showed them the church marking the spot where Paul supposedly threw a viper into the flames and another where the Governor Publius was reported to have welcomed him.

At any other time, Cleo would have delighted

in both the scenery and the history of this tiny island. She and her father had traveled to so many countries during his years with USAID that she made a habit of gathering interesting tidbits about people and places and squirreling them away to savor later.

This time she barely registered the passing view. Her mind was too busy with the tangled events that brought her to this sleepy resort town on Malta's north coast…and with the mysterious woman who resided in the house set on the far curve of St. Paul's Bay.

The villa looked modest when the driver first pointed it out. It was flat-roofed in the Mediterranean style, with a buttery tan exterior. Then a bend in the coast offered a view of the house's rear. Cleo took in a cascade of glass walls, rooms that stair-stepped down the rocky cliffs and garden terraces jutting right out over the sea.

The driver pulled up at a set of iron gates and buzzed for entry. A moment later the gates swung open. As the limo wound along a driveway that hugged the cliffs, Cleo detected a camera tucked into the branches of a gnarled olive tree and the tiny, unwinking red eye of a sensor planted amid mossy ferns.

A uniformed maid answered the doorbell and escorted them through a living room done in soothing cream tones that showcased a stunning collection of modern art. Sliding glass doors gave onto an upper balcony. A short flight of stairs wound down to the terrace. It was there, against a backdrop of bright red geraniums and glorious turquoise sea, that their hostess greeted them.

Floating across the terrace on a cloud of amber chiffon, she held out her hand. "Well, Ms. North, we meet again."

"So we do," Cleo replied. "Let's hope we don't have to dodge any bullets this time."

"I rather think we won't."

Her cool smile stayed in place as Cleo made the introductions.

"This is Jack Donovan, an associate of mine. Diane Walker, also an associate. And this is…"

"Marcus Sloan. Yes, I know."

When the woman offered Marc her hand, Cleo could have kicked herself for not making the connection sooner. Diane had hit the nail smack on the head. Johanna Marston was a female version of Marc. Her eyes were more slate-blue than gray and her chin lacked the dimple that characterized his. But they shared the same high, chiseled cheekbones and firm lips, as well as a distinctly aristocratic nose.

"How do you do, Mr. Sloan?"

Marc shook hands politely, but his feelings were anything but gracious as he stared into a face that rolled back the years and stirred turbulent memories.

He could still recall the morning the general had summoned his six-year-old sons into his study and informed them they'd been adopted at birth. He'd assured the twins it made no difference, none whatsoever, in how he and their mother felt about them. He simply wanted them to understand that medical issues might arise someday they couldn't deal with unless they knew the truth.

That was the general. Blunt. Straightforward. Fully aware he'd rocked his sons' world right off its foundation. Fully expecting them to adjust.

Alex had, and far more quickly than Marc. He'd always been the smart, agile twin. The straight-A student. The star center on the basketball team. The hotshot air force pilot destined for greatness, like his illustrious father.

Marc had tried to fit into the good-son mold. More or less. He'd aced those classes that interested him, copied Alex's homework in those that didn't. He'd played sports more to work off energy than anything else. He'd accepted an appointment to the Naval Academy, fully intending to make a career of the military, but opted out after serving his tour to swim with the financial sharks.

As a consequence, he'd never quite measured up to the general's exacting standards. There had always been that distance, that degree of separation, as well as unanswered questions about his biological parents.

The general disclaimed all knowledge of his sons' birth parents, but Marc knew damned well he wouldn't have taken in two babies without checking their bloodlines. By the time Marc had the resources to hire investigators to trace his real parents, though, the lawyer who'd arranged the adoption was dead. Marc petitioned the court to unseal the records, only to find the birth certificates and affidavits supplied by the attorney were clever forgeries.

The trail dead-ended in that courthouse, but Marc's determined attempt to trace his roots had driven another wedge between him and the man who'd adopted him. They'd rarely seen each other in the general's later years, and then only when Alex had arranged a family gathering.

Now, as he looked down into this woman's face, Marc had to fight to keep the old hurts and a sharp, new anger from seeping into his reply. "You have the advantage of me, Lady Marston. You obviously know who I am. I don't have a clue who you are."

Her smile took a mocking slant. "Mother referred to me as the middle sin."

"I beg your pardon?"

"I'm your sister, Mr. Sloan. According to our mother, I entered the world red-faced and howling some eight minutes after Alexander and twelve before you."

"The hell you say!"

He'd figured cousin. Or half sister, maybe. A daughter born later and not given up for adoption, as the inconvenient twin boys had been. He sure as hell hadn't expected to hear this tall, elegant woman say she'd shared a womb with him and Alex.

"A bit of a shocker, isn't it, Mr. Sloan?"

"A bit," he ground out.

He wasn't the only one stunned by the news, he saw. Diane's incredulous glance kept swinging from Marc to their hostess. Cleo eyed the woman with intense speculation. Donovan cut right to issue of most concern to him.

"Sloan and his brother are identical twins. That means they share one hundred percent of their DNA. Just where do you fit into that DNA equation?"

The brunette pulled her gaze from Marc. "You're very direct, Special Agent Donovan. I've heard that about you."

Donovan stiffened, but before he could ask just how the heck he'd popped up on this woman's radar screen, she responded to his question.

"Identical siblings occur when an egg is fertilized by a single sperm and the embryo subsequently splits. Fraternal siblings result when the mother releases two or more eggs which become fertilized. It's extremely rare for both to occur simultaneously, but that's evidently what happened here. Thus Marc and Alex share one hundred percent of their DNA, but only fifty percent with me—the same ratio as any other set of siblings. I must admit," she added with a lift of one perfectly shaped brow, "that made it difficult for me to use his DNA signature to access your Afloat Prepositioning database."

The cool admission elicited a curse from Marc and a swift, indrawn hiss from Jack.

Cleo's hand slipped inside the zipper of her purse. Her instincts told her this woman posed no immediate threat, but the mere fact she knew about the APP upped the ante considerably. Lady Marston observed the movement with another lift of her brow but addressed herself to Donovan.

"Then, of course, I realized Marc couldn't have used his own DNA *because* he and Alex are identical. Nor could he supply DNA belonging to another living person to establish access, as that would violate your security requirements."

"You seem to know a lot about our system requirements."

"Yes, I do."

"Care to tell me just how you came by that knowledge?"

The brunette's glance slid to Diane before returning to Donovan. "I couldn't contact you until I notified my superiors of your arrival. I had just received clearance to speak with you when Marc and Ms. Walker showed up. Her presence required additional coordination."

"You had to get the green light from C?"

Her laughter rippled out, light and amused. "A clever pun, Mr. Donovan. And spot on."

Cleo caught the reference immediately, but Marc was obviously still struggling with the fact that he and this woman sprang from the same mother. He didn't understand the oblique reference and made it clear he didn't like being left behind in the conversation.

"What the hell are you two talking about?"

"Your sister is with the British government," Donovan informed him. "MI6, unless I miss my guess."

"Jesus!"

Marc shoved a hand through his hair. Cleo felt a distinct sympathy for the executive. This meeting was delivering one punch after another. While her client tried to unscramble his thoughts, she regarded their hostess with new approval.

"So you're SIS. That explains that bullet you put between the shooter's eyes in the cathedral."

"Not to me." It was Diane's turn to demand clarification. "C. SIS. MI6. Will someone *please* clue me in?"

"SIS is the British Secret Intelligence Service," Cleo explained. "MI6 is its foreign-intelligence division, the counterpart to our CIA. It's the successor to the Secret Service Bureau founded by Sir Mansfield Cumming in 1909."

"Very good," Lady Marston murmured. "You paid attention when you went through your air force intelligence training, Ms. North."

"Yes, I did. Sir Mansfield signed himself as 'C' and used only green ink," Cleo continued for Diane's benefit. "Supposedly, all SIS chiefs since have continued the tradition."

"They have," the brunette confirmed. "A silly practice, one must admit, but the stuff of legends."

"Okay," Diane said, "I get it. Green ink, green light. I still don't understand how you gained access to a classified database using the DNA signature Marc had established, though."

Marc's gaze bore into the woman. "There are a few things *I* don't understand, either. Like how you knew about Alex and me. And why we never knew about you."

"It's rather a complicated tale." She gestured toward the table set with a massive silver tea service. "Shall we have a spot of tea or coffee while I explain?"

"Do you have anything stronger?" Marc muttered as he hooked a hand under Diane's elbow. "This is turning out to be one hell of a morning."

Marston's laughter spilled out again, light and silvery. "As it happens, I do."

Lady Marston wielded the heavy silver pot with an expertise that suggested she'd performed this ritual at any number of afternoon teas and garden parties. Coffee and tea poured, she passed a three-tiered plate of puff pastries. Cleo was more than happy to sneak two flaky tidbits onto her plate as her hostess reached for a crystal decanter almost hidden behind the teapot.

"You prefer single malt Scotch, don't you?"

"Yes, I do. How did you know?"

She poured a stiff shot and met Sloan's eyes. "You owe that to the general, I would guess. Mum indicated he developed a taste for it during his tour in England."

Sloan froze with his hand stretched halfway across the table. "Wait a minute. Are you saying your mother..." He broke off, took a breath and started again. "Are you saying our mother was acquainted with the man who adopted Alex and me?"

Sympathy softened the high, clean lines of Marston's face. "Yes, she knew him. In the biblical sense, as it turned out. Major General Harrison Sloan was my biological father."

"But that would make him Marc's...!"

Cleo's startled exclamation was lost in the crash as Sloan exploded out of his chair and sent it crashing to the tiles.

"*My* biological father, too," he finished on a snarl.

"That's correct." Quiet empathy filled Lady Marston's voice. "I found the original birth certificate among my mother's papers after she died last year. I brought you a copy."

Fury blazed from Sloan's eyes. "The bastard! He adopted his own sons. All those years, he let Alex and me believe we were some other man's discards and we were his own sons."

Whirling, he strode across the terrace and turned his face to the sea. Diane started to rise and go to him. Lady Marston waved her back down.

"Please," she murmured. "Let me."

As she joined Sloan, the breeze off the ocean teased her hair into silky black wings and molded the amber chiffon to her slender figure. She spoke softly, most of her words lost to the wind and the waves slapping against the rocks below the terrace.

Whatever she said, Marc wasn't buying. He stared at the sea, his face a stone mask. Cleo could only imagine what it would feel like to have your entire life ripped off its foundations. Finally, his sister laid a hand on his arm and pulled him around. Her voice took on a tart note that carried clearly across the terrace.

"The general *wanted* his sons. He went to the trouble to arrange an adoption and give you and Alex his name. That's more than he did for his daughter."

Sloan held her eyes for long moments before covering her hand with his. "You're right, it was."

The touch was tentative, the response even more so. American caution meets British reserve, Cleo thought with a little pang for both of them.

She'd grown up with only one parent. But Patrick North had closed the hole made by his wife's death with a lifetime of fierce bear hugs, loud smacking kisses and efforts to make sure his daughter knew she was loved. Judging by Marc's previous comments, the general had hardly qualified as a warm, loving parent. She felt for Sloan as he tried to bridge the forty-year gap between him and the stranger who shared his blood.

"I don't know about you," he said gruffly, "but I could sure use that whisky now."

"So could I."

Once they were back at the table, a worried Diane searched his face.

"Are you all right?"

"I'm getting there."

When his sister passed him the whisky, he offered her a silent salute and tossed back the contents. Lady Marston did the same, thereby earning Cleo's instant approval. Anyone who could shoot with such deadly accuracy and down two fingers of Scotch in one smooth swallow qualified as okay in her book.

Lifting his chair back onto its legs, Marc settled beside Diane. His fury had cooled, but tension still showed in the stiff set to his shoulders.

"Tell me about your…" He gave an impatient shake of his head. "About our mother. How did she and the general meet?"

Cleo caught Jack stealing a glance at his watch. They had a helicopter inbound and a cargo ship loaded with munitions to fly out to. He hid his impatience, though, as Lady Marston responded to Sloan's question.

"They met in York, actually. The general was on leave from his embassy duties. He'd motored up to research the old Roman fort at Chesters, stopped for a pint in York, and ended up tumbling into bed with a university student he met in a pub."

"A student?"

"She took honors in Roman history at Oxford."

Sloan gave a bark of laughter. "I would imagine that gave the general a real boner."

"Yes, quite. I didn't learn any of this until last year," Johanna continued with a shrug. "I always knew I was illegitimate, but Mum claimed she'd never tried to track down my father. I certainly never knew I had brothers. I didn't discover that until I was going through her papers and found the letter the general had written in response to one she posted to him, advising him she was pregnant. She knew she was giving birth to triplets. Knew two were boys. She also knew she couldn't care for three nippers without financial assistance. The general very graciously offered to relieve her of some of that burden by adopting the two boys. Apparently he didn't have any use for a girl."

"Bastard," Marc said again.

His sister smiled. "I rather thought so, too. I had planned to tell him so to his face and was quite crushed to learn he'd died years ago."

"Why didn't you contact Alex or me?"

"I intended to. I did quite a lot of research about you both, but—" a shadow rippled across her face "—Barty was diagnosed with liver cancer shortly after Mum died."

"Barty?"

"My husband, Sir Bartholomew Marston. Such a dear, dear man. I miss him dreadfully. I don't know what I would have done if the Firm hadn't kept me so busy."

"That's the SIS," Cleo explained in an aside to Diane. "They're known as the Firm, just as the world knows the CIA as the Company."

Diane shook her head, as if to indicate all this cloak-and-dagger stuff was out of her league. The reference provided just the opening Donovan had been waiting for, however. Sliding his china cup to one side, he leaned forward.

"Just what is it you do for the Firm, Lady Marston?"

Her glance shifted to Jack. Cool. Assessing. Deliberate. When she replied, Cleo guessed her superiors had vetted the response well before the four of them had shown up at her front door.

"I do the same thing you do for the United States Air Force, Mr. Donovan. Collect intelligence and run covert operations."

"Does that include collecting intelligence on the movements of a United States munitions ship?"

"It does when that ship is in my area of operations and may be the target of a possible hijacking."

"SIS couldn't just notify the CIA and let our own people work it?"

"Actually, my superiors inform me such notification was made," she replied. "But our intelligence at that point was vague and nonspecific. The threads didn't begin to come together until the *Pitsenbarger* made port here in Malta and I, ah, ascertained the cargo she carried."

"By hacking into a classified air force database."

She had the grace to look embarrassed. "I do apologize for that. But when I researched the ship and saw that Sloan Engineering had retrofitted it to meet the new NOx emission-control standards, I couldn't resist."

"How did you break the DNA code on my access signature?" Marc asked.

"I knew you couldn't have used your own DNA, since you and Alex are identical twins. Nor could you use the DNA of another living person, as that person could be compromised. On a hunch, I tried a sample from our father."

Cleo was having awful mental images of forty-year-old excrement again when Lady Marston explained the source of her sample.

"I extracted the DNA from the letter our father sent our mother, offering to adopt you and Alex. I guessed, correctly as it turned out, he licked the envelope flap and left some of his tongue skin cells in the glue."

That was almost as bad as excrement.

Jack wasn't as concerned with the how as with the why. "What made you zero in on the *Pitsenbarger?*"

The British agent's face reflected the same grim intent as Donovan's. "For almost a year now I've been on the trail of a shadowy international contraband broker both our countries would very much like to unmask."

"Domino," Jack growled.

"Domino," she confirmed. "I thought I had him when one of my agents stumbled across information indicating he had offered to act as intermediary on a massive armaments deal. My agent heard rumors that the source of those arms might be the *Pitsenbarger.* That's when I began to gather specific information on the vessel."

Her glance flicked to Cleo.

"Unfortunately, this operative blew his cover and took a bullet in the back before he could confirm the rumors."

The three others swiveled in their seats. Cleo threw up both hands in defense. "Hey, all I did was show a photo at the Café Corinthia. I didn't know the waiter was an undercover British agent."

"I blame myself for that," Johanna admitted, her cool facade cracking long enough to reveal bitter regret. "I'd heard you'd arrived in Malta, Ms. North, and was checking into the reasons behind your visit. I didn't expect you to move so quickly."

"You moved pretty fast yourself in the cathedral. I owe you for that one."

"Yes, well, you can repay me by—"

The chirp of a beeper halted her in midsentence. She slid a hand into the pocket of her caftan, glanced at the beeper's display and rose with a fluid grace.

"I must make a call. Please excuse me."

She disappeared in a cloud of amber chiffon, leaving her guests to digest their coffee, puff pastries and the startling information she'd just shared.

Cleo helped herself to another flaky offering stuffed with nuts and caramel. Diane slipped her hand into Marc's and murmured something for his ears alone. Jack shoved his chair back, got up and paced the terrace.

Everything he'd uncovered in the past few weeks pointed to the *Pitsenbarger* as a potential target. Johanna Marston's intelligence pointed in the same direction. He needed to get out to the ship, talk to the captain, assess the need for increased defenses.

Jaw set, he shot another look at his watch. He was about to tell Cleo they'd have to leave when his cell phone rang. Flipping up the lid, he saw he had a secure transmission. A push of a button unscrambled the brief message.

"Great," he muttered. "Just what I need. Another female to keep on a leash."

Cleo strolled across the terrace, licking sugar from her fingers. "What's up?"

"I just got a message from the Old Man. He's in direct communication with SIS."

"'Bout time."

"As a result, he's cleared Agent 316 to accompany us out to the *Pits*."

"Agent 316, huh? What do you want to bet that's Lady Marston?"

Jack's gaze swiveled to the left. "Yeah," he choked out, "I'd say it is."

Cleo threw a puzzled look over her shoulder. One glance provided an explanation for Donovan's sudden loss of speech.

Lady Marston had shed her layers of chiffon. Also her air of aristocratic sophistication. The woman who strode toward them wore boots and a black jumpsuit that looked as though it had been painted on. She also had a small, lethal semiautomatic tucked in a holster under one arm.

"Headquarters informed me you're choppering out to the *Pitsenbarger*. They've requested and received authority for me to accompany you. You should receive a communiqué from your headquarters directly."

"I just got it."

"Excellent. Then we're good to go."

Sloan and Diane had picked up on the conversation.

"I'm coming, too," Sloan stated. "I know the ship," he added before either Jack or his sister could protest. "I climbed all through her during the retrofit. And I've got the necessary security clearances—unless you still consider me a suspect in the APP breach."

"I think we've resolved that issue," Jack said with a wry glance at his British counterpart.

He wasn't too keen about hauling a civilian out to the *Pits*. On the other hand, agents in the field had to make instant decisions based on best available intel and their gut instincts. Jack's gut was telling him Sloan might be a good man to have as backup.

"All right," he conceded, "let's get this show on the road."

22

Diane wasn't happy about being left behind.

The wash from the chopper's whirling rotor blades whipped her hair around her face as she stood beside the limo and glowered at the four people cutting across the tarmac to the helo pad.

They couldn't have looked less like a team. Marc wore the dress slacks and the hand-tailored blazer he'd donned for coffee with Lady Marston. His sister was zipped into a black jumpsuit that only a woman with her figure—and utter self-confidence—could wear in public. Special Agent Donovan was in jeans and his rumpled sport coat. Cleo blazed in bright jungle colors that ended mid-thigh.

She'd traded her spiky sandals for a pair of sneakers borrowed from Lady Marston, though. Diane wouldn't have imagined the Englishwoman would even *own* black-and-white high-tops. But then Diane hadn't imagined she'd be standing beside a chopper pad in Malta, either, watching Marc prepare to chase off after a cargo vessel on the high seas.

He was at the hatch, about to climb aboard, when he suddenly turned and ducked under the blades again. Diane's mind clicked instantly into executive-assistant mode. Holding back her whipping hair, she pushed away from the limo.

"What is it? What did you forget?"

"This."

The kiss was hard and fast and potent. She was breathless when he yanked open the limo door and thrust her inside.

"Go back to the hotel and stay there."

The glow faded. Evidently she wasn't the only one who'd slipped back into their previous mode of operation.

"Yes, sir. Right away, sir. Any other orders, sir?"

"Just one. Call the office and clear our calendars for the next few weeks…or however long you think it will take us to formalize this new partnership of ours. We're not flying back to Charleston until we do."

There, Marc thought as he ducked under the blades once more. At least that was settled. Given the way his world had turned upside down in the past few hours, he refused to zip across a hundred miles of open sea without letting Diane know she was one constant he couldn't let go of.

A seaman in a navy flight suit reached down a hand to help him aboard the SH-60 Seahawk. Shouting to be heard over the whine of the engines, he directed Marc to a seat beside Cleo.

"We'll power up and be on our way as soon as you strap in, sir."

Nodding, Marc hooked the harness. The young flight engineer waited until he was settled to hand him a headset.

"You key the mike to transmit," he yelled. "And this button to switch channels. Channel one will get you the flight deck. Channel three is the intercom if you folks want to talk to one another."

"Got it."

Marc didn't tell him he'd logged more than a few hours aboard SH-60s during his years in uniform. A seagoing version of the army's Blackhawk and the air force's Pavehawk, the twin-engine, medium-lift Seahawk was the workhorse of the navy. Its missions included everything from anti-submarine warfare, drug interdiction and cargo lift, to search-and-rescue and Special Ops. The two powerful General Electric engines gave it a max speed of one hundred and eighty knots and a cruising range of almost four hundred nautical miles, depending on the load.

The helo also packed a hell of a punch in terms of armaments. Marc was eyeing the two .50 caliber cannons mounted at either side hatch when Cleo's voice floated through his headset.

"Do those babies bring back memories?"

"As a matter of fact, they do."

"Have you ever fired a cannon that size?"

"Once or twice. How about you?"

"Once or twice."

"I hate to disappoint you two," Jack drawled into the mike, "but we're not going in with guns blazing. The last communiqué from the captain of the *Pits* approved our request to set down aboard his ship and extended a hearty welcome."

All business now, Cleo keyed her mike. "What have you got on the captain and crew?"

Jack hunched forward. The other three did the same. Elbows on knees, he briefed the small, intent circle.

"The captain is Eric Kobe. He has some twenty-two years in the merchant marine under his belt. The crew consists of three deck officers, a chief engineer and three assistant engineers, and a radio operator, plus assorted deckhands, cooks and oilers."

"Whatever those are," Cleo muttered.

Marc caught the comment and flashed her a quick grin. "They work for the engineering officers below decks, lubricating gears and shafts, reading pressure and temperature gauges, repairing equipment."

"Sounds like fun."

"It is, if you don't mind oozing grease from every pore."

Cleo wanted a number. "So that makes what? Eighteen, twenty aboard the ship?"

"Twenty-three," Jack confirmed.

"Did you run background checks?" Johanna Marston asked.

Cleo could have told her Donovan *always* ran detailed background checks when preparing for an op. He probably knew the captain's shirt size, astrological sign and preferred sexual position. Jack confirmed her guess with a succinct report.

"All but three of the crew are clean. One popped in NCIC for a drug bust seven years ago, another for a failure to pay court-ordered child support. The third got drunk and busted up a waterfront dive in San Diego a couple years back. Took four cops to subdue him."

"Just your typical sailors," Marc observed dryly.

Fully airborne now, the Seahawk banked into a sharp turn. Cleo's stomach banked with it. Grabbing a side strap, she hung on until the deck leveled beneath her borrowed high-tops.

"No links to any smuggling rings or stolen cargoes like this guy Domino likes to broker?" she asked Jack.

"None that I could find."

"If pirates are seriously considering hijacking the *Pitsenbarger*'s cargo, they'd have to have someone on the inside," she argued. "Maybe several someones."

"They could be planning to come aboard in Cyprus," Jack countered, "when the *Pits* takes on fresh water and fuel."

"Taking over the ship might be more difficult than it would seem at first blush," Johanna commented. "The International Ship and Port Facility Code that came into force in July of last year requires every ship to develop a security plan to guard against terrorists and pirates. Has the *Pitsenbarger* implemented such a plan?"

"It has," Jack confirmed, "and it's been tested twice. Once by the port of Charleston and once by the Navy Sealift Command. The ship passed both tests."

Considerably relieved by that information, Cleo slumped back against the webbed seatback. The two puff pastries she'd scarfed down at Johanna Marston's seaside villa were already wearing off. Unfortunately, the Seahawk didn't come equipped with a galley. Not even box lunches or Meals Ready to Eat. Those MREs would taste pretty good right now.

Maybe when they touched down on the *Pits* one of its cooks could serve up a little snack. Buoyed by that hope, Cleo spent the rest of the hour-and-a-half flight alternately huddled with the others and visiting with the crew up in the flight deck.

Cleo's first view of U.S. Motor Vessel *A1C William H. Pitsenbarger* was through the cockpit windshield. It came as a severe shock.

After being wowed by the size of the army ship at Sunny Point, Cleo expected to see a vessel the size of three football fields chugging across the Mediterranean. This speck on the horizon looked positively microscopic.

Granted, she was viewing it from a perspective of two hundred feet above sea level and three nautical miles out. Still, the sight wasn't reassuring. Just a tad nervous, she keyed her mike.

"I don't want to question your navigational skills, guys, but are you sure that's the *Pits?*"

"That's her," the co-pilot confirmed.

"And we're going to put down where?"

"On the helo pad near the bow, well forward of the deckhouse."

Cleo spotted the pointy-ended bow. She spotted the tall deckhouse at the stern of the ship. She *didn't* spot anything remotely resembling a helo pad.

As the Seahawk drew closer, though, the ship assumed more majestic proportions and the miniscule pad attached to the bow swam into view. So did the air-conditioned, dehumidified pods Sergeant Stevens had told her about. The huge, square pods crowded every inch of the upper deck and housed the shipping containers that wouldn't fit below. Every one was packed with bombs or missiles or other high-explosive devices.

Gulping, Cleo returned to her seat. She strapped in, sincerely hoping the pilot put his craft down gently and didn't scrape or bump any metal against metal, thereby generating a few wayward sparks.

To her intense relief, the Seahawk hovered over the ship like a curious mosquito and inched downward. The skids hit the pad with only a small thud…then immediately lifted again as the *Pits* plunged into a trough and the deck dropped away.

The Seahawk's pilot kept his craft in a hover until the deck rose. The skids hit again. No gentle thump this time, but a solid whack. Cleo's stomach flattened and her face must have turned a little green because the young flight engineer was grinning when he jumped out the side hatch to attach the tie-downs.

"Watch your step," he warned as he helped his passengers exit the craft. Grasping his gloved hand, Cleo stepped out.

"Holy crap!"

Funny what a difference perspective could make. Looking *up* from the dock at Sunny Point at some ten or twelve stories of black hull was one thing. Looking *down* from a tiny landing pad perched on the bow of a ship plowing through swells some ten or twelve stories below was something else again.

Hanging on to the lifeline the flight engineer passed her, Cleo inched her way across the helo pad and down the steps to the deck. It rolled and pitched beneath her feet as an officer in khakis with the collar insignia of the U.S. Merchant Marine came forward to greet them.

"I'm First Officer Westerbeck."

His keen glance took in Marc's expensive slacks and blazer, lingered for a moment on Johanna's jumpsuit, and got stuck on Cleo's spandex and high-tops until Jack produced his credentials.

Dragging his gaze away from the jungle print, Westerbeck barely glanced at Jack's ID.

"We received a communiqué you were coming, Major Donovan. Welcome aboard."

"Thanks."

"The captain is waiting for you on the bridge. Follow me, please."

The smile was polite, the greeting courteous. Cleo had trouble placing the accent, though. Jack's background brief had indicated all the ship's officers were U.S. citizens. They had to be to wear the uniform and insignia of the U.S. Merchant Marine. First Officer Westerbeck's faint, almost indiscernible tendency to elongate his vowels sounded European to Cleo, though. He could be a naturalized citizen, she reasoned.

Then again…

Casually, she let her hand slide down the shoulder strap of her purse to rest lightly on the half-open zipper. Just as casually, she brought it back up again. The idea of pumping off a shot surrounded by all these pods crammed with explosives popped out tiny beads of sweat on her temples.

The pods were stacked along the entire length of the deck—huge, square blocks arranged in double rows, three high and eight or ten deep. Hoses snaked from one end of the pods, sucking damp air out and pumping cool air in.

Cleo tried to do the math as they made their way along the port side of the ship. Or maybe it was starboard. She never had been able to keep them straight. Sergeant Stevens had said the *Pits* could haul more than nine hundred containers. Seven hundred or so below deck, the rest above deck in these pods. That meant each pod sheltered around thirty containers. More or less.

Abandoning the calculations, she focused instead on the three massive yellow cranes that hovered over the pods like long-legged storks. One was set amidships, the others at either end of the cargo deck. Those cranes gave the *Pits* the ability to offload its own cargo—very useful for a munitions ship that might have to pull into ports with minimal to nonexistent dock facilities.

She also noted the extensive array of radar and radio towers atop the high-rise deckhouse at the stern of the ship. Judging by that array, the *Pits* could no doubt pick up everything from precise global-positioning navigational data to just-released movies beamed in via satellite for its crew.

"This way, please."

Holding open a hatch, Westerbeck ushered them into the deckhouse. It was narrow, barely one room wide so as not to sacrifice cargo space, and straight up and down.

Cleo caught the scent of fried onions drifting from below and guessed the galley must occupy a lower deck. Her stomach took due note of the tantalizing aroma as she chugged up flight after flight of stairs, passing the crew quarters, the officers' deck, the captain's quarters, the radio room and—finally!—the bridge.

Huffing slightly, Cleo stepped into the gleaming white operations center. Glass panes circled the bridge, providing the captain a sweeping view of his ship and the sea. Radar consoles, navigational equipment and computers ticked and beeped and glowed beneath the windows.

Captain Eric Kobe was waiting for them with his radio operator. The radio operator was short and pudgy and gave them a friendly smile. The captain was tall and spare and nowhere near as welcoming as his subordinate. Offering them a mere dip of his head instead of a handshake, Kobe acknowledged each of his visitors briefly before zeroing in on Jack.

"I understand you have vital information regarding my ship, Major Donovan."

Cleo sympathized with the man. She'd probably cut right to the chase, too, if she were hauling five million pounds of explosives across an ocean. Still, a mug of the coffee sloshing around in the coffeemaker at the rear of the bridge would have been nice.

The captain caught her glance and issued a terse command. "Some coffee for our guests, Mr. Westerbeck. If you please," he added curtly, as if the courtesy pained him.

The first officer accepted orders for two black coffees and one with cream. Johanna declined refreshment. As Westerbeck moved away, the plump radio officer edged closer. Curiosity gleaming in his dark eyes, he took up a position just behind his captain's left shoulder.

Kobe folded his arms. A frown creased his forehead. Eyes narrowed, he addressed Jack. "Now, Special Agent Donovan, what have you heard regarding the *Pitsenbarger?*"

"Unfortunately, nothing specific, sir. But we have reason to believe it may be targeted for possible hijacking."

The captain's jaw set. Brows lowering, he blinked several times and glared at Donovan. "By whom?"

"We haven't been able to pin that down."

"Well, hell, man! What *have* you been able to pin down?"

"An individual by the name of Adrian Mustafa Moore entered the United States three months ago using a false passport issued under the name of Frank Helms. We've linked him to an employee at Sloan Engineering...."

The captain's eyes cut to Marc. "Sloan Engineering. Is that you?"

"It is."

"Your company did the NOx emission-control design and retrofit on the *Pits.*"

"Yes, we did."

"And you're telling me an employee of yours got involved with someone who entered the U.S. under a false passport?"

"Yes."

His eyelids twitched again, furiously. "I don't like what I'm hearing here."

Marc frowned and left it to Jack to answer.

"Neither did we. Particularly after Sloan's employee turned up dead and we determined someone had used her password to access the engineering schematics of the *Pits*."

"Someone?" Kobe echoed, as his first mate returned with a fistful of mugs. "That's the best you can do?"

"We traced Adrian Moore to Malta, where we lost him. We traced the computer query to a server in Cyprus, your next port of call." Jack hesitated a moment, as if reluctant to add mere gossip to his thin pile of facts. "We've also picked up some chatter indicating a willingness by a certain broker to negotiate the sale of any cargo off the *Pits*."

"Give me a name," the captain snapped.

"We don't have one, sir. Only a handle. He goes by Domino."

Kobe's face folded in disgust. "I've heard rumors about the man."

"I've heard rumors about him, too," the radio operator put in. He had a soft, almost girlish voice, a puppy-dog face and milk-white hands. "Some people refer to this Domino as a modern-day pirate," the radio operator added on a giggle. "A real swashbuckler."

"He's a damned scavenger," the captain countered coldly, "feeding off the sweat, blood and bones of honest seamen."

Put in his place, the radio man hunched his shoulders and stepped back a pace. He would have looked abashed if not for the twinkle in his dark eyes. Cleo guessed he took a tongue-lashing regularly from this stern, unsmiling captain.

"I tightened security onboard ship after your initial communiqué," Kobe informed them. "We're in constant communication with the Military Sealift Command's Crisis Operations Center. They inform me that both the air force and the navy are prepared to fly cover for the *Pits* should I request it."

"That's correct, sir. We're also flying a detachment of marines into Cyprus. They'll be guarding the dock when you steam into port."

That was news to Cleo. Jack hadn't mentioned that the Old Man was sending in the marines, but then Donovan rarely showed his whole hand.

Kobe accepted the news with another dip of his head. Johanna, who'd remained silent up to this point, voiced the concern of the British government.

"We're cooperating with the Americans in this, Captain. Adrian Moore is a British subject. We'd like to find him and learn his role in the recent death of one of our agents."

"I assure you, I would very much like you to find him, too."

"You mentioned you've tightened security aboard the *Pitsenbarger*," Jack said. "Perhaps we could review your plan and offer an outsider's perspective."

"Are you qualified to assess the safety of a ship at sea, Special Agent Donovan?"

The question came from the first officer, but the captain appeared keenly interested in the answer.

"I've some experience to draw on, Mr. Wester-beck. So does my British colleague. And Ms. North is one of the top private-security consultants in the business."

Cleo kept her jaw from dropping. Barely. Jack never passed out compliments—unless they had to do with lace-trimmed boxers.

"With Mr. Sloan's expertise in ship design," Donovan continued, addressing himself to the captain, "we can bring a fresh set of eyes to your protective approach."

"With all due respect, sir, I don't think…"

Kobe silenced his first officer with a frigid look. "We can never be too cautious when it comes to the safety of this ship, Mr. Westerbeck. Please escort our guests to my wardroom. I'll notify the second officer and have him brief you on our security arrangements before taking you on a tour of the ship. Perhaps you'd like some lunch while you review the plan?"

Yes!

The first officer's lips folded. Obviously piqued that a clutch of landlubbers would question plans put in place by men with saltwater running through their veins, he shot a look behind the captain's back at the radio operator.

The pudgy little seaman was standing to the captain's rear, barely within Cleo's field of view. His response to his first officer's look was so slight she almost missed it. Not quite a nod, not quite a shrug, it was just enough to drive every thought of food right out of her head.

She'd hung up her military uniform years ago. Unless customs and courtesies had changed drastically, though, officers didn't wait for approval from subordinates before complying with orders from their superiors. Every nerve in her body kicked into overdrive as Westerbeck herded his visitors toward the stairs. Marc started for the companionway and pulled up short at the high-tech radar display.

"This is one of the new Sperry Rascar Touch Screen systems, isn't it?"

Westerbeck gave an impatient nod. "Yes, it is."

"I knew the system was being installed in the *Pits*, but this is the first time I've actually seen it in operation."

Marc dallied by the blipping, beeping screen, fascinated by its colorful display. "The Rascar combines two radars," he informed the others. "An S-band ten centimeter and an X-band five centimeter. Both radars are used for collision avoidance and navigation."

Cleo couldn't have cared less about S- or X-bands. Her goosey feeling was gathering speed and momentum with every passing second. She needed to get Jack aside, tell him about that little exchange she'd just observed.

Johanna started down the stairs. Cleo followed, then Jack. With an impatient glance at Sloan, the first officer exited the bridge. Marc lingered at the radar display for another moment, feasting on its blips and beeps, before he, too, hit the stairwell.

The small cavalcade descended one level and began moving to the next. Cleo was halfway down when she heard the unmistakable thud of a fist crunching bone.

23

Dropping into an instinctive crouch, Cleo whirled just in time to see Westerbeck's eyes bulge and his cheeks puff out like birthday balloons.

Jack stood one step below him and had his fist buried in the man's midsection. Marc was one step above. He'd evidently just bounced the edge of his hand off the first officer's neck...and was now feeling the effect. While Donovan caught the crumpling Westerbeck, Sloan winced and shook his hand a few times.

"That's not as easy as it looks," he muttered.

"Takes practice," Jack agreed, lowering the unconscious man to the deck. Swiftly, he patted him down.

Cleo blew out a breath, came up from her crouch and flashed a look at Johanna Marston.

The brunette was observing the proceedings with interest but no evidence of surprise.

"What tipped you off?" she asked her brother. "The captain's nervous eye tic?"

"That wasn't a tic." Still grimacing, Marc cradled his hand. "It's been a while since my navy days, but I can still read Morse code when someone flashes it in my face. The captain was signaling an SOS."

"And an X-band radar is three centimeters, not five," Jack added, extracting a small, lethal semiautomatic from the first officer's pocket. "Our friend here certainly should have known that."

The fact that *Donovan* knew it impressed the hell out of Cleo.

"The radio operator is in it with this character," she said, helping Jack haul the first officer over his shoulder. "I think he's running the show. I saw him give the nod to Westerbeck to take us downstairs."

"They must have gotten to the *Pitsenbarger's* crew," Jack said grimly. "God knows what they did with them."

"If they're alive," Marc supplied, "they'll probably be confined below deck in one of the cargo compartments. Each compartment can be sealed off individually."

Grunting, Donovan hefted the first officer's dead weight. "Let's get this guy inside the captain's cabin and stow him out of sight while we search the ship. Lady Marston, you take the lead. Cleo, watch our six."

With Cleo duly performing rear-guard duty, they descended the last few stairs to the deck housing the captain's quarters. Johanna went first, Marc second, then Jack and his burden just ahead of Cleo. She kept her weapon trained on the stairs above them, but no one popped out of the bridge.

Marc's knowledge of the ship proved invaluable. Following his lead, they moved in single, silent file down a passageway lit with bright lights and ducked into the captain's private quarters. Cleo skimmed a swift glance around the two spacious staterooms fitted with gleaming teak and brass while Jack dumped his still-unconscious burden and began stripping off the khaki uniform.

"Find something to restrain this guy," he instructed Cleo. "I don't want him coming to and sounding the alarm while we're searching the ship."

It was on the tip of her tongue to ask him if he'd run out of plastic when Marc volunteered his leather belt.

"Use this. I'll take his uniform. I'm about his build."

Within moments, Jack had Westerbeck down to his shorts, gagged and strapped into a chair bolted to the deck. Marc shed his own clothes and donned the khakis with speed and precision. Thrusting the brass tongue of the web belt through the buckle, he gave it a quick tug to align it with his zipper. Gig line set, he settled the first officer's bill cap low on his brow.

"We need to tell our respective headquarters that the *Pitsenbarger* has been taken," Jack advised Lady Marston.

"And alert the crew of the Seahawk," Cleo added, thinking of the chopper still perched on the bow of the ship.

Marc nixed the use of their satellite cell phones. "Those high-powered antennas you saw on the deckhouse will pick up any signal emanating from aboard ship."

Jack thrust his phone back into his pocket. "We'll have to use the Seahawk's radios, then. Sloan, you and Lady Marston can take care of that while Cleo and I search for the *Pitsenbarger*'s crew."

"I'm familiar with the ship's layout and design," Marc argued. "I also know how to operate the hatches in the cargo hold. I'll go with Cleo while you call in the marines."

Before Jack could argue the point, Johanna intervened.

"I'm perfectly capable of making my way to the helicopter on my own. The three of you conduct the search. I'll send the alerts."

They started out in single file, but Marc stopped at the door and swung back. "I forgot something."

Rummaging in the pocket of his discarded blazer, he extracted the shellacked starfish. His eyes were iced-over granite when he came back across the stateroom.

"Let's roll."

* * *

Silent as three shadows, Cleo, Marc and Jack descended two more levels to the deck housing the engineer's quarters. They found one man wearing the insignia of an assistant engineer sacked out on a bunk, another with his pants around his ankles, perched on the head. Their reactions when they spotted the newcomers tagged them instantly as unfriendlies.

Engineer Thug put up a short, if vicious, fight. No-Pants Guy didn't get the chance. Within moments, the two men were strapped ankle and wrist in chairs bolted to the deck. Engineer Thug proved unresponsive to the gun barrel Jack screwed into his right temple, but No-Pants went rigid as Cleo aimed the .38 at the shriveled dick and hairy sack splayed out between his naked thighs.

"How many of you are there?" she asked him.

"*Femmina!* You cannot…"

She didn't appreciate being called a bitch in Italian any more than she did in English. Coolly, she thumbed back the hammer of the snub-nosed Smith & Wesson.

"How many?"

"*Jesu!* There are ten!"

Once he'd started babbling, No-Pants spilled his guts. Disguised as deckhands, nine pirates had come aboard when the *Pitsenbarger* refueled and resupplied in Malta. The pudgy radio operator had been there to greet them and had hidden them in a cargo compartment until the ship was well out to sea. They'd crept out at night and taken the ship.

A skeleton crew from the *Pits* was in the engine room, keeping the ship under steam and on course. One seaman was in the galley. The rest had been confined in a compartment on the third cargo deck, just forward of the engine room.

"Are they alive?"

The man's mouth clamped shut. He threw a quick glance at the bloodied face of his companion, who barked something back in a dialect Cleo couldn't catch. She took two steps forward and rammed the .38's barrel between No-Pants' thighs.

"Are they alive?"

"Some!" he screeched. "Perhaps."

She was tempted to make him a eunuch right then and there. She settled for crashing the revolver's butt down on his skull. Jack put the second hijacker to sleep with a squirt from the spray he produced from his pocket.

They encountered another pirate on the crew deck. Marc was in the lead and used the momentary confusion engendered by his uniform to plant his fist in the man's face. Jack followed up with a puff of the subduing agent.

"That's four down counting Westerbeck," Cleo murmured as they dragged the unconscious hijacker into a crew cabin and stuffed him in a locker. "Only six more to go."

The tension knotting her stomach gave way to

some serious rumbling as they descended to the mess deck. With each step the aroma of garlic and fried onions that had tantalized her since coming aboard the *Pits* grew stronger.

The officers' mess was empty, but a tight-jawed cook scraped a spatula across the griddle in the galley. A crewman in jeans and a T-shirt sat at one of the tables. Cleo recognized the face printed on the T-shirt: Andre Shevchenko, the sexy Ukrainian soccer hero who played forward for Italy's team and had recently made *People* magazine's list of the ten most gorgeous men in the universe. But it was the face above the T-shirt that grabbed her full attention.

It registered surprise, shock and instant panic. Jolting upright in his chair, the mariner scrabbled for the gun resting on the seat beside him. Before any of the newcomers could respond, the cook flung a spatula full of sizzling onions in the man's face.

Screaming, the highjacker pumped out a wild shot. The cook went down, Marc cursed and Jack fired. With an inarticulate grunt, the soccer fan slid under the table.

Thankfully, the first bullet had just grazed the cook's skull. Jack propped him in a chair and squatted in front of him while Cleo wadded a towel against the wound.

"Do you know the status of your fellow crewmen?"

Dazed, the cook blinked away the blood dripping into his eyes. "No. But I was told…" He swallowed, pressed the towel to his head and tried again. "I was told to cook for half the number I usually do since these pigs came aboard."

Cleo lost her appetite. From the sound of it, most of the *Pitsenbarger's* crew had been shut up in a cargo compartment without food or water since Malta. Radio Operator and friends were due some serious payback for that.

And for Trish Jackson. Marc hadn't forgotten. Neither had Cleo. The young woman's face hovered before her as Marc led them down into the bowels of the *Pitsenbarger*.

"A container ship is basically an empty hull," he muttered, his voice low and tense. "Bulkheads separate the hull into watertight compartments. The containers are stacked on movable cross hatchers inside each compartment."

Putting his shoulder to a hatch, he pushed it open and stepped into a dim, dank canyon. Cleo and Jack followed, alert for any movement, any sound other than the hum of the metal decking under their feet as it vibrated to the beat of the engines.

Once through the hatch, though, she stopped dead. Her rational mind told her she was only seeing a small portion of the cargo area, just one compartment full of containers. The knowledge didn't blunt the impact of those metal boxes stacked as high and as far as she could see in the faint glow of the lighting system.

Gulping, Cleo eased her finger away from the trigger of the .38. The Smith & Wesson didn't have a safety, and the mere thought of accidentally popping off a round made her palms feel cold and clammy.

"The engine room is down one more deck," Marc said. "Close to where we're standing."

"How many ways in and out?" Jack asked.

"Three. The stairs we just came down. Another set aft of the main propeller shaft. And an escape hatch. There's one in every compartment. The one over the engine room should be right about…"

He strode along the gangway that cut between the containers, passed through one compartment, entered another. Mid-center, he stopped beside ladder rungs welded to a support column.

"Here."

Kneeling, Jack examined the mechanism that screwed down the hatch. "Can they open this from below?"

"They can." Hooking a thumb, Marc indicated a similar hatch directly above them. "Just as we could open that one to access the upper cargo deck."

Donovan didn't take long to formulate a tactical strike plan. That was one of the things Cleo admired most about him. When she wasn't totally pissed at him, that is.

"All right, here's the plan. Sloan, you guard this escape hatch. North, take the rear stairs. I'll go forward and enter via the front. Give me five minutes to get into position." He squinted at the lighted dial of his watch. "At my hack. Five, four, three, two…"

Jack looked up from his watch and flashed Cleo a grin.

"One. Let's go get 'em."

Jack made a frontal assault on the engine room. Cleo burst in through the rear.

She formed an instant impression of massive turbines, pumping pistons and at least seven crew members frozen in surprise.

One of them was a husky female in a grease-spattered T-shirt and dungarees. She glanced at Cleo, gave an inarticulate roar and brought the wrench in her hand crashing down with lethal force against the skull of the man hunkered on a stool behind her, a pistol in his hand.

When the dust settled, three hijackers lay face-down on the deck. Two had their arms and legs spread wide. Blood poured from the gash in the third's head. The *Pitsenbarger*'s senior oiler had laid his scalp open down to the bone. Chest heaving, she clutched the bloody wrench in her fist.

"The sons of bitches killed our chief engineer," she panted over the thump of machinery. "Sliced his throat right in front of us to make sure we understood they meant business."

"Threatened to cut up another of our shipmates every time we balked at following their orders," another machinist's mate snarled.

"They won't be slicing up anyone else," Jack promised. Three quick puffs put the hijackers out of action indefinitely. "Let's go find your shipmates."

Cleo was on her way out with the others when she remembered Sloan. "We left Marc guarding the hatch. I'll let him know the engine room is secure."

While Jack and the engine-room crew went in search of their remaining crew, she raced up the stairs she'd crept down just minutes ago. The stink of oil and diesel fuel followed her when she ducked through the hatch into the dank recesses of the cargo hold. She had just started down the narrow passageway between the containers when a figure in khakis appeared in the next compartment.

"Marc!" she called softly. "The engine room's secure. We need to…"

The figure spun around. Cleo barely had time to register the face of Adrian Mustafa Moore, aka British-Accent Guy, before he whipped up the sub-machine gun he had tucked under his arm.

"Don't be crazy!" she squawked, flinging out a hand to encompass the containers crammed with explosives. "You can't fire that thing down here!"

He spit out a curse and, to her infinite relief, lowered the weapon.

"I know you. You're the American who came to the Café Corinthia asking questions about me."

The words echoed in the cavernous compartment. Cleo edged closer, not about to let the bastard retreat.

"My brother radioed the ship and told us you had come to Malta." Hate blazed in Moore's thin face. "He was the man in the Co-Cathedral of St. John. The one you killed."

"The one who tried to take me out?" Cleo shot back, her gaze never leaving him. "Like you did Trish Jackson?"

"Pah," he said in sheer disgust. "That stupid cow wasn't even worth a bullet."

His utter contempt got to Cleo far more than his words. Fighting a wave of fury, she took another step toward him. "I saw what was left of her body. Did you know she was pregnant?"

"Of course. She called me from her doctor's office." His lip curled. "She said she had to meet me. At our 'special place.' She babbled on about how she loved me, how I had to marry her, how she would do anything for me. I wanted only one thing from her, though."

"You slimy prick! You used her pregnancy to worm her password out of her."

"It took little worming."

They faced each other across ten yards of steel gangway, surrounded on all sides by stacked containers, each dead certain the other wouldn't leave the cargo hold alive.

That became clear when Moore reached for the small of his back and produced a six-inch blade. The naked steel didn't worry Cleo as much as the Heckler & Koch still tucked under his right arm. She gathered her muscles, went up on the balls of her feet. She was ready to spring when another figure lunged out of the shadows between the containers.

"Eat this, you murdering son of bitch."

Moore whirled, threw up his arm, but couldn't block the vicious thrust. Snarling, Sloan stabbed the point of the shellacked starfish into his throat.

Red spewed from the wound in a glistening arc, drenching both attacker and attacked. Choking, gurgling, strangling on his own blood, Moore slashed at Marc.

Sloan danced to one side to avoid the blade, jerked the starfish free and stabbed again.

The hijacker staggered, then went to his knees, the starfish embedded in his jugular. With a last choking gurgle, he raised his weapon.

Cleo leaped forward but couldn't close the distance in time. The bastard fired, either from reflex or intent.

She knew one instant of absolute terror as bullets pinged off metal containers. Another when a stray shot hit some vital ship's organ and plunged the entire hold into darkness.

"Marc!"

Totally blind, she thrust out her arms and started to feel her way forward.

"Where are…?"

She broke off, wincing, as a Klaxon began to scream. In the next instant, the hatchways between the watertight compartments began to thud shut.

Now blind *and* deaf, Cleo didn't dare move forward. She stood frozen for a moment, then grabbed her purse and pawed through it.

The key chain was there.

She knew it was there.

Somewhere.

Ears aching under the siren's violent assault, she fumbled in the darkness. She was almost weeping when her fist closed around Doreen's souped-up penlight.

The high-intensity beam pierced the darkness. Flinging up an arm to shield her eyes from the reflection off the metal containers, she directed the beam down the center of the hold. A solid wall of steel separated her from Marc. With a sinking sensation in the pit of her stomach, she spun around.

Yep, there it was. Another eight or ten inches of solid steel, standing smack between her and the stairs.

And that damned Klaxon wouldn't stop shrieking.

Fighting the urge to fire a few desperate rounds in the general vicinity of the siren, Cleo tried to remember Marc's crash course on the *Pitsenbarger*'s layout.

Every watertight compartment came equipped with an escape hatch. Sloan had guarded the one over the engine room. All Cleo had to do was locate the one in this compartment, scramble up the ladder and crawl out onto the deck.

She found the ladder easily enough. Holding the penlight between her teeth, she even managed to climb the rungs and wrestle the iron latches securing the hatch free of their flanges.

The heavy cover took all she had, though.

Scrunching around, she put her shoulders to the reinforced lid and shoved upward. The first heave dislodged it. The second sent it flopping back. Wedging her hips through the narrow opening, Cleo scrambled onto the deck.

The wind whipped at her hair. Salt spray needled her face. She gulped in several deep breaths, dropped the forever light into her purse and turned in a circle to get her bearings. The tall, air-conditioned pods blocked her view of everything but the antennas and glass eyes of the bridge.

Still deafened by the shriek of the Klaxon, she rounded the far pod and started for the deckhouse.

The sight that greeted her at that point shoved the breath back down her throat. The radio operator leaned against the rail halfway down the deck. He had a rocket launcher propped on one plump shoulder and the muzzle aimed at the Seahawk still perched on the pad.

Cleo saw the pilot through the bubble of the cockpit, his hands on the throttle. Saw one of his crewmen dive for the .50 mm canon. Saw Lady Marston spring out of the side hatch and drop into a two-fisted shooter's stance.

Johanna was too far out of range. All the way at the bow of the ship. Cleo registered that fact even as she herself leapt forward, shouting wildly.

"Hey! Radio Man!"

His head whipped around at the same instant the rocket launcher's target-acquisition indicator light went from red to green. Setting his fleshy lips, Radio Man whirled and aimed the muzzle at the chopper once more.

Cleo didn't hesitate. Blanking out any thought of the explosives stacked all around her, she brought the .38 up and fired.

24

The bullet took Radio Man in the shoulder and spun him around. Cleo had all of half a second to congratulate herself for spoiling his aim before a sleek white missile erupted from the launcher.

"Oh, shit."

Horrified, she watched the lethal cylinder fly straight for the *Pitsenbarger*'s bridge. Glass splintered. Metal shrieked. The missile disappeared.

For a delirious instant, Cleo thought the thing must have pierced right through the bridge and splashed harmlessly into the ship's wake. The thought had no sooner formed than the entire upper portion of the deckhouse blew.

Shock waves from the explosion threw Cleo against a storage pod. She hit with a thud that jarred every bone in her body, remained flattened against the container for a second, then slid to the deck.

She sat there, legs splayed, ears ringing. Black spots danced in front of her eyes. With every thud of her heart against her ribs, she expected the pods surrounding her to blow.

Radio Man must have expected the same thing. When the spots cleared enough for Cleo to focus, she saw the horror on his tubby face as he stared at the flames now engulfing the upper half of the deckhouse.

Tossing aside the launch tube, he whirled and ran for one of the lifeboats. Before Cleo could stagger to her feet, he'd ripped off the orange cover, scrambled inside and began frantically cranking the davits to swing the boat over the rails.

She didn't spare the little creep another glance. Her first priority right now—her *only* priority—was finding Jack and Marc and the others before the fire reached the cargo deck.

She raced along the rail, aiming for the nearest hatch cover. Marc was in the next compartment. He had to be. And Jack... He was heading forward with the crew. Or was it aft? Cursing, Cleo tried to remember.

A panting Johanna Marston came racing toward her. "Where are Marc and Donovan?" she shouted over the still-shrieking Klaxon.

"Below. Somewhere."

"Sod it! I assume that bloody Klaxon means the emergency systems have activated and the cargo compartments are sealed off."

"Right."

She whipped a glance at the row of hatch covers stretching the length of the ship. "So the men will have to escape through one of those hatches."

"If they can locate them! It's pitch-black down there."

The British agent cursed and threw a look at the flames and smoke pouring from the upper deckhouse.

"You take this one. I'll get the next."

She was already off and running as Cleo dropped to her knees beside the nearest escape hatch. The deck that had looked no bigger than a postage stamp from two hundred feet up now seemed to stretch to infinity. Thirteen compartments from stem to stern, all with heavy, stubborn hatch covers to wrestle off.

Cleo attacked the first, twisting the flanges, popping the cover, shoving it to the deck. She poked her head into the opening and screamed into the inky darkness.

"Sloan! Donovan! Anyone!"

There was no answer except the scream of the siren. Heart pounding, Cleo pushed to her feet.

Panting, she and Johanna Marston leapfrogged down the deck. The iron latches scraped the skin from Cleo's palms. The heavy covers ripped her nails off at the quick.

"Donovan!"

The flames roared higher, hotter. She remembered the hijackers they'd left bound and gagged in the lower portion of the deckhouse. Jaw set,

Cleo shoved the thought away. Jack and Marc and the *Pitsenbarger*'s crew came first.

Particularly Jack.

Mostly Jack.

The awful, agonizing fear that Donovan might die locked in a dark cargo hold sent her racing to the next hatch. The ship couldn't blow until she'd found him. It *couldn't!*

Every pulsing shriek of the Klaxon spiked into her skull. Heat blistered her skin. Smoke seared her throat. Nails bloodied, she ripped at another hatch cover and screamed into the blackness.

"Donovan! Where the hell are you?"

"Right here."

The white blur of a face popped out of the darkness. When five or six others crowded behind it, Cleo sat back on her heels and gulped down a lump the size of Texas.

Shooting her a grin, Jack hauled himself up. "'Bout time you showed, North."

"Yeah, well, things got a little hot up here on deck."

When he caught his first glimpse of the flames shooting from the deckhouse, his grin dived straight south.

"Jesus H. Christ! What did you do?"

"Radio Man fired a missile. He was aiming for the Seahawk, but I, uh, got in the way."

"What?"

"I'll tell you about it later. Right now I think

we should just concentrate on getting the hell off this ship."

Jack agreed. Kneeling beside her, he reached down to help a filthy, bearded seaman through the hatch.

Crew loyalties died hard, Cleo discovered when she and Jack got the small, ragged band on deck. None of them wanted to leave their ship-mates behind. Nor could Cleo or Jack abandon Sloan and his sister.

One of the crew who'd climbed through the hatch was the second engineering officer. He sported a bruise the side of a grapefruit on one side of his face and his nose was a pulpy, swollen mass, but Cleo guessed he'd been kept alive be-cause he was needed to operate the ship's sys-tems. Turning a grim face to the flames, he assessed the situation.

"We've got ten, maybe fifteen minutes before the fire reaches the lower deckhouse. Who's left inside?"

Thank God she'd kept a running tally. "Last time we saw Captain Kobe, he was on the bridge. The radio operator—or the man disguising him-self as a radio operator—has already hit the lifeboats. We left one of the hijackers trussed to a chair in the captain's cabin, two more on the thirds' deck, another on the crew deck."

"Fuck 'em. What about McCauley, our cook's mate?"

"He took a bullet and was too woozy to walk. We left him in the galley."

"Powers, you and Handerhand go for Mc-Cauley. Jerrold, you come with me. We'll try to find the captain. The rest of you, launch the lifeboats and abandon ship."

"We've still got two of our own aboard," Jack said. "We have to—"

"Is that them?"

With a jerk of his chin, the engineer indicated the figures plunging out of the smoke. Lady Marston had Marc's arm draped over one shoulder. Bowed under his weight, she half carried, half dragged him across the deck.

Jack hurried to relieve her of the burden, his jaw tightening at the glistening red splashes on Sloan's borrowed khakis. "Did you take a shot?"

"No," Marc croaked. "Just came up...on the windward side and...swallowed some smoke." Despite the smoke still rattling around in his lungs, he managed a small, savage smile. "The blood isn't...mine."

"Marc put Trish's killer out of business," Cleo said, getting a shoulder under Sloan's other arm. "Come on, let's get you two into a lifeboat."

With the electrical systems out, the crew had to manually crank the davits to swing the boats clear of the rail and lower them to sea level. Jack hefted Sloan into one already full to overflowing and steadied Johanna Marston as she climbed in behind her brother.

"Take her down!" Jack shouted to the man at the crank. "We'll go for the next one."

Two of the gaunt crew members were already ripping the cover off the next lifeboat. Cleo took a couple of steps, skidded to a halt and saw the decision she'd just come to reflected in Donovan's blue eyes.

"They're scum. I know they're scum. But we can't let them fry."

"Get into the lifeboat, Cleo. I'll go after them."

She didn't bother arguing with that women-and-children-first absurdity. Spinning on one heel, she raced for the deckhouse.

"You take the engineer's deck," she shouted above the crackling flames. "I'll take the crew quarters."

The smoke wasn't as intense as she'd expected. The wind was sucking it up through the deckhouse like a chimney, Cleo realized, and blowing it back over the ship. But the heat was blistering.

"Use this to shield your face." Jack flung his sport coat at her. "And don't touch the rails. They'll sear the skin off your palms."

Ripping off his shirt, he wrapped it around his face and head and sprinted up the stairs three at a time. Cleo threw a last look at his bare back and ducked into the crew quarters.

She found the unconscious hijacker still folded into the locker where they'd stuffed him. Cursing the potency of Donovan's subduing agent, she hauled the man across her shoulders in a fireman's lift and staggered back down the stairs.

The flames must have consumed another deck. Cleo could hear them above her, hissing and spitting. Close. Too damned close to those tons of explosives on the upper cargo deck.

"Get him into the boat!"

Dumping the unconscious man at the feet of the crew manning the davits, she whirled and started back for Jack. She was a few yards from the deckhouse when the hatch flew open and No-Pants Guy burst out.

Wide-eyed with terror, he raced for the lifeboat. Leaving him to make it on his own, Cleo wrapped Jack's coat around her head and fought her way back into the inferno.

A half deck up, she was almost bowled over by the *Pitsenbarger*'s second engineer. He carried a body slung over one shoulder. Captain Kobe, she saw in a quick, frantic glance.

"Found him on the thirds' deck," he shouted over the roaring flames. "Bastards put a bullet into him, but he's still alive."

"Did you see Donovan?"

"Yeah. Said there was one more, up in the captain's quarters."

Dammit! He'd gone for Westerbeck.

"You'd better get the hell out of here," the engineer warned, his boots thumping on the stairs. "You've got to put some blue water between you and the *Pits* before the flames reach the cargo deck."

Right! As if she needed the reminder!

Mouth and nose masked, eyes streaming, Cleo

peered up through the well in the center of the deckhouse. All she could see were smoke and flames.

Leaving the hijackers to fry was one thing. Frying along with them wasn't on Cleo's immediate agenda. If that was anyone but Donovan up there...

She started up the stairs, only to discover frying wasn't on Jack's agenda, either. He came barreling down, grabbed her hand on the run and yanked her after him.

"Couldn't reach Westerbeck," he shouted. "The officers' deck is ablaze. Let's get the hell out of Dodge."

They shot out of the deckhouse and saw they were alone. The crew had evidently decided a hijacker wasn't worth getting blown apart for. They were already in the water and firing up their boat's engine.

Cursing a blue streak, Jack and Cleo raced for the last remaining lifeboat. Cleo tore off the orange cover, then flopped into the boat. Donovan followed and cranked away. The bow tilted, dropped at a sharp angle and almost sent her splatting into the water. She wrapped both arms around a seat and hung on for dear life.

Swearing, Jack reversed the crank and gave it another couple of turns. This time the back end of the boat plunged straight down. Cleo's arms were almost wrenched out of her shoulder sockets before he got the craft relatively level.

They jerked and humped and seesawed downward. When they hit the water, the force of impact rattled her teeth and sent waves crashing over the gunwales. Blinking the salt from her eyes, Cleo dived for the latch securing the cables. She got the forward cable free and tore off what was left of her fingernails struggling with the rear cable.

"We're clear! Fire her up."

The engine kicked over after only one false start. Absolutely certain that first abortive attempt had turned her hair a snowy white, she collapsed onto a seat while Jack shoved the throttle up to full power.

The boat lurched, gathered speed, took off. Cleo risked a glance over her shoulder and sincerely wished she hadn't. The flames had reached the cargo area. Snaking out from the deckhouse, they licked at the pods stacked one on top of the other.

"Faster, Jack. Puh-leeez, just a little faster."

He couldn't hear her. Nor did he look back. The angle of his jaw told Cleo he knew their chances were slim to nonexistent.

She started making lists of all the things she should have done before zipping off to Malta. Like update her will to include six months' severance pay for Mae. Bequeath the antique samurai sword she'd picked up in Japan to Goose. Set Doreen up with an unemployment fund of sorts. Call Wishy-Washy Wanda and offer some advice on wallpaper.

Say goodbye to her dad.

The idea that Patrick North might very well get a phone call informing him that his only daughter had died in a fiery explosion in the middle of the Mediterranean Sea was *not* something Cleo wanted to think about.

Instead, she wrenched her thoughts back to Jack. If she had to be blown out of the water, she couldn't think of anyone she'd rather be blown out with. She figured this was as good a time as any to tell him so.

"Hey! Donovan!"

"What?"

"I just thought you should know. I think you're Sierra Hotel."

His grin flashed out. Cocky. Irresistible. All Donovan.

"You're pretty hot yourself, North."

"In case I don't get a chance to tell you so later, you're forgiven for the plastic restraints."

"Don't be too hasty. I'm planning on a second round after we—"

The explosion blew the rest of his sentence all to hell. It also blew him halfway across the boat.

He slammed into Cleo, knocked her off her seat and went down with her. Wrapped in a tangle of arms and legs, they rode wave after wave of percussive blasts.

With each blast, the lifeboat lifted out of the water. Slammed down. Rocked from side to side. Water poured in, leaving Cleo awash and snorting out salty spray. Debris rained down around them.

Finally, the explosions were reduced to a series of hissing electrical spurts. The waves subsided. Jack's heavy weight, however, did not.

It pinned Cleo to the bottom of the boat, smooshing the air from her lungs. It had also, she realized as she tried to wedge her arms between their chests, protected her from the falling debris. When he pried himself off her, they sat up to view the drama unfolding behind them. Shoulder to shoulder, they watched a cloud of black smoke spread across the sea and the column of flames that used to be the *Pitsenbarger* sink slowly into the Mediterranean.

"Jesus."

Jack's soft murmur raised the hairs on the back of Cleo's neck. She huddled closer while debris popped up like odd-shaped corks. The less-buoyant pieces soon sank out of sight. Bits of plastic and wood and foam continued to bob on the surface long after an eerie stillness had enveloped the lifeboat.

In a voice that reverberated with both awe and chagrin, Jack shattered the moment. "When you blow things up, you do it right, woman."

"For the record, I did *not* cause the *Pitsenbarger* to blow. Radio Man did."

"After you 'got in his way.'"

"It was either that or watch the Seahawk take a direct hit from a shoulder-launched missile."

"Helluva choice," Jack agreed, slewing around.

The movement sank him back into the seawater and tipped Cleo onto his bare chest again. He settled her more comfortably, stroking her hair as the smoke swirled across the surface of the sea.

She was so busy soaking in the comfort from Jack's solid bulk, it took her a while to realize she needed to give as well as receive. Lifting a hand, she traced a fingertip over the old bullet wound in his right shoulder. Just the feel of that scar generated a rush of memories of another firefight, another close escape. It also stirred a sharp, primitive need.

Part of it was beating the odds. All she had to do was glance at that black pall of smoke to feel a shivery thrill race along her veins.

But most of it was Jack.

"How long do you think it will take search-and-rescue to find us?" she asked.

"Not long, once I activate the lifeboat's homing device."

"We've got a homing device?"

"It's required by maritime law for any lifeboat carrying more than four passengers."

"Funny, I only see two in this boat."

She could tell the instant both her touch and her comment registered. His muscles went taut under her hand and his voice tipped into a low drawl.

"Now that you mention it, that's all I see, too."

He eased her down, stretching his long length out beside hers. Water sloshed over them, unheeded. Smoke blocked the sun, the sky, everything but Donovan's crooked grin.

"Ever do it in a lifeboat, North?"

"No. You?"

"No. But I'm game if you are."

She was game.

She was most definitely game.

Particularly after Donovan slid his hand under the jungle print and worked a hand inside her boxers.

25

A return to reality came with the whap-whap-whap of the Seahawk. The chopper circled through the smoke, marking the location of the various lifeboats that had sped in all directions to escape the explosion.

It was followed a short time later by the buzz of search planes scouring the area. By then Cleo's stomach was expressing serious displeasure at having been deprived of sustenance for so long. The growls had gathered enough volume to almost drown out the slap of the waves against the boat and the distant drone of aircraft.

"Think we should activate the homing device?" Jack asked lazily, a smile in his voice.

"Mmmm."

"Is that a yes?"

Cleo waged a brief internal war. She lay stretched out beside Jack on the nest they'd made from the inflatable lifejackets stashed in the boat. Her head was pillowed on his shoulder. Splashy red-and-green spandex once again covered the more vulnerable portions of her anatomy. The silk boxers were sloshing around in the bottom of the boat, though, buried under several layers of life vests.

Unfortunately, her pesky conscience had already started nattering at her with the same annoying frequency as her stomach. She knew Sloan and his sister had made it into a lifeboat and departed the *Pitsenbarger*. He was still technically her client, though, and Cleo needed to wrap things up with him.

Then there was the matter of the ship.

They'd face a barrage of questions. The air force would conduct a board of inquiry. The navy, as well, since the Naval Sealift Command had contracted for the ship.

And, Cleo thought with a sinking sensation, the U.S. Merchant Maritime Authority, since they licensed the crew and manned the ship. Then, of course, there was the Coast Guard, which regulated the Merchant Marine. She was pretty sure the Department of Homeland Security would get into the act, too.

The list was endless. To someone who tended to annoy, antagonize or generally piss off officialdom without even trying, it was also horrifying. Shuddering, Cleo curled up against Jack.

"Forget the homing device! Let's sneak away and head for the Greek Isles."

Donovan played with her hair, curling a damp strand around his thumb. She could hear the laughter and the regret in the answer that rumbled up from his chest.

"As tempting as that sounds, the Old Man's probably bitten through several pipe stems by now."

Oh, God! She'd forgotten about General Barnes. The Greek Isles wouldn't put enough distance between Cleo and her former boss when he heard about the *Pitsenbarger.* She was thinking Antarctica when Donovan reminded her that his investigation was far from over.

"I need to brief Barnes on the hijacking. I also need to follow up on the gut feeling that this character Domino is more than just a broker."

Wiggling upright in the orange nest, Cleo shoved her tangled hair out of her eyes. "I got that feeling, too. The hijacking was organized and well funded. Someone masterminded it from the start. It makes sense that someone would be the person who stood to profit most by it."

Jack came up on one elbow and let his eyes drift over the bits of debris still floating on the darkening sea. "I want him, Cleo. I want him bad."

"So do I."

The survivors from the *Pitsenbarger* were flown to the navy base at Naples. Some of the mariners were in pretty bad shape and had to be treated for various injuries, as did a number of the hijackers.

To Cleo's profound disgust, the pudgy little radio operator wasn't among them. The ships and planes combing the Med had found no trace of his lifeboat. Not surprising, since one of the other hijackers admitted that particular lifeboat had been outfitted with special radars and a high-speed engine to facilitate just such a quick escape.

They didn't admit much else, though. Jack grilled them for hours through interpreters before leaving them to the navy JAGs, who would work their extradition back to the States for crimes committed against a ship flying the U.S. flag.

Donovan looked like hell warmed over when he rejoined Cleo, Marc and Johanna Marston. Johanna had already arranged transportation to London. Like Jack, she had to brief her superiors.

Unlike Jack, however, the British agent was traveling via a Royal Air Force transport laid on especially for her. Donovan would zip back to the States aboard Sloan Engineering's corporate jet. With her usual efficiency, Diane Walker had packed them all up and settled the account at the Auberge St. Georges. She was due to arrive in Naples within the hour.

Johanna said goodbye on the veranda of the hospital. Night had settled in perfumed splendor over the base perched on a curve of the Bay of Naples. The bright lights of the Italian city winked across the bay. The darker shadow of Mount Vesuvius loomed beyond the lights.

Cleo and Jack waited in an alcove while brother and sister made their farewells. With all that had happened, it was a jolt to remember that Sloan and Lady Marston had met for the first time only that morning. They obviously felt the oddness, too. Cleo could see the tug of emotions in their faces, so alike now that she knew the connection.

Svelte and eye-catching in that black jumpsuit, Johanna clasped her brother's hand. "I have a country house in Kent. You must bring Diane and come for a visit. Perhaps you might bring Alexander, too. I should like to get to know you both."

"I'd like that, too."

She hesitated a moment before offering a word of advice. "I must say I was quite impressed with Diane. It's none of my business, of course, but I do think you should marry the woman."

"I couldn't agree more. I've been trying to convince her to formalize our partnership. She's proving surprisingly stubborn."

Johanna smiled at the irritation buried in his reply. Obviously, the handsome executive wasn't used to being rebuffed.

"Try harder," his sister advised. "As I learned from the loss of my dear Barty, one simply cannot take life—or love—for granted."

Johanna's advice rattled around in Marc's head as the driver he'd hired whisked him, Cleo and Donovan out to the airport. The Gulfstream had already touched down and was waiting at the private jet terminal. Diane was waiting beside it.

When they climbed out of the car, the rock-steady assistant who'd helped him build a corporation from the ground up started toward him. Within two steps, she'd broken into a jog. Before Marc could pay the driver, she was racing across the tarmac. Tears streaming down her face, she threw herself into his arms.

"I heard about the explosion on the radio. They said there were casualties. I couldn't reach you. I couldn't reach anyone! I thought... I was so afraid..."

"I'm sorry. I had them contact you as soon as we got picked up."

Noisy, gulping sobs shook her. She thrust back, elbows stiff, skimming his face with anxious eyes. "Are you hurt? Your throat... Your voice..."

"I'm okay. I just swallowed a little smoke."

She dropped onto his chest again. Marc folded his arms around her, feeling a fierce rush of love tinged with more than a touch of guilt. Trish's tragic death had brought him both a sister he never knew he had and this incredible woman he was only now getting to know.

He couldn't—*wouldn't*—squander that legacy.

"Cleo, you and Donovan take the Gulfstream back to the States. I have some business to attend to here in Italy."

Swallowing her sobs, Diane pushed out of his arms again. "You didn't tell me," she gulped, struggling for composure. "I didn't make any arrangements or reservations."

"I'll take care of the arrangements."

"But…"

"All you have to do is say *si*."

"What?"

"That's Italian for yes, isn't it?"

"It is, but I don't…"

"When the priest or magistrate asks for your response, all you have to do is say *si*. Think you can manage that?"

She opened her mouth. Drew in a deep breath.

Anticipating another refusal, Marc preempted any further discussion by the simple expedient of covering her mouth with his.

The kiss was long and hard and put him in a fever of impatience. Without another word to Cleo or Jack, he yanked open the passenger door of the limo and thrust Diane inside.

"The Amalfi coast," he instructed the driver.

"But where on the coast, *signor?* Sorrento? Ravello? The ferry to Capri?"

"Just drive. I'll tell you when to stop."

With a shrug that spoke volumes about Americans with more money than sense, the driver climbed into his seat and put the car in gear.

"That was interesting," Cleo commented as the taillights disappeared around a hangar.

"Very," Jack agreed. "Think Diane will agree to go before that priest or magistrate?"

"Not before she lays down some very specific ground rules. I'm guessing Marc's past is about to catch up with him."

Cleo couldn't dodge her past, either. It smacked her right in the face some forty minutes after the Gulfstream glided into D.C.'s Reagan National Airport. Jack had been instructed to report to Andrews Air Force Base immediately upon landing to brief General Barnes. He argued and cajoled and, finally, blackmailed Cleo into accompanying him.

As payback for sending her into the line of fire, he promised to keep her advised of the continuing search for Domino.

"Advised, hell," she countered glumly as the taxi sped them to Andrews. "I want in on it."

"Why don't we talk specifics after you hear what the Old Man has to say?"

"I've got a good idea what he's going to say. I also have a good idea I'm not going to enjoy hearing it."

She didn't.

Big and bristling in his blue uniform, the OSI commander pointed her to a seat with the stem of his pipe and started with the fact that she'd jetted off to Malta without consulting Special Agent Donovan. He then proceeded to excoriate his former employee for stirring the pot at the Café Corinthia, made a scathing reference to the two dead bodies, and finished with the small matter of an entire shipload of air force armaments disposed of in a single flash.

Cleo countered with the same polite, stubborn smile that had caused more than one of her air force supervisors to lose his hair along with his cool.

"That's better than having those munitions sold to the highest bidder on the black market. Which is what might well have happened if I hadn't uncovered a link between Trish Jackson, Adrian Moore and the *Pitsenbarger,* then jetted off to Malta to stir the pot."

"All right. I'll give you that. The link proved useful."

"Excuse me?"

His brows snapped together. "Don't push it, North. The air force is still missing one munitions ship."

"And the man who put the missile through its deckhouse," Jack put in smoothly. "Maybe when we find the radio operator, he'll lead us to Domino."

Barnes swung his scowl toward his agent. "Why do you think he'll know anything more than the other hired thugs who came aboard the ship in Malta?"

"Because he was *already* aboard."

Cleo leaned forward. She and Jack had used the long flight back to the States to compare specific details and spin out possibilities.

"The second engineer told us Radio Man joined the crew before the ship left the States, as a last-minute replacement. He also told us the man carried papers issued by the U.S. Merchant Marine

Authority. They were probably forged or stolen, but along with those papers he had to have some working knowledge of radio operations to get the crew to accept him until his friends came aboard at Malta. He also seemed to be in charge of the hijacking operation."

Barnes set aside his pipe, all business now. "So what's the theory? This radio operator orchestrated the hijacking with the intent of brokering the goods through Domino?"

"Either that," Jack answered, "or he's Domino's trusted lieutenant. His man on the scene."

"There's another possibility," Cleo tacked on. "He could be Domino himself."

She wasn't sure where that idea had come from. Nothing about the giggly radio operator suggested a man of wealth and power...except for that nod he'd given Westerbeck. He'd clearly been in charge aboard the *Pits*.

The general grunted. "We don't throw out any possibilities at this point. You stand to make a billion or so off the sale of the world's most sophisticated armaments, you want to make sure you get delivery of those armaments. You have a name?"

"We have his physical description and the name listed on the crew manifest. We figured we'd start with those and see where they take us."

"We?"

"We," Jack repeated.

The pipe went back into the general's mouth

with a clatter of clay on enamel. The brows came down again. His gaze sliced to Cleo.

"Am I to assume we're paying your usual consulting fees?"

The small matter of a sunken munitions ship still hung in the air. She figured she could afford to be magnanimous.

"This one's on the house."

Jack suggested Cleo accompany him when he went to claim his vehicle at Base Ops. That suggestion naturally led to another.

"I'm wasted. What do you say we head back to my place, order in, grab a shower and rack out for a few hours before starting the hunt for Radio Man?"

"Rack out, as in sleep?"

"That, too."

The offer was too tempting to resist. So was the urge to see Donovan's private lair. Cleo had never been to his Washington, D.C., condo. Their brief, cataclysmic affairs had occurred in more exotic locales like Honduras, Santa Fe and Malta. She wanted to view him in his native habitat.

It matched the man, she decided when he stood aside for her to enter the third-floor apartment overlooking the Potomac. Neat, minimal, no fuss, with only a few mementos to mark the place as home to a military officer. The cracked ceramic mug emblazoned with the OSI's logo. The AF sweatshirt tossed over an arm of the couch. A small, framed five-by-seven of Jack and the previous president, gathering dust and almost hidden behind a stack of Tom Clancys and John Grishams.

"There's beer in the fridge," he told her, sliding open the balcony doors to let the stuffiness out and the spring morning in.

Cleo scooped two longnecks out of the fridge. It was only a little past 10:00 a.m. Washington time, but cocktail hour in the eastern Med. Not that the time mattered. Her body clock was too screwed up at this point to know whether it was a.m., p.m. or FM.

Closing the fridge, she popped the tops on the bottles and followed Jack into his office. Like the kitchen and living room, it was strictly no frills. The modular desk sported a combination phone/fax/copier and a sleek laptop she suspected was plugged into every law-enforcement database in the free world. Circulars, memos and hand-scribbled notes crowded the bulletin board set at convenient eye level above the laptop. The chair was sturdy, ergonomic and Donovan-size. Definitely a working office, she thought, handing him his beer.

"Here's to a successful hunt," he said, clinking his bottle against hers.

"I'll drink to that. And to... Hey! Is that me?"

She leaned over the desk to get a better look at a glossy magazine ad almost hidden under a list of OSI contact numbers.

That *was* her. Much younger and much barer. Best she recalled, she'd earned two hundred dollars for modeling those French-seamed bikini briefs. Major bucks at the time. Enough to keep her in Big Macs and pizza during the summer session between her sophomore and junior years at the University of Texas, anyway.

Turning, she tipped Jack a wicked grin. "I didn't think copies of that ad was still floating around."

"They pop up every now and again."

Smugly pleased that he'd pinned her to his bulletin board, Cleo amused herself by checking out his bookshelves while he punched the button on his answering machine.

"You have seventeen new messages," the recorder chirped.

Cleo listened with half an ear as the messages played. Two were official, requesting return calls. One was from a tailor saying the pants he'd left to be hemmed were ready for pickup. Then came a string of calls from a woman Cleo guessed immediately was Donovan's ex-wife.

"Jack? It's me. I need to talk to you."

"It's Kate. Call me."

"Where are you this time, Jack? Africa? Singapore? I need to talk to you. Call me when you get this message."

Her next messages came at rapid intervals and showed increasing signs of anger and desperation. They'd been recorded late yesterday afternoon, while Cleo and Jack were still bobbing in a lifeboat.

"I can't do this alone. Please, call me."

"Dammit, why aren't you ever there when I need you?"

"Where the fuck are you?"

"Jack, please. I can't reach my counselor. I have to talk to someone."

That one ended on a dry, racking sob that clutched at Cleo's heart. She could only imagine what it did to the man staring down at the answering machine, a muscle working in the side of his jaw.

The next call included a background buzz of conversation and the unmistakable clink of glasses.

"This is your fault, you bastard. You're never—" a boozy hiccup burped over the line "—when I need you."

The last was recorded early this morning. Cold and merciless, it instructed Jack to ignore the previous messages. She'd survived the night, no thanks to him.

Jack hit the Erase button.

Cleo ached for him. She was a trained investigator. She'd seen the depths the human spirit could sink to. She knew, as well, how often those broken or depraved spirits dragged others down with them. The fact that Donovan hadn't resorted to an unlisted number to avoid his ex-wife's calls told her he had yet to climb out of the pit.

"Sorry you had to hear that," he said, his jaw still tight. "What do you want to eat?"

"Jack…"

"We can order Thai. The restaurant around the corner delivers. Or Chinese."

"She's wrong to blame you for her problems with alcohol. Surely her counselors have told you that."

"Yeah, they've told me. Problem is, *they're* wrong."

His eyes were emptier that she ever remembered seeing them. And infinitely more weary.

"Kate has it right, Cleo. I wasn't there when she needed me. Two miscarriages. The day she was awarded her masters. The time she stepped on a wasp's nest, took more than fifty stings all over her body and went into shock. I think I was on temporary duty in Iceland that time. Correction. That was the Azores. What do you want to eat?"

Okay. All right. He didn't want to talk, she wouldn't push.

"Thai sounds good."

26

Cleo took charge of ordering dinner. Her teenage years in Bangkok had given her a taste for sour, spicy and hot. She took pity on Jack's less-sophisticated palate, though, and added crispy fried noodles, green papaya salad and kai yang chicken to the curried fish cakes and tam sung beef.

The order was delivered twenty minutes later, barely enough time for Cleo to shower away the effects of the flight home and purloin a freshly laundered shirt from Jack's closet. Rolling up the sleeves, she let the tails flap against her bare thighs as she joined him in the living room.

He'd changed into sweats, too hungry to take a turn in the shower. They ate sitting cross-legged on the floor, right from the containers. Jack insisted on trying the beef despite Cleo's cautions. The first bite probably scorched his mouth all the way down to his tonsils. The second left his taste buds permanently scarred, or so he stuttered before she stuffed a taro ball soaked in coconut cream between his lips to douse the flames.

"I warned you."

The glutinous mass muffled his answer. It didn't sound friendly, though.

Grinning, Cleo forked up the last of the fish cake. The curry was potent enough to send air hissing through her nostrils. She refused to think what it did to her breath.

It took a few minutes for the *bau loi phauk* to work its magic. Gradually, Jack's eyes stopped watering and the purple receded from his cheeks. He also lost most of that tight, closed look he'd worn since listening to those damned phone messages.

Cleo was determined to erase the rest. Sincerely hoping she never came face-to-face with the former Mrs. Donovan, she laid aside her fork.

"You think the *tam sung* was hot? Wait till you taste the special dessert I have for you."

Wariness narrowed his eyes. When she popped the top button on her borrowed shirt, though, suspicion gave way to instant joy.

With a choke of laughter, Cleo popped another button. "God, Donovan, you are *so* easy."

She'd make this sweet and slow, she decided. So sweet he'd forget the guilt his ex had carved into his heart. So slow, he wouldn't have the strength afterward for anything but the sleep she knew his body craved.

That was the plan, anyway. It pretty well fell apart when he hooked a hand around her wrist, gave it a tug and tumbled her onto her back.

"Let's consider this round two."

The sharp, stinging nip at the base of her throat told her Jack was in the mood for a tussle. That was fine with Cleo. Sliding her hand inside his sweats, she threaded her fingers through his groin hair and wrapped them around him.

She loved the feel of him. Smooth and hot and hard, like suede over steel. Loved the way he never bothered to hold back his hunger for her. It was right there, surging from greed to need with the tight bunch of his muscles.

She used her hands and tongue and teeth. He used all of those *and* his knee. It got wedged between her thighs somewhere between their tongue-swallowing contest and the tumbling, limb-tangling roll that left her smushed against the coffee table. Skin slicked against skin as he eased her up so he could feast on her breasts. The friction both above and below her waist soon had Cleo writhing. She tried to give as good as she got. She honestly tried. But when he contorted enough to substitute his mouth for his knee, she lost any semblance of control.

Gasping, she spread her legs. His tongue flicked and probed and pleasured and tortured. She could feel the gathering pressure. Feel the tight spasms spreading in concentric circles. Groaning, she tried to hold back, to prolong the pleasure. It was like trying to hold back the flames that had consumed the deckhouse. She detonated with at least a million or so short tons of explosive force.

It took a while to gather the strength to raise one eyelid. "Okay, Donovan. Round two is yours."

Jack un-contorted. "Not yet."

In one smooth move, he had her under him. With another, he rammed home.

Jack transferred Cleo to the bed just before the carpet left a permanent imprint on her bare butt. By then she was a half grunt away from total unconsciousness. She flopped onto the mattress, buried her face in the pillow and blanked out like the lights in the *Pitsenbarger*'s cargo hold.

Jack stretched out beside her, but his body wouldn't give in to the exhaustion weighing him down. Neither would his mind. The best he could manage was a couple of short catnaps. In between, the same thought kept surfacing.

Cleo wasn't Kate.

She wasn't anything like Kate.

His intellect got it. His body sure as hell got it. All he had to do was look at her to see the differences, for God's sake!

She sprawled across the sheets, hogging more than her share of the mattress. Her dark hair feathered across the lower portion of her face, the ends lifting with each breath. Her skin was sleek and smooth and tanned in patterns unique to a woman who spent as much time outdoors as in. She was issuing an occasional puffy snort, the kind she always vehemently denied making, punctuated by a sporadic mumble or twitch that indicated her mind was still at work although her body slept.

That was Cleo. All energy. All stubborn determination. All hot, sexy female.

But the dark corner of Jack's soul still scored by guilt and regret countered every rational message he tried to send it.

So she wasn't clingy and insecure? So she had a full, demanding life that didn't include him? If this thing between them went where it seemed to be heading, there'd come a time when she'd want more than a quick tussle between the sheets or backup during an op.

The very real possibility that he'd be on the other side of the world when she needed a shoulder to cry on or someone to rant at punched a hole in Jack's gut. It also had him thinking harder about his options.

He could leave the air force. God knew the irritations outweighed the excitement at times. But only at times.

Under the petty annoyances and everyday hassles lurked the absolute certainty he was part of something important. Jack never talked about it. None of the men and women he worked with did. It was too schmaltzy, too clichéd. Too red, white and blue.

It was there, though, buried deep inside the

ever-present awareness that he played his own small role in the defense of his country. That was why he'd gone into Afghanistan with the first on-the-ground OSI cadre. Why he now plowed through case files at headquarters, when he craved the action and excitement of the field. Why he...

"Not in the locker room!"

Twitching, Cleo thumped his shin with her heel. "You're going down, Gooz."

The ache around Jack's heart eased enough for him to slide into a smile. He'd met Cleo's tattooed trainer during their recent stint in Santa Fe. If Goose went down, he wouldn't go easy.

Dragging his arm out from under his head, Jack checked his watch. He was wiped, but that hot, sweaty session with Cleo had recharged his batteries enough to send him back to work.

She was still fighting her dream battles when he emerged from the shower. Pulling on a pair of jersey sweats and a V-necked exercise shirt, he padded into the kitchen and filled the coffeemaker.

He was at his desk, downing his third cup, when she came out of the bedroom. She'd brushed her hair, scrubbed her face and buttoned herself back into the shirt she'd lifted from his closet.

"Is that real coffee?"

"Starbucks' own."

"Thank God!"

Spinning, she aimed for the kitchen. Jack allowed himself the pleasure of watching his shirttails flap against her bare ass before returning his attention to the screen.

She was back a few moments later, cradling a mug in both hands. "What have you got?"

"The *Pitsenbarger*'s crew registry lists the radio operator as Henry Walls. He was hired just three months ago as a replacement for the operator who had served aboard the *Pits* for almost four years."

"Four years, huh? Why did he quit?"

"He didn't." Donovan angled her a look. "He was flattened by a hit-and-run driver while on shore leave."

"Well, hell! Why didn't that interesting fact come up when you had your guys run background checks on the crew?"

"Because I had them run the crew. Not their predecessors."

Hitching her hip on the credenza, Cleo downed a slug of caffeine. She could see Jack wasn't happy about the miss.

"You said Radio Man joined the crew of the *Pits* three months ago. That's about the time Adrian Moore entered the U.S. under a false passport."

"Yeah, it is."

"If they had a man aboard ship, why did they need Moore to get cozy with a Sloan Engineering employee?"

"My guess is they wanted a breakdown on the specific weapons package aboard the *Pits*. They were probably looking for a way to get into the

Afloat Prepositioning database to find out exactly what was in which containers."

"Wouldn't that information be included on the ship's manifest?"

Hands locked behind his head, Jack tipped his chair back. "The exact weapons breakout was classified, remember. The ship's manifest showed only general tonnage and the number of sealed containers."

"So you're guessing they didn't want the entire cargo, only specific portions. That makes sense. It might be kind of difficult to find buyers for five-thousand-pound bunker busters."

"Not as difficult as you think. The GBU-28 hard-target penetrator proved its stuff in the first Iraqi war. It also drove bin Laden out of his hole in Afghanistan. Think what it could do if it was targeted against, say, Moscow's subway system or underground command-and-control facilities."

She knew him too well. His response was too even, too controlled. She thunked her mug down and skewered him with an I-mean-business-dammit glare.

"Okay, Donovan. Spill it. What the hell was aboard that ship?"

He hesitated just long enough for Cleo to know he was trying to find a middle ground between his military security clearances and her civilian, no-need-to-know status.

"The program is still in the research-and-development phase."

"What program?"

Still he hedged. "Have you read anything in the technical press lately about tungsten rods?"

Cleo didn't bother to tell him her main access to technical matters these days was her *Simpsons*-addicted step-cousin-in-law.

"All I know about tungsten is that it's heavy."

"Very heavy. It also has the highest melting point and lowest vapor pressure of all metals."

"So?"

"So we've been looking at using tungsten rods as space-based weapons that wouldn't violate the no-nukes-in-space treaty."

He scrubbed a hand over his jaw, still cautious, still measuring his words. Even with her. That was Donovan for you. Jump your bones one minute, put you on the other side of his shield the next.

"They've been dubbed the Rods from God. They're about twenty feet long, one foot in diameter. The idea is to put them on a high-altitude orbiting platform and satellite guide them to targets. They could be launched within minutes and would strike the earth at speeds of up to twelve thousand feet per second."

Cleo swallowed a sigh. The world ran on numbers. "Is that faster or slower than your everyday, average satellite guided bomb?"

"These aren't bombs. Not in the technical sense. They don't contain any explosives. Their speed and weight alone supply enough force to penetrate and destroy even hardened targets, yet leave everything outside a twenty-five-foot radius untouched."

"Whoa! That's like laser surgery from the sky."

"Exactly. Our aviators tested the no-explosives principle with concrete bombs. They took out tanks hidden behind mosques and hospitals in Iraq."

"So now we're going with tungsten?"

"We were," he said dryly. "The first shipment of test rods is now at the bottom of the Mediterranean."

"Hooo-boy! No wonder the Old Man went apoplectic on me."

Jack grinned. "He wasn't too happy with me, either. His last bit of advice was to find this bastard who engineered the hijacking or forget about pinning on my silver oak leaves."

"Donovan! Are you on the lieutenant colonel list?"

"Yeah, but that's not supposed to be common knowledge."

She wrinkled her brow, struggling with numbers again. "Isn't this early for you?"

"A couple of years."

"That calls for a celebration."

Sliding off the credenza, she landed in his lap. The kiss was loud, smacking and filled with joy for him. Cleo knew how much the air force meant to him. Knew, too, that he was one of the OSI's best and brightest. If anyone deserved to be promoted ahead of his peers, it was Donovan.

One celebration could easily have led to another

if Jack's computer hadn't chosen that moment to ping. He darted a look at the monitor, saw the flashing icon and shifted Cleo around in his lap.

She nestled between his thighs while he hit Receive. The plump face that emerged on the screen had her sucking in a breath.

"Little bastard."

The face looked out from a license, she saw. Issued by the Federal Communications Commission.

"What's this?"

"Walls passed himself off as a radio operator for three months aboard the *Pitsenbarger*. All radiotelephone operators aboard vessels of more than three-hundred gross tons have to be licensed by the FCC before they can be certified by the U.S. Maritime Authority."

Jack stretched his arms around her waist and scrolled down the screen.

"According to this, Walls qualified for both a GROL and a GMDSS/O. Whatever the hell they are."

Further scrolling revealed GROL stood for General Radiotelephone Operator License. A GMDSS/O was an operator licensed to maintain and operate the newer, satellite-based Global Maritime Distress and Safety Systems intended to phase out the old Morse code radio systems.

"Radio Man could have hacked into the FCC computers and forged those licenses."

"He did," Jack confirmed, still scrolling. "Looks like he hacked into a few other computers, as well."

His chubby face appeared on four additional licenses, all issued under different names on different dates in different countries. A beard covered his cheeks and chin on one. His hair was blond on another. The squidgy eyes and simpering smile were the same, though.

"Australia, Ghana, Dominica, Zimbabwe," Jack read. "Little bugger got around."

Cleo skimmed the list again. "Those are all predominantly English-speaking countries. Our boy must not be fluent enough in other languages to pass himself off as a citizen of another nation."

That set her mind off and running. With Jack's bristly chin scraping her temple, she scowled at the face on the screen.

"You said this Domino character brokered deals on all kinds of contraband, stolen artifacts, human cargo. If Radio Man is one of his key lieutenants, we should run a list of all such incidents involving ships flying the flags of nations where English is the official or predominant language. Maybe we can narrow their field of operations. Or get a vector on their activities to date."

Jack planted a wet, sucking kiss on her neck. "It's a start. How many countries are we talking about?"

"I don't know. Thirty or forty."

"Hell!" He blew out a breath. "I'll have to go through State or the CIA to get the information from thirty or forty different maritime agencies. This could take a while."

She couldn't think of any way to expedite the process. Beanie Doreeny was a near genius when it came to computer games and hacking into databases. But Cleo doubted even she would be able to milk information from forty systems, each with its own architecture, any faster than Jack's pals at State or the CIA could retrieve it.

"Tell you what. You work the world of official-dom and I'll go nuke the leftover kai yang chicken. I think there are some noodles left, too."

"Anything but that beef."

She returned his kiss with a smacking one of her own and pushed off his lap. He was at the keyboard, clicking away, before Cleo hit the door to his office.

The distinctive chime of her cell phone stopped her halfway through the living room. Her purse was still on the chair where she'd dropped it earlier. She got to her cell on the third ring and carried it with her to the kitchen. A quick glance at the number displayed on the LCD screen sent pleasure spurting through her.

"Hiya, Pop."

"Cleo, it's me."

Her pleasure sputtered and went out. "Hi, Wanda. What's up?"

"I just wondered…" The pause was nervous, hesitant, all Wanda. "Where are you?"

"I'm in D.C."

"Could you…could you come home?"

"I'm a little busy at the moment."

Way too busy to grit her teeth while Wishy-Washy Wanda dithered betweens stripes and murals.

"If this is about the paper for the den, why don't you get Doreen to—"

"It's not about the den. It's about your dad."

Cleo went still. "What about Dad?"

When Cleo swooped back into the study five minutes later, she was fully dressed and carrying her tote.

"That call was from my stepmother. My dad's been having chest pains. I'm catching a flight out of National in fifty-five minutes."

"Jesus! Is he in the ER or ICU?"

"Neither. My stepmom says he keeps insisting they're just twinges. He didn't even tell her about them until she caught him popping a nitro. The man is so damned stubborn."

Jack hooked a brow but refrained from comment. Her face was dead white under its tan. She didn't need his smart-ass suggestions that she came by her own hard head naturally.

"I'll drive you to the airport."

She was at the door before he'd shoved out of his chair. "I've already called a taxi. And you've got work to do."

"Cleo! Call me! Let me know how he is."

"Yeah, I will."

The front door slammed. Frowning, Jack stood in the silence she'd left behind.

His laptop sat ready. The queries he'd just

begun formulating needed to be sent. He should probably brief Barnes, too, get him to throw the weight of his stars behind the requests to make sure they didn't lie buried on some action officer's computer desktop.

Yet all he could see was that pallor of sick fear under Cleo's tan. She hadn't looked that scared in Honduras, with half a dozen heavily armed dopers chasing her through the jungle. Or aboard the *Pitsenbarger*'s lifeboat, with tons of munitions about to blow right behind them.

"Fuck it."

Whirling, Jack slammed down the lid on his laptop and scooped it off the desk. He hadn't been there for Kate when she needed him. He'd damn well be there for Cleo. He could finish formatting the queries on the plane and zap them off after they landed and she'd taken care of her father.

He'd made it to the front door before he remembered he was still barefoot and in his sweats.

27

Jack caught up with Cleo at the Delta counter at Reagan National. The fact that she showed more relief than surprise at his sudden appearance told him he'd made the right decision.

She kept her hand locked in his for most of the flight to Dallas. The bone-cracking hold and white lines at the corners of her mouth gave Jack a new insight into the complex creature that was Cleo North. Despite her tough outer shell, she had her Achilles heel.

Gently, he probed the soft spot. "Does your father have a history of heart problems?"

"He's had a couple bad bouts of angina. The first led to his retirement and brought him to Texas. He had another episode last year. That's when he had the stent put in."

"A stent is good, isn't it? Better than open-heart surgery, from what I've read."

"That's what they told us. Surgery might come, though, if his cholesterol-lowering medicines don't work and his arteries continue to harden."

Her hand crabbed under his, the knuckles showing white. Jack took the pain without flinching. His laptop was tucked under his seat, but the queries could wait. Cleo needed to talk out the fear that was gnawing at her.

"Your father used to work for the government, didn't he?"

"Right. USAID. We lived in a dozen different countries before I started high school."

"Must have made filling out the paperwork for your air force security clearances fun."

"Damned form ran to twelve pages."

To Jack's infinite relief, some of the worry left her face. She didn't let go of his hand, but she did slump back against her seat.

"Pop's a lot like you," she said after a moment.

"Big, handsome and sexy as hell?"

She managed a small choke of laughter. "A and B, anyway. Wanda will have to vouch for C."

"Wanda being?"

"My stepmother. She and Pop met up and got married last year."

"You and a stepmom." Jack shook his head. "The woman has my sympathy."

"Hey, I've stood on my head to be a good daughter and make her feel welcome."

"As I said," he drawled, "the woman has my sympathy."

Indignant, Cleo proceeded to enumerate her efforts. Most of them centered on what appeared to be Wanda's favorite sport, redecorating her new home. Satisfied he'd brought some color back into Cleo's cheeks, Jack sat back and let her grumble about hours spent choosing curtain rods and carpets.

During the taxi ride from the airport, Cleo tried to call home but got no answer. When no one answered the doorbell at her dad's condo, either, her stomach lurched.

"Do you have a key?" Jack asked calmly.

"Yes."

"Let's check inside. They knew you were on the way. They may have left a note."

Right. Cleo sucked in a steadying breath. Even Waffling Wanda wouldn't depart for the hospital without leaving some kind of word. Disgusted at the way her hands shook, Cleo dug her key ring out of her purse.

"Dad? Wanda?"

The keys cut into her palms as she hurried down the hall. Jack closed the door and followed. Cleo didn't spare a glance at the smirking cherub her stepmother had bought to replace Elmer the croc, a beady-eyed souvenir from her dad's sojourn in Egypt.

The carved African masks still decorated the walls of the den, though. Right above the worn leather sofa, where Patrick North sat stiff and unmoving. Wanda huddled beside him. Her face was red and splotchy from weeping. His was closed and tight.

Cleo's heart dropped like a stone.

"Pop! What's wrong?"

She rushed into the den. And pulled up short. Hard on her heels, Jack almost collided with her. His vicious curse rang in her ears as she stared at the squat figure seated behind her father's desk.

He held a silenced semiautomatic in one hand. The two men flanking him on either side were similarly armed. Given that lethal firepower, the gunman's high-pitched giggle scraped like fingernails on a chalkboard.

"Two for one. I didn't anticipate it would be this easy."

"What are you doing here?"

Jack had to growl the question. Cleo was shaking too hard with rage to do more than hiss.

"You two cost me a great deal of money. A very great deal. I had two potential purchasers in a bidding war for the Rods from God."

Cleo hissed again, more audibly this time. "So you're Domino?"

"I am."

Radio Man giggled once more, clearly delighted to have his genius recognized.

"I know, I know. I hardly look like the mastermind of an international-crime syndicate. I truly believe that's part of the reason I've been so suc-

cessful. But only part. I'm very thorough, as I suspect you've already determined. I can also be very
ruthless when necessary. I'm afraid this is one of
those times when it's necessary."

His sigh was as dramatic as it was false.

"I knew when you came aboard I'd have to deal
with you. You and Sloan and that Marston
woman. I'd intended to arrange a helicopter crash
after you departed the ship, all souls lost at sea. So
tragic, to have you all just disappear off the radar
like that. You must tell me how that fool, Westerbeck, tipped our hand."

"Yeah, right," Jack growled. "Like that's going
to happen."

Above his limpid smile, Radio Man's eyes narrowed to slits.

"Oh, it'll happen. As soon as I put a bullet
through Ms. North's shoulder, as she did mine. Or
perhaps you'd rather I start with your father, Ms.
North. The data I collected on you told me he
would be your only vulnerable spot. I was right,
wasn't I? You certainly came running fast
enough."

Cleo would be a long time forgiving herself for
that. She saw her mistakes now with the sharp
brilliance of a lightning bolt. If Wanda's call hadn't
shaken her so badly, she would have contacted
Mae or Goose or even Doreen and had them
strong-arm her father into his cardiologist's office.
She would also have insisted on talking to Patrick
herself, maybe picked up on the nuances in his

voice she missed completely in Wavering Wanda's.

Cursing herself for the fear that had sent her running blindly into a trap, she dug the keys deeper into her palm, using the pain as a spur to clear her mind. She needed to think. Needed to pick up the silent signals she was sure Donovan was sending her.

Needed to shield her father and Wanda.

She couldn't make a move, couldn't let Jack make a move, until she got between them and the men by the desk.

"Let's talk about this, Walls. Or whatever your name is."

"Walls will do."

She moved farther into the den. One step. Two.

With each step, her mind raced.

Neither she nor Jack was armed. They hadn't had time to clear their weapons through Security and catch the flight. All Jack carried was the soft-sided briefcase with his computer. All she had were her keys.

"This is between us, Walls. You. Me. Donovan. My father and stepmother don't know anything. They couldn't tell the authorities who you were if they wanted to."

"Perhaps not," Radio Man said, "but their only usefulness to me was as bait to lure you here. They'll have to be disposed of, I'm afraid."

He sighed again, making Cleo ache to gouge out his eyes with her keys. That was when she felt the penlight thump against the heel of her hand.

Her pulse spiked. Doreen's forever light had lit up an entire cargo compartment on board the *Pits*. More to the point, it had damned near blinded Cleo the first time her techno-geek cousin had demonstrated its potency.

Radio Man and his two goons were within a few feet of each other. Maybe, just maybe, the beam would throw enough wattage to catch all three.

Her heart thumping, she palmed the penlight. Sweat dampened her hand. Her thumb was slick on the cylinder. So slick, she worried she'd miss the switch. Or take two or three tries to activate it.

Panic turned her blood to water. She could face down armed dopers or take out the knife-wielding husband of a battered client with icy nerves and swift moves. But her pop's life was riding on this one. And Jack's. And Wanda's.

Surreptitiously swiping her thumb against her side, Cleo screwed her face into a plea.

"Please. Just think about this, Walls. You can't believe you'll get away with a quadruple murder in a north Dallas suburb."

"I sold an entire cargo of teenage Sri Lankan girls. This presents far fewer difficulties."

"Yeah? Well, I have only one thing to say to that, you sick bastard. *Tachi dao.*"

The giggle came again, sounding so much like a teenage Sri Lankan girl that Cleo almost gagged.

"*Tachi dao?* What's that supposed to mean?"

Cleo sliced a look at her dad. At his imperceptible nod, she turned a smile on Radio Man.

"It means, asshole, that you're a dead man."

The high-intensity beam stabbed across the den, searing in its intensity. Radio Man shrieked and threw up his gun arm to shield his eyes. The man to his left spun away from the light, then dropped like a lumberjack when Donovan's briefcase smashed into his head.

The goon to his right squeezed his eyes shut at the same instant as he pumped off several rounds. Cleo couldn't stop to see where they hit. She'd already launched herself through the air.

When the red haze cleared, Cleo had dropped goon number three, Jack's briefcase had put a crease in goon number two's skull, and Radio Man was lying in a crumpled heap on the floor. The fist Jack had plowed into his face while he was still blinded by the forever beam had sent him south.

Bullets had stitched a seam across the den wall. One African mask hung at a crazy tilt. Another had splintered. Wanda was crushed under Patrick's sheltering body, screaming hysterically.

"It's okay," Patrick huffed, trying to calm his bride. "Wanda. Baby. It's okay."

She wouldn't believe him. Either that or she couldn't hear him over her own screams.

"Pop! For God's sake, you're crushing her."

While Jack collected the scattered weapons and mounted guard over Walls and his accomplices, Cleo helped her father and stepmom up, then dialed 911. She had to put the phone to one ear and a hand to the other to shut out Wanda's hysterics, but managed to get her message across.

Less than ten minutes later, three squad cars came tearing up the street, sirens wailing. When Jack let the police in and Patrick led his wife upstairs, Wanda was still gulping back sobs.

28

It was late, almost midnight, when Cleo mumbled into the speaker beside her front door.

"Little Miss Muffett sat on a tuffet."

She would just as soon Jack hadn't heard that. Short of directing him to stand on the sidewalk while she muttered into the speaker, there was no way to avoid it.

Sure enough, his eyes held a wicked glint when the door of her home-slash-office clicked open. "Real sophisticated code you use there, North."

"Sophisticated enough. The system only recognizes selected voice prints."

Jack gave the box another once-over. "I didn't realize they were putting out reliable voice-recognition systems for home-security systems."

"They're not. My stepcousin-in-law rigged this one. I gave her a hefty bonus for it. It won't come anywhere *near* the one I plan to give her for this little baby, though."

Jiggling the penlight on her key chain, Cleo led Jack inside.

"I have to meet this woman," he commented.

"You probably will. If you plan to stay more than a night or two, that is. She usually parks on my living room couch during working hours." Cleo dropped the keys on the counter and turned to face him. "Do you, by the way? Plan to stay more than a day or two?"

"Am I invited?"

Oh, yes, he was invited. Into her home. Into her heart. She owed him for dropping everything to come with her. Big time.

"Well, I can't see any reason for either of us to rush back to Washington. We've bagged Domino. We won't have to appear before any boards of inquiry for at least another week or so. And we have at least one more round to decide yet. We were going for two out of three, remember?"

"I remember."

Grinning, he hooked a hand in the waistband of her jeans and yanked her forward.

Cleo's heart did a joyful little dance against her ribs. She caught his hands, though, and held them still before he could work the snap.

"Thanks, Jack," she said softly, "for being there when I needed you."

"You're welcome."

As single-minded as most males, he had only

one thing in his head at the moment. The snap popped. Her zipper came down.

"This time, we go the full count, babe. We don't answer any phones. We don't answer doorbells. No clients. No bosses. As long as it takes."

It took a long time.

All that night.

Most of the next day.

Well into the third day, when Jack had to fly back to Washington.

Cleo followed two weeks later. As she'd feared, she had to testify at so many different hearings and boards of inquiry she soon lost count. Every agency with an interest in the *Pitsenbarger* wanted the details on how and why she went down. The air force. The army. The navy. The Coast Guard. The U.S. Maritime Authority. The Department of Homeland Security.

The *Pitsenbarger* incident turned out to be merely the tip of the iceberg. Jack's queries about Radio Man had reopened dozens of cases the International Commercial Crimes Service maritime division had put in the cold file. He was soon up to his ass unraveling a string of hijackings and illegal shipments that stretched back for years and involved every country from Australia to Zimbabwe.

Cleo returned to Dallas, where her stepmother was still trying to recoup her shattered nerves and Doreen was enjoying the flat-screen TV she'd purchased with her hefty bonus. She'd mounted the screen high on the wall in Cleo's living room. She could now stretch out all two hundred plus pounds and cackle away in total comfort.

Given all Jack had to do, Cleo figured she'd hear from him in a month or so. She was surprised to get a call from OSI headquarters less than two weeks later. Even more surprised that it wasn't Jack on the other end of the line. It was a harried-sounding officer who identified himself as General Barnes's exec.

"Would you hold for the general, please? I'll put him on the line."

Despite herself, Cleo went into a mental brace.

"North?"

"Yes, sir."

"Are you available to work a case for us?"

"That depends. What is it?"

"Someone pumped two bullets into a United States Air Force captain stationed at RAF Lakenheath last night. We have reason to believe there may be international implications. At the request of the British government, I'm pulling Donovan off the Walls investigation and sending him over."

"And you want me to assist?"

A warm glow spread through Cleo. It felt good to be considered part of the team again. Better than she would ever have imagined.

"No," Barnes barked into the phone, bursting her bright bubble. "The British Intelligence Service, in the form of Lady Marston, wants you to assist. She seems to think you and Donovan make a helluva team."

He paused. Cleared his throat. Rattled his pipe stem against his teeth.

"So do I. When can you jump a plane for D.C.? I want to brief you before you leave for London."

Jack. London. Murder. What more could a girl ask for? Cleo's heart was already halfway across the Atlantic. Her feet stayed firmly rooted in her business.

"There's the slight matter of payment for services to be rendered to be discussed first."

Barnes made a noise halfway between a sigh and a snort. "Your standard fee, plus expenses."

"Color me gone, Chief."

Join Cleo North for another action-packed adventure in

THE LAST BULLET

by Merline Lovelace
Available from MIRA Books
June 2005

Please turn the page for an exciting preview

"I've got to jump a plane to D.C. in a few hours, then I'm off to London," former USAF investigative agent turned private security consultant Cleo North announced as she breezed out of her office. "The air force wants me to work a murder case."

Mae, her part-time office manager, looked up from the latest issue of *Golf Digest* and gave an absent smile. "Your passport is in the safe. I'll go get it."

"And I'll go pack."

The call had come from her old boss, General Sam Barnes, commander of the USAF Office of Special Investigations. Cleo and the OSI chief had parted on somewhat less than amicable terms six years ago. Barnes had accepted her resignation with grudging words of praise for her ability to bust cases. He'd then tacked on rather scathing and, Cleo had thought, completely unnecessary comments about her hardheaded independence and tendency to bend the rules.

Her relationship with the Old Man hadn't improved over time. And matters had taken a definite turn for the worse when the ship-hijacking Cleo had recently helped foil had ended in an explosion that destroyed tons of air force munitions.

As if it was her fault the bullet she'd put into one of the hijackers had spun him around at the precise moment he'd decided to launch a shoulder-held missile? At least she'd saved the Navy Seahawk helicopter the bastard had been aiming at, along with its crew…and the British operative who'd just climbed out of the chopper.

Now that operative wanted Cleo to investigate the murder of an American officer stationed in England.

Cleo's flight landed at Reagan National just past 2:00 p.m. Washington, D.C., was decked out in its best spring finery. The cherry trees surrounding the tidal basin had shed their blossoms, but still wore the feathery green leaves of May. The white marble columns of the Jefferson Memorial sparkled in the sun, as did the clean lines of the federal buildings in L'Enfant Plaza. Construction around the plaza slowed things to a crawl until the exit for the Capitol Street Bridge. Crossing the Potomac once more, they zipped along the Suitland Parkway.

Security was extremely tight at Andrews. Understandable, as the base was home to the 89th Airlift Wing, which flew Air Force One and other VIP support aircraft. The driver did a careful zigzag around strategically placed concrete barriers. At the sandbagged gate, Cleo was asked to provide two sources of identification. Even with a military driver, she had to wait while the security force specialist called OSI visitor control to verify her appointment.

Once cleared, the driver angled right and followed the perimeter road to the boulevard of flags leading to the 89th wing headquarters. The semicircular building also housed a number of tenant units, including the headquarters for the United States Air Force Office of Special Investigations.

Charged with providing professional investigative services to air force commanders, the OSI conducted criminal investigations and counter-intelligence operations around the globe. To accomplish that mission, it fielded more than eighteen hundred federally credentialed special agents. And Cleo had once been one of them.

Cleo was escorted into the general's office. Barnes was a tall, spare man who carried every one of his years of service stamped on his craggy face. Today he wore a set of the new blue-and-gray striped camouflage utilities Cleo had heard were being tested for wear by air force personnel in the field.

"'Afternoon, sir."

The *sir* was instinctive. So was the urge to whip up a salute. Damn! There was more of the military officer still skulking around in her than she wanted to admit.

"What's good about it?" Barnes growled.

Uh-oh. Things were not going well in OSI-land.

"Get Donovan in here," he barked at his exec. Gesturing Cleo to the chair in front of his desk, he shoved a folder in her direction. "While we're waiting, you might as well take a look at this."

This was an OSI file on one Captain Douglas Caswell, tanker pilot, currently deceased. Cleo absorbed the details like a sponge sucking up water. Born, Minneapolis. Graduated University of Minnesota near the top of his class. Completed undergraduate pilot training in 1997, tanker training the following year. Upgraded to command pilot in minimal time. Earned an Air Medal and one oak leaf cluster during initial Afghanistan surge, another cluster for support of Iraqi operations.

Pretty impressive, until you got to the index of cases in which Caswell was named as either a contact or a possible suspect.

"Busy guy," Cleo murmured, skimming the executive summaries. "Investigated for possible black marketeering in Turkey. Named as suspect in a computer porn case, but never charged. Believed to be the instigator of a regularly occurring poker game."

Her brows lifted.

"Since when does the OSI investigate poker games?"

Barnes shifted the Meerschaum from one corner of his mouth to the other. "Since Captain Caswell relieved a senior senate staffer of roughly six thousand dollars during a Congressional junket."

Her lips pursed in a silent whistle. The captain played for high stakes. Flipping the file open, she was treated to a digitized image of what she assumed was formerly Doug Caswell's skull.

"We're waiting for the autopsy report," Barnes informed her. "Preliminary indications are he took two .45 slugs to the back of his head."

Ouch! One would have done the trick very nicely, thank you. Whoever put the captain down had wanted to make damned sure he never got up again.

"The shots were fired at close range, from a silenced pistol."

"Where and when?"

"Monday night, between seven and eight p.m., London time. Caswell was at his flat a few kilometers from Royal Air Force Base Mildenhall."

"Any witnesses?"

"No."

"Suspects?"

"None so far, but given the captain's extracurricular activities, the list could turn out to be a long one."

"What about forensics?"

"The Brits are still working the ballistics on the bullets. They also lifted fingerprints and DNA from the flat, but I suspect this shooter was too smart to leave his behind. I don't suggest you hold your breath."

Cleo didn't intend to. Nor did she intend to go into any situation blind. "There's an OSI detachment at RAF Mildenhall. They have responsibility for working a case like this in conjunction with the local constabulary. Why did the Brits request reinforcements?"

The pipe made another shift. The general's eyes narrowed to a skin-searing laser. "That's what I'm sending you and Donovan to find out."

As if on cue, the exec rapped on the door and stuck his head in. "Major Donovan's here, sir."

He stepped aside and Jack strode in—tall, tanned, with tawny hair and those ridiculously thick, gold-tipped lashes fringing his blue eyes. Like the general, he was in BDUs, but his were the standard green and brown that looked baggy on most everyone else but molded Donovan's muscular frame. The pants were neatly bloused in his shiny black boots, the sleeves rolled up to reveal the scattering of sun-bleached blond hair on his arms.

Cleo's stomach did a funny little flip-flop. Pretty ridiculous, considering she'd spent several quality hours with the man just two weeks ago. Maybe the fact that they'd both been naked and breathing real hard at the time had something to do with her suddenly constricted blood flow.

"Sir."

Donovan tipped a nod in his boss's direction, but his eyes were all over Cleo. A happy sound thrummed at the back of her throat. It stayed there until Barnes yanked his pipe from his mouth and lanced the stem at her like a sword.

"The last case you worked cost the air force a cargo ship and tons of munitions, North. Don't blow anything up on this one!"

There's nothing like finding the body of
your boyfriend's wife in your hotel suite

ROBYN CARR

Runaway

MISTRESS

Convinced she's next on her boyfriend's hit list, Jennifer Chaise
takes off down the Vegas Strip armed with only her wits and a
Kate Spade bag full of money. Giving herself a drastic makeover—
complete with a new name—she lands herself a waitressing job in
a nearby town. Jennifer settles in very nicely, but sooner or later
she's going to have to deal with her past....

> "Robyn Carr writes books that touch
> the heart and the funny bone."
> —*New York Times* bestselling author
> Debbie Macomber

*Available the first week of May 2005
wherever paperbacks are sold!*

www.MIRABooks.com

MIRA®

MRC2174

Merline Lovelace

32075 UNTAMED	___ $6.50 U.S.	___ $7.99 CAN.
66871 THE COLONEL'S DAUGHTER	___ $6.50 U.S.	___ $7.99 CAN.
66707 A SAVAGE BEAUTY	___ $6.50 U.S.	___ $7.99 CAN.
66649 THE CAPTAIN'S WOMAN	___ $6.50 U.S.	___ $7.99 CAN.

(limited quantities available)

TOTAL AMOUNT	$ _____
POSTAGE & HANDLING	$ _____
($1.00 FOR 1 BOOK, 50¢ for each additional)	
APPLICABLE TAXES*	$ _____
TOTAL PAYABLE	$ _____

(check or money order—please do not send cash)

To order, complete this form and send it, along with a check or money order for the total above, payable to MIRA Books, to: **In the U.S.:** 3010 Walden Avenue, P.O. Box 9077, Buffalo, NY 14269-9077; **In Canada:** P.O. Box 636, Fort Erie, Ontario, L2A 5X3.

Name: _____
Address: _____ City: _____
State/Prov.: _____ Zip/Postal Code: _____
Account Number (if applicable): _____

075 CSAS

*New York residents remit applicable sales taxes.
*Canadian residents remit applicable GST and provincial taxes.

MIRA®

www.MIRABooks.com

MML0505BL